The U.S. Navy's ⋯ a world ⋯

This story takes you into that world and gives you an authentic glimpse of military life.

Meet Lori Sepanik—aka Jo Marche—one of the most memorable characters in recent romance fiction. Join her as she discovers what Fleet Hospital is all about. And meet Captain Michael McLowery, the man in command....

They're both people with secrets. They're both stubborn and individual and self-possessed. They're both working—sometimes at cross-purposes—to solve a murder.

When *they* fall in love, sit back and watch the excitement!

* * *

I would like to dedicate this book to all those who offered
medical aid after the 9-11 terrorist attack.

I also dedicate it to our best friend, Hospital Corpsman
Second Class (USN Retired) Thomas Anthony Tindall.
Hugs from all of us at Camp Pendleton and Balboa Naval
Hospital who were touched by your life and mourn
your death. You made the world a better place.
We miss you, Tonyota. Love from Ogre and Row-ger.

Books by Anne Marie Duquette

HARLEQUIN SUPERROMANCE

644—FINDING FATHER
700—SHE CAUGHT THE SHERIFF
759—IN THE ARMS OF THE LAW
787—SHE'S THE SHERIFF
849—HER OWN RANGER
975—CASTILLO'S BRIDE

SILHOUETTE DREAMSCAPES

NEPTUNE'S BRIDE (February 2002)

Fleet Hospital
Anne Marie Duquette

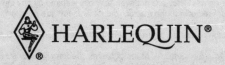

TORONTO • NEW YORK • LONDON
AMSTERDAM • PARIS • SYDNEY • HAMBURG
STOCKHOLM • ATHENS • TOKYO • MILAN • MADRID
PRAGUE • WARSAW • BUDAPEST • AUCKLAND

ISBN 0-373-71055-0

FLEET HOSPITAL

Dear Reader,

The tragedy of the destruction of the World Trade Center in New York City has led many media commentators to claim that the U.S. just "wasn't prepared." Regarding the deaths, injuries and destruction, this is certainly true. However, our country *was* prepared in one way—in the readiness and heroism of our rescue personnel.

The U.S. Navy maintains hospital ships and containerized field hospitals that can be deployed at a moment's notice. The unfortunate wounded are fortunate in one sense. These ships have the most state-of-the-art medical technology available and some of the best-trained medical personnel in the world. Two of our country's leading medical institutions, Bethesda Naval Hospital in Maryland and San Diego Naval Hospital in California, along with their support units, train the finest medical caregivers in the military.

Those who watched the news about 9-11 might remember the U.S. Naval Hospital ship, *The Comfort*, based out of Maryland, ministering to the New York City wounded. The Navy also maintains *The Hope*, berthed on the West Coast.

Another facet of field training for the U.S. Navy Medical Department is the *Fleet Hospital*, located at Camp Pendleton military base in California. Not only is this the largest military base, in actual land area, in the world, but San Diego County, where it's located, holds the highest concentration of military and support bases. San Diego is an important place when it comes to the training of our military and medical heroes.

My own husband, a retired U.S. Navy Hospital Corpsman, spent his last five years in the military at Fleet Hospital. While the story, the characters and the murder mystery in this book are entirely fictitious, Camp Pendleton itself and the training of students to the very highest level of medical preparedness are not.

Mobile hospitals with skilled staff are a strong tool in the fight against terrorism. Many injured who might have become fatalities owe their lives to the real medical heroes with their caring, compassion and intense training. They save lives under the most harrowing of conditions. I hope you enjoy my portrayal of them.

Best,

Anne Marie Duquette

CHAPTER ONE

Pearl Harbor, Hawaii
Early October 1967, afternoon

TEN-YEAR-OLD MICHAEL James McLowery yawned, squirmed and scratched at the neckerchief of his Cub Scout uniform. Sweat trickled through his crewcut and down his face, dropping onto the cafeteria table. Where he sat was hot. Hot outside. Hot inside. Hot everywhere. He wished he was at the officers' pool with his father and baby sister, instead of at school. When they came to pick him up—thank goodness that would be soon—they'd be nice and cool. Not like Michael. Hawaii sure was roasting....

Not like Boston, Dad's last duty station. Once more Michael checked his black "Glows in the dark!" Seiko watch, a smaller version of his father's, and groaned. Half of Saturday was already gone, and where was he? At Navy housing's elementary school, working on his first-aid merit badge. If that wasn't bad enough, his mother, in her starched white nurse's uniform, was teaching the badge class. Dutiful boys filled in the blanks on mimeographed handout sheets.

His mother was even more boring than his history teacher. He couldn't believe it. This day was one big gyp. He'd never wanted to be a Scout. He wanted to go out for Little League and become the next Carl Yastrzemski, but Dad said it was too much driving for a family with only one car. Stupid Navy only shipped one car to Hawaii, instead of their two from Boston. No sense buying another, Dad told him. The same rules worked when leaving Hawaii. Stupid Navy.

The boy sitting next to him, older and looking just as bored, was doodling on his first-aid sheet. Maybe Dennis Klemko was good for a game of hangman or ticktacktoe. Michael, ready to latch on to anything to pass the last ten minutes of the class, leaned over for a quick peek. His breath caught.

On the handout was a surprisingly lifelike sketch of his mother, complete with big pointy titties, rounded thighs—and no clothes but her nurse's cap, Navy gold-braid rank bands across the brim.

Michael promptly delivered a hard sharp elbow to the artist's ribs and grabbed the paper with its disgusting picture. The other boy grunted and rubbed his side.

The Scoutmaster's voice from the front of the room made Michael and Dennis jump. "What's going on there?"

Neither boy answered. The Scoutmaster waved at the sheet of paper in Michael's hands.

"Do you have something to share with the rest of the troop, young man?"

Michael's face burned. "No, sir!" He crumpled the paper into a tiny ball and held both hands behind his back while everyone stopped filling in blanks and stared at him.

"He's drawing dirty pictures," Dennis Klemko said. "I caught him doing it, but he wouldn't give me the paper."

"You turd! Mom, he's lying! *He's* the one who drew it!"

The older boy's taunting grin infuriated him even more. Michael searched for and found the worst insult his parents could deliver to family, friend or foe. "You're a disgrace to your uniform!"

His mother and the Scoutmaster exchanged long-suffering looks, then marched his way, hands outstretched. The matching expressions on their faces promised trouble. They actually believed he could do such a terrible thing? Michael bit his lip. He could defy the Scoutmaster, even kick him in the shins if he had to, but he couldn't do that to his mom. Nor could he let Mom see that picture—or worse yet, let the Scoutmaster see it. Michael had only one choice.

Retreat!

He bounded from his seat and alternately ran and leap-frogged on and across the other tables until he got close to the door and big exit sign. He jumped; his red sneakers made a loud smack, and he dashed outside. No one could catch him now!

"Stop him, boys," the Scoutmaster yelled. "Get that paper!" The boys, as bored as Michael and as eager to escape, poured out the door after him.

Michael ran full tilt, looking for a trash can. He had to get rid of the crumpled drawing in his fist. He couldn't litter—littering was a Bad Thing, a disgrace to the uniform. If the Cubs caught up, they could easily take the paper from him—or from any trash can he'd thrown it in. He had nowhere to hide. This school was the pack's territory, as well as his own; every boy knew all the good hiding places. And most of them were older, with longer legs. They were catching up.

Michael made the sidewalk. He was off school property now. His legs and arms pumped, his heart pumping even faster in the tropical heat. The boys closed in. It was no longer a game to them. The honor of their pack was at stake. Already Michael's side was aching.

"Daddy!" he screamed in desperation...and was rewarded. Moving along the opposite side of the street was his father's car, a 1964 steel-blue Plymouth Deuce, headed toward the school to pick him and his mother up.

Jaywalking was a Bad Thing, too, but his father would understand. Dad said that sometimes a sailor had to break the rules. Dad flew jets where he wasn't supposed to, drove cars faster than he was supposed to and drank harder than he was supposed to. Dad said it kept lives and sanity intact. He learned that in Vietnam. This was Michael's day to break the rules. Dennis Klemko, that rat fink who'd started the disaster, was almost upon him—and across the street was a storm drain with bars.

Michael raced toward it to rid himself of the drawing. Arms flailing, he waved his father down. "Daddy, help! Stop the car!"

Lt. Commander Patrick Andrew McLowery took in the scene before him in a fraction of a second. He hadn't survived two tours of bombing the Ho Chi Minh Trail without damn good reflexes. He slammed on the car's brakes and whipped the steering wheel to the right. The car fishtailed in the gravel. Its front end missed his son by six inches; the back end missed his son's pursuer by a whisper and skidded away.

Michael hurled the balled paper at the storm drain even as he avoided the moving car. With reflexes almost as sharp as his father's, he saw that his aim was true but had no time for a moment's relief. At the same instant the drawing flew from his hand, his two-year-old sister flew out the open passenger window of his dad's car.

The brand-new "latest, safest model" child seat, its plastic and aluminum ends hooked over the top of the Plymouth's front bench seat, had been no match for the car's centrifugal force. Baby Anna Mary McLowery's head was no match for the road. Her blood spread over the scorching black asphalt like lava from a volcano.

On that hot summer day, despite the presence of a whole troop of Scouts trained in first aid, the troop's nurse instructor and the nurse's husband, Michael James McLowery watched his sister die.

ANNA'S OPEN-CASKET funeral Mass was held in the Navy chapel. On such short notice, none of the relatives from Boston had made it to see Anna for the last time, wearing her new white gown and lacy bonnet. In full dress uniform, Lt. Commander McLowery and his wife, Lieutenant Junior Grade McLowery, sat alone with their son in the front pew. Michael was too scared to look at his sister's body, although he pretended he wasn't. He just refused to look. He also refused to pray out loud. A bunch of mumbo-jumbo prayers weren't going to bring back his dead sister, but Mom said he couldn't stay home. He was mad at Mom, mad at Dad, mad at Anna, mad at the whole world.

His fury built, but Michael managed to keep it in check—barely—until his entire Scout troop arrived, dressed in formal uniform, just like him. Right behind the Scoutmaster, leading the line of silent boys, was Dennis Klemko, who'd dared—actually *dared*—to show up.

Michael's fury exploded. Flying out of the pew, he

barreled headlong into the dirty traitor, knocking him over. Michael pinned him to the aisle carpet.

"You killed her! It's your fault!" Michael screamed again and again, his fists pounding at Klemko before the horrified faces of the chaplain, his parents, the Scoutmaster, even his father's and mother's Commanding Officers and Executive Officers.

It took three strong enlisted men to pull Michael off Klemko. Two female Nurse Corps officers supported his mother while Michael screamed, "He drew you naked, Mom! He drew you and said I did it! Ask him! Ask him! Tell everyone what you did, you fink!"

Michael again lunged for Klemko. The enlisted men's hands tightened on his arms, but Michael scored with a hard kick at Klemko's face. Nose broken, Klemko screamed and collapsed into a wailing lump of agony.

"He drew it, Mom! Not me! He was going to let the whole troop see you naked! I grabbed the paper so he couldn't! That's why I ran away! That's why Anna got killed! It's all his fault!"

His mom took a step, went limp and dropped out of Michael's sight below her pew. More Nurse Corps officers swarmed around her. Others swarmed around Klemko and worked on his bloody nose and cut eyebrow. The CO and XO rallied to his dad's side.

The Navy chaplain came straight to Michael and said, "Let the boy go." The enlisted men released him. "Come on, son, let's talk this over."

"I'm not your son!" Michael shook off the chaplain's hand and looked for his mother. "Mom! You believe me, right, Mom? Where are you?"

She rose from behind the pew. Her arms were wide open and shaking. Michael felt dizzy with relief. His mom wanted to hug him! She believed him! He tried to reach her, tried to push aside all the people in the aisle to get to her, but couldn't. Mom left her pew and staggered toward Anna's open casket. She lifted the stiff rouged corpse, hugged it tightly to her chest.

Michael froze in place. "Mommy?"

The chaplain left Michael and tried to take Anna from his mother. Mrs. McLowery screamed, whirled away from everyone and ran up onto the altar, the only place where there were no people. Michael broke free and ran for his mother. Anna was so tiny. Surely there was room for him, too, in his mother's arms.

Up the steps he ran, one, two, three, in between the Stars and Stripes, Navy and Hawaiian flags on the left and the two flags with the Cross of Christ and the Star of David on the right. His mother hunched protectively over Anna, accidentally catching Michael with her hip. Michael fell backward down the steps, three, two, one. Some woman he didn't recognize caught him.

She took him outside, away from the pandemonium. He'd stopped yelling by then, but Mom and some of the Scouts hadn't. The lady who'd caught him smelled pleasantly of mint, instead of stinky perfume. She sat down on the curb and pulled his trembling body onto her lap.

"Want a Certs?" she asked. Michael didn't answer, but she peeled off a "Two! Two! Two Mints in One!" and held it in front of his mouth. "Open up, little bird."

He opened.

"Close," she said.

He already had. The candy tasted good. The woman popped a Certs into her own mouth and hummed and rocked him while they both sucked on their bits of sweetness. After a while she asked, "Want another?"

Michael realized he'd broken his communion fast. He

shouldn't have eaten anything. Now he couldn't offer his communion grace for his sister's soul. Not that it mattered, since he and Klemko had killed her. According to catechism classes, he was damned, anyway. One more Bad Thing wouldn't make any difference. He wiped at the tears on his face, then held out his still-trembling hand.

"Here, sweetheart. Take the whole roll."

When his father came to get him, Michael cried some more, and after the first surreptitious mint, ate the rest of the Certs in the front pew in full view of God and country. He sat between his parents, and they didn't seem to notice.

Michael saw that Anna's little coffin was now closed and latched. "Is Anna back in there?" he whispered to his father.

Dad nodded.

"Are you sure Mom didn't hide her somewhere?"

Dad nodded again.

"Positive? Can I see?"

His wet-cheeked father murmured, "Trust me," and took his hand. Michael's dry-eyed mother, watchful nurses on the other side of her, didn't touch him, didn't even look at him. Michael swiveled around to check out the pews and saw Klemko was gone. So was the Scoutmaster. Good riddance. They didn't deserve to be in the same room with Mom and his poor baby sister. He wished he could see Anna one more time. He should've looked at her earlier when the coffin was open. Now it was too late. He'd never see her again. It wasn't fair. Nothing was fair. He started crying again and ate another Certs.

The service didn't last long. The Navy chaplain rattled off that funeral faster than Michael's father drove on a Friday-night payday.

THE HEAT CONTINUED the next day and the next and the next. The sun beat down with a fierceness Michael hated. Only one thing made it bearable—he was allowed to sweat at home, instead of in school. His parents were on compassionate leave and home from work. It felt strange. *He* felt strange.

His mom insisted on going back to the hospital three days after Anna's funeral. Michael clung to his father when she announced her decision. He didn't want her to leave. The house was too quiet with Anna gone. His parents were too quiet with Anna gone. It frightened him, especially at night.

He was glad his father said, "Honey, don't go."

"You two can finish watching the baseball playoffs on television."

"But, Mom—"

"Michael, don't talk back. If I don't do something, I'll go crazy," she said. She wore her white nurse's uniform with her Navy officer's cap.

"The last place you need to be is in surgery," Patrick argued. "You're in no better shape to be working the OR than I am to be flying."

Mrs. McLowery shook her head and the Red Sox game continued to play on the television. "I already talked to my CO. She'll let me have morgue duty. I can't do any damage there. It's all paperwork."

"You hate morgue duty!" Patrick McLowery said. "Every time you work it, you have nightmares about getting trapped in the freezer."

Michael shivered. He hated nightmares, and he'd been having a lot of them lately.

"You won't even go near the morgue without a corpsman on the outside and one on the inside."

"I don't care!" she shrieked.

Michael winced at the nails-on-chalkboard sound of her voice.

"This heat is killing me! I have to get out of the house!"

"Fine. We'll take a drive to the Ala Moana Mall for ice cream. We can walk around there and cool off."

"No. I'm going to work."

"The hell you are!" Michael's father rose to his feet, almost tipping over the box fan whirring on the floor. "The last thing you need to be around is a bunch of you-know-whats!"

Bodies. Dead bodies. Like Anna's.

"I need some quiet, Patrick," she said. "I made dinner for you and Michael. There's a chicken potpie in the oven. Listen for the timer. I mixed up some cherry Jell-O and bananas for dessert. It's on the second shelf in the refrigerator."

"For God's sake, sweetheart—"

"I already ate. It's time for me to leave or I'll be late."

"At least let me drive you in!"

"No, Patrick, I'm fine. Really I am. Keep the car. I'll take the bus." She bent to grab her purse. She didn't even kiss Michael or Patrick goodbye. "I may work an extra half shift, so don't wait up."

Michael didn't see his mother again that night.

He didn't see her in the morning, either. Dad said he could stay home from school once more. Michael was on his hands and knees out front, driving his red Tonka truck full of green plastic Army men through the grass, patiently waiting for the base bus Mom took home. It always stopped at the corner, three houses down.

An official military car, gray with blue lettering on the side and government plates, drove up and stopped at his house. Two men in uniform climbed out. Automatically Michael checked the men's collar insignias. One of them wore a cross.

Right then he knew. Every military kid knew what it meant when two uniforms came to your house and one of them was a chaplain. Dad was home from Vietnam— safe inside the house. He'd just seen him. Anna was in the ground. That meant...

"Dad!" he screamed. One of the men started toward him. Michael backed away. "Daddy!" Michael screamed even louder.

He dropped the toy truck and the Army men, ran into the house and hid under the kitchen sink, his spine jammed against the hard metal J-pipe. His father called him. He heard the front screen door slam, heard nothing for a while, heard the door again, then his father calling him over and over.

Michael didn't answer. He couldn't talk. Couldn't move. Couldn't breathe. All he could do was shiver amidst the slightly rancid fumes of sacked potatoes and onions, the antiseptic smell of cleanser and dish soap, the commissary grocery bags stored in his hiding place.

His father opened the cupboard doors, found him and pulled him out. He told Michael what he already knew.

"Your mother's dead, son. The night crew found her."

"At the hospital?"

"Yes. The chaplain said she was...she got trapped in the refrigeration unit at the morgue."

"Dad, they're lying! She'd never get locked in there!"

Michael fought to escape from his father's arms, his father's words. He couldn't escape either.

"Listen to me, Michael! The next shift found her inside. They tried to revive her, but…" His voice cracked.

"Where was everybody? Where was the corpsman?"

"Gone home, I guess. She had her car keys and purse with her."

"Why was she in there?" Michael sobbed. "She hated that place!"

"She wasn't in her right mind."

"It's because of Anna, right? She didn't want to come home."

"Everyone says it was an accident," his father said.

"It wasn't an accident, was it?" Michael forced himself to ask.

His father looked away. "At least she had the decency to take off her uniform before she went in. She didn't disgrace it," he choked out. Tears rolled down Patrick's cheeks.

Michael had his answer. Mom was really dead. She'd killed herself. He started to cry, his sobs harsh and violent. Patrick picked him up and, on the kitchen floor amidst potatoes and cleanser, rocked him the way Mom used to rock Anna.

THE SAME CHAPLAIN they'd had for Anna's funeral droned on and on during his mother's closed-casket service. With two deaths in the family, Michael thought he'd blab less. Then again, maybe the chaplain wanted to make up for Anna's short sermon. Whatever the reason, his mother's took forever.

Michael's whole Scout pack—minus rat fink Dennis

Klemko—wore their uniforms to the second funeral. Michael flatly refused. He hated Scouts. He hated everyone who'd ever been a Scout.

Without a uniform, he had nothing formal to wear. His father said he wasn't up to taking him shopping and didn't even know Michael's new size. Michael had outgrown his old church suit ages ago, and the Scoutmaster's wife couldn't get off work to take him shopping, either. So the Certs lady—his Scoutmaster's single sister-in-law with the silly name of Sunshine Mellow and sillier plastic go-go boots—guessed his size and showed up at the last minute with a new black suit and white shirt from the Navy Exchange. Apparently it was paid for by the Scout troop, which made Michael almost want to reject it.

When the Certs lady dropped off the suit bag, Michael asked her if she'd sit with him at his mother's funeral. Michael knew Sunshine didn't meet his father's standards. She wasn't Irish, she wasn't even Catholic and she had a "hippie" name, but Michael liked her, anyway. She said he had to ask his father; she'd wait in the car while he did. Michael ran back inside.

"Please, Dad, can she? She brought me a suit. So can she?"

His father, busy phoning relatives from both sides of the family, phoning Navy staff above and below him at the flight line, planning the second funeral and arranging for Michael's make-up schoolwork, agreed. Once again Michael sat in the front pew of the Navy chapel, this time flanked by his father and the Certs lady.

All through church, his father held Michael's right hand, and Sunshine held his left—in between Certs after Certs. She adjusted his old bow tie, which made him itch and scratch. It was too tight for his neck, but the base exchange was out of new ones. Michael didn't mind, really he didn't. He *wanted* to be dressed right for Mom.

At least his tie wasn't some stupid neckerchief. Michael sucked on his candy, ignored the communion line Dad was in and leaned a salt-wet cheek against Sunshine's Protestant shoulder. He wondered if Mom was rocking Anna in heaven. Mom *had* to be there—she was a good mom, and she hadn't disgraced her uniform. He wondered who'd take care of him and Dad. He knew he'd never see Mom and baby Anna again, not even in heaven. If he hadn't been such a baby himself and called out for his father when the boys were chasing him, Anna would still be alive. He'd gotten rid of the drawing; he should have taken the beating like a man. Now, he was damned to hellfire and worms forever.

Unless… Michael slowly inserted another Certs into his mouth. Unless he got a new uniform, started over and never disgraced that uniform again. He was the son of uniformed parents. He knew about duty. He was no rotten quitter. Michael sat up a little straighter in the pew. He could wear a new uniform with a new Scout troop, and a Navy uniform later, like his mom's.

On his honor, Michael vowed to do his best…to do his duty to God and his country…to help other people at all times…and to never do another Bad Thing again. Starting now. He shoved the rest of the Certs into his pants pocket.

On his honor.

CHAPTER TWO

MEMO

TO: All Personnel
FROM: U.S. Naval Training Program Office
SUBJ: FLEET HOSPITAL Mission Description

1) Is a Department of Defense standardized, modular, deployable, rapidly erectable, relocatable shore-based medical facility.

2) Provides Fleet Commander in Chief with fully mission-capable combat medical treatment facilities in support of combat forces at risk.

3) Deployed in three phases: Air Detachment, Advance Party and Main Body.

4) Assembled rapidly at prepared sites in five to ten days with 100-bed or 500-bed combat zone hospital.

5) Unlike Army MASH units, Navy FLEET HOSPI-TAL units are essentially *self-sustaining*.

6) Once FLEET HOSPITAL facilities are erected and provided with 60 days of supplies, FLEET HOSPITAL is *on its own*.

Naval Fleet Hospital Training, FHOTC (Fleet Hospital Operations and Training Command)

Camp Pendleton Marine Corps Base
Day 1

TABLOID WRITER Lori Sepanik, pen name Jo Marche, stepped outside into Southern California's July sun and the noon heat of the fenced desert compound. It was the day's second muster. Located directly to the north of the Fleet Hospital Command, the training class within the fenced area offered no frills—or even basic comforts. The assembled students, sweating in heavy green cammies, black boots and starched covers, tried to ignore the humming of Admin's air-conditioning outside their barbed-wire fences and guarded gates. Judging by the looks on their faces, Jo decided they were failing miserably. She knew *she* was.

Air conditioning existed for the staff's administration computers only and the few staff personnel lucky enough to work in the regular buildings. Typewriters were used in the Fleet Hospital's actual training area, and the frigid air wasn't needed there. Everyone not in FHOTC's Admin building, from instructors and students to civilian guests like her, sweated. Their only relief was drinking potable water outside the huge tent "hospital" that served as their classroom. No soda, soft drinks or pop, depending on one's regional vernacular. In Jo's case, it was a Midwesterner's "soda." She'd kill for one right now. No such luck. She was stuck inside the compound, sweating and waiting for the training exercise's first "casualties."

Jo had been admitted onto the marine base as an Associated Press reporter. However, the credentials she had were as phony as her pen name. If she was lucky and able to write a decent story, instead of her usual tabloid trash, she just might get away with what she hoped was the last lie she'd ever have to tell. Face it, tabloid reporters were pretty much professional liars—if you considered the lousy substandard pay she received for her articles "professional." But so far, she hadn't found even the hint of a real story at Fleet Hospital.

I'll never get a decent job with a decent newspaper at this rate. She hadn't managed to get an interview with the Commanding Officer, a Captain McLowery. Not yet, anyway. AP rarely bought feature stories without a diversity of interviews. In this case, that meant officers and enlisted, high ranks and lower ranks, men and women, and people of varied ethnic backgrounds. Unfortunately, an interview with the high-ranking McLowery wasn't happening so far, despite a quick conversation with him earlier in the day.

Not needing to worry about the muster, Jo stepped back into the shade and consulted her notes as the roll call droned on in the blinding light. She had to find a story, so she might as well go where it was cooler and start with some of the low-ranking officers.

Luckily for her, the CHC—Chaplain Corps—worked inside the hospital, a huge complex of connected canvas tents, which all the students learned to assemble. The hospital air-conditioning operated only in critical areas— Surgery, Intensive Care and the Expectant area, which was what they called the cordoned-off area for those expected to die. Those three sites, especially the latter two, were chaplain territories, she read. Chaplains would be praying over the dead and dying.

"Nothing like fake blood on bandages to spice up a dull shot," Jo murmured. She felt for her camera at her side and stayed in the shade as she searched the mustered ranks for the chaplain participating in this exercise. She had a gift for both words and photography—although she rarely needed photos when it came to the tabloids. Celebrity stories used stock shots, and fake stories used computer-generated photos, like those used to show readers supposed alien-human babies born in Roswell basements near Area 51.

She ought to know; she'd written a series of alien-baby stories herself under her Jo Marche byline. They sold almost as well as Elvis sightings and features on the British royals' latest affairs—whether they'd actually happened or not. Jo had always wanted to be a nonfiction writer, but for some reason only the tabloids bought her stuff, and that sort of writing could hardly be classified as true reporting.

She winced at the thought of some of her past work, although she had more scruples than many of her colleagues. She flatly refused to write tabloid trash about celebrities, royals or any real people. But her aliens, ghosts, vampires, zombies and other weird creatures in the midst of suburbia were pure fiction and so, fair game. Those stories hurt no one—except Lori Sepanik and her professional reputation, even if they did pay the bills.

Hence her pen name, Jo Marche, with the intentionally added "e." She was an avid reader who'd used books to escape from a poverty-ridden childhood, and Jo March of Louisa May Alcott's *Little Women* became Lori's favorite heroine. The fictional Miss March had escaped the world of lurid fiction to become a famous writer. Even as a child, Lori had pretended she was Josephine March, the famous writer. In her version, Jo married the handsome Laurence, even though the pretty younger sister ended up with him in the book, and she vowed to follow Jo March's example. Sadly, young Lori's plans for herself hadn't panned out, and rather than sully the innocent name of the fictional Miss March with trashy tabloid fiction, the adult Lori had added an "e" to her pseudonym, vowing to drop it when she finally became legitimate—as in publishing an AP or UP story. The name change might be slight, but it made her feel…less guilty.

She'd left her old neighborhood in St. Louis four years ago and moved to Las Vegas, hoping to cover the entertainment news. But not once had she ever been in the right place at the right time with the right "connections" to get to the really big stars. With some college education, a little money and a couple of "you're almost there" rejection letters to spur her on, she'd moved south from Las Vegas to Southern California. Writing about California's "four seasons"—earthquakes, droughts, fires and mudslides—helped supplement her income, especially since Hollywood stars tended to be even more guarded than those in Vegas. And San Diego, so close to the border, didn't make a big deal about people who lived out of their cars in trailer parks, river washes or the interstates' many "rest areas." As long as there were no sanitary or trash problems, the police left her—and others living the not-so-glamorous California dream—alone. At least she could shower and keep clean until another sale afforded her enough money to stay at a cheap motel. She hadn't hit San Diego's definable rock bottom yet—living on the beaches or in the parks year-round and fishing through trash for redeemable bottles and cans.

Luckily Jo had talent, determination and, at age thirty-three, enough of her youth plus enough maturity to keep reaching for her star. A Fleet Hospital story might provide her with enough money to go legitimate for a real newspaper and find an apartment where she could live and date like a normal person. Maybe even get married eventually and have a kid or two. She refused to consider herself homeless—just struggling—but a 1968 Chevy Impala back-seat bedroom wasn't exactly a good place for children.

Jo had a game plan. No one knew a thing about Fleet Hospitals. No one had written about them, not even the big papers like the *Los Angeles Times*. Maybe she could get enough material for a features article in Sunday's nationally syndicated *Parade* section. With luck, she might be able to get enough info to write a TV sitcom, too. Everyone loved *M.A.S.H.*, the TV show, which was still going strong in reruns.

So what if the odds were stacked against her? Except for her quick brain, the odds had been lousy since the day she was born. Fleet was better than alien stories; something, *anything* was needed to feed her creative mind—and her nearly empty bank account.

She intended to write a piece establishing herself once and for all as a woman going somewhere. A woman with a future in legitimate journalism. Either that, or she'd be stuck composing her next tabloid story: "Shape-shifters locked in guarded Fort Knox vaults. Military denies all knowledge."

Right now Jo had everything on the line. Someone had broken into her car and stolen her used but serviceable laptop and the trash bag holding most of her clothes, leaving behind the few dirty clothes she hadn't washed yet. Another female resident of the trailer park where Jo stayed had almost been raped in the showers; she'd escaped only because her attacker had slipped on the slimy mildew-covered tile. Still, he'd succeeded in getting away before the police arrived.

Jo now had a limited wardrobe, an empty stomach and a backpack that served as her camera case, suitcase and purse. She discovered that she wasn't bouncing back from life's little problems the way she used to. The trailer park was getting too scary, even for a lifelong veteran of trashy neighborhoods, and she didn't know which felt worse, the lousy mattresses in the lousy motels or the back seat of her Chevy, with its broken springs and torn vinyl upholstery. Being at Camp Pendleton meant a cot, and since she was a reporter—an invited civilian guest—her meals were free.

None too soon. She'd paid almost all her money to a Los Angeles forger for two fake IDs, both in her pen name: one a bogus driver's license, the other an Associated Press card that had gotten her permission from the Marine Base General to report on Fleet Hospital. All she had now was a stash of about a hundred bucks to hit the thrift shop for some new clothes—if there was anything left after renting a computer to type out her story and then fax it in.

But first she had to *find* that story. She'd better start interviewing as many people as possible—and that meant she could stay in the shade for a while. Anyone who had any sense would join her after mustering.

"Finally!" she murmured as roll call ended. She scanned the crowd again. She needed to locate the handsome CO, Michael James McLowery, and then that boring-looking chaplain. What was the guy's name and rank? She checked her notes one more time. Oh, yeah, there it was....

HERE HE WAS, Daniel Preston, Lieutenant, CHC, USN, a chaplain straight out of OIS—Officer Indoctrination School in Newport, Rhode Island—and about to undergo an exercise that would teach him about dealing with the dead and dying. His years in the Navy Reserves hadn't acquainted him with a chaplain's most solemn duties, which was why he'd finally made the jump to full-time sailor. Like most of the population in a wealthy country usually at peace, he'd never seen an adult die. In fact, he'd never seen anyone die…

Except for a small child. Anna McLowery. That was back when he was Daniel Klemko, Jr., known as "Dennis." But his father, Daniel Senior, had died in 'Nam, from friendly fire, no less, and his mother had remarried and let his new stepdad adopt him. He became Daniel Preston, minus the Jr.

The memory of that little girl's death had stayed with him, made his new name welcome and had later driven him to bars, booze, women's beds and, finally, to the ministry. He doubted he had any genuine calling as a man of God, but he could certainly identify with other tortured sinners. So here he stood, an honest-to-goodness military chaplain, expected to counsel, pray with—or pray for—moulaged military personnel made up with eerie Hollywood expertise to look like dying patients.

Soon "the enemy," the instructors and support staff, would quit mustering them and start the attack. He'd been waiting for it since early morning. Two hundred personnel from all over North America were also waiting.

"Back to your stations. Disssssss-missed!"

Everyone except the armed on-duty compound guards at the gate fell out and shuffled back to the two hospital entrances, either Triage and Casualty Receiving or the main hospital entrance to the command center.

An African-American female with an M-16 slung across her back and a radio attached to her shoulder fell out beside Daniel. She reached up to adjust the security earpiece/radio she wore, swiped at the sweat on her face, then stared at her hand.

"Damn heat's melting my mascara—" She broke off at the sight of Daniel's subdued black lieutenant's garrison emblem on the left of his uniform collar and the Cross of Christ emblem on the right. "Sorry, sir. Didn't mean to swear, sir."

Daniel read her Second Class rank on her collar and her Master-at-Arms rank, rate and name, A. Jackson, by the embroidered badge on her pocket. "I've heard worse, MA2." He reached into his pocket for the ever-present wad of tissues he carried. Prayers and Kleenex, a chaplain's stock in trade. He gave her a handful and gestured toward another area of mascara on her skin.

"Sorry, sir," she said again. He noticed—couldn't help noticing—Jackson's flawless feminine features and trim but voluptuous body. Her accent was as thick and heavy as her weapon. Thanks to his internship in the South, he'd bet money she was a Bible Belt Baptist.

"People act as ridiculous around chaplains as Friday-night drivers do around MPs," he said. "I get tired of it—don't you?"

"Yes, sir. It's a...pain, sir."

"You can stop with all the sirs, too."

She grinned, the smile definitely making her feminine and attractive despite the unflattering uniform and the melted mascara still speckling her cheeks.

"Missed a spot."

She scrubbed at her face with the wadded tissue. "All gone, Chaplain?"

"It is now, Petty Officer Jackson."

"Thank you, sir. Duty calls, sir."

He watched her military-trot toward the guard shack.

From behind Daniel, a pleasant voice commented, "Now that's an oxymoron—a military chaplain."

Daniel swiveled around to find another woman. Her face was more pretty than classically beautiful, and there was little delicacy in this sassy lady. A lightly tanned white civilian in scruffy jeans, she didn't bother with a cap to shade a head of untidy, shoulder-length dark-blond curls. Her gray-eyed gaze met Daniel's. He noted the two cameras slung over one trim shoulder. A piece of masking tape hand-printed with "Press" was stuck to her shirt below the neck with its two open snaps. He observed she had a very nice bust line, the only part of this woman that didn't seem to need fattening up.

She caught the quick flick of his eyes. "Judging by that look, I'd say you're not a Catholic chaplain. Or a married Jewish one."

She had seen his cross. Jewish chaplains wore the Star of David, not that religious insignias mattered to a dying sailor. As with all military chaplains, Daniel had been trained in the rites and prayers of the three major religions, and was expected to use them.

"Protestant chaplain, right? Single, too."

"Yep." Not that he could've bypassed that figure even if he had been married. The smiling woman before him was in her early thirties and was as sexy as the MA2 was businesslike. Daniel warmed to this woman's sensuality as quickly as he'd warmed to Jackson's honest personality. The cross on his collar didn't cancel out his masculinity, and as Ms. Reporter had noted, he wasn't bound by a Catholic priest's vow of celibacy.

However, as a chaplain, he *was* bound to marital sex only. He wasn't married, and his days in strange women's beds were long over. He was only human, however, and sometimes that human side overcame his spiritual calling. Breasts were breasts, even if he refused to ogle them. But he had no plans for a girlfriend, fiancée or wife.

"Lt. Daniel Preston, CHC."

She held out a friendly hand, which he shook. "I'm Jo Marche—that's Marche with an 'e'—AP. That's Associated Press."

Daniel knew what AP meant.

"I'm here to cover the training exercise, starting with you."

"Me?"

"Yes. Everyone does stories on the poor wounded men and the Florence Nightingales who treat them."

She didn't sound disparaging in the least, but as a good citizen in uniform he couldn't help commenting. "That's what war's about—death and destruction, wounded men *and* women."

"Sadly, yes," she said with real feeling, apparently not offended by his correction. "However, this is a training exercise, not a real war. I thought I'd get some different angles—a chaplain's angle, for one, and you're the only Chaplain Corps personnel assigned. You're the first person I plan to talk to, since Michael McLowery is unavailable at present. Until I can get near him, I'd appreciate an interview."

Despite the blow to his pride, Daniel admired her frankness. He still wasn't eager to volunteer as her subject. His experience as a chaplain wasn't vast enough for her to report on, and he certainly didn't consider himself representative of the Navy norm. Ever since he'd graduated from divinity school seven years ago in New York, his experience had been mostly with paperwork, not people. Even his years with Navy Reserves, serving a weekend once a month, plus two weeks in the summer, wasn't enough to learn his trade…or maybe he just wasn't very good at it. Best to tread cautiously here.

He also intended to call as little attention to himself as possible. He'd been deeply shocked six weeks earlier, when he'd received his orders for Fleet Hospital. The CO's name, Michael McLowery, had been printed in big bold letters. So far, McLowery hadn't recognized him. Daniel had decided not to press his luck. For everyone's sake, he'd decided not to reveal their childhood connection until the training exercise had concluded—if at all. No sense in rocking the boat.

"My job isn't that exciting from a media point of view."

"Oh, but it is. I did my research in the base library right here. I read about those two chaplains who each received our country's Medal of Honor—Capodanno and O'Callahan, right?"

"They were both Catholics," he said, impressed at her knowledge. She had brains, as well as looks. "I'm Protestant."

"So tell me, are you Protestants cowardly? Or just smarter than Catholics? I can't tell. I'm nondenominational myself."

Witty, too, it seemed. No way would he touch that remark. "Chaplains don't earn medals in training exercises."

"Such an interesting fact. I'd better write it down."

Was she mocking him or flirting with him? He wasn't sure. The woman whipped out a notebook and scribbled in it, then slipped it back into her jeans pocket. Maybe forced was a better word. There wasn't a lot of room between that tightly rounded buttock and the thin denim. Despite her intelligent professional air, he decided it was time to abandon Ms. AP's ship. Michael McLowery was welcome to her.

"Please accept my apologies, Ms. Marche, but maybe you should find someone else."

"But it's so hot out here," she moaned. "Ordinarily I'm not such a wimp, but I definitely need a break—and an interview. The guard shack and ordnance areas aren't air-conditioned, so I'm not interested in interviewing their staff until it cools down later on, and I can't get near the CO. The hospital *is* air-conditioned, and since you're assigned there, why don't you make things easier for me?" She smiled with an easy sensuality.

He had no good answer to that question, either. "I suppose I could walk you through the place this afternoon, if nothing comes up in the line of duty."

"Great. I'll stick close for the next few days. I do have the command's permission to stay for the full two weeks of training."

"In writing?"

She promptly showed it to him. Damn, she did have it.

"How about if I agree to the interview just for today? You won't need more time with me than that."

They headed toward the Triage entrance, empty except for stretchers.

"Sounds as if you're trying to get rid of me."

He shrugged. "I'm here to work, and you'll get bored," he warned her. "I doubt there'll be much for you to see. Casualties filter through Triage, Surgery and Post-op first. I don't get them until ICU, Recovery or the Expectant area." At her look of confusion, he explained, "Expectant—death and dying area."

"No problem. I can wait."

Her persistence didn't bother him as much as his own

lack of experience. "I doubt a photo of me reading my Bible is going to win a Pulitzer prize," he said with undisguised sarcasm.

She leaned his way, her camera brushing his hip. "Tell you a secret, Preacher Man. Heavy casualties will be on the way soon."

Daniel slowed his pace, unwilling to touch her camera, or anything else. "What makes you say that?"

She winked. "The command gives civilians like me the whole exercise script in advance. This lull is to get everyone off guard before the shit hits the fan. I'll get you a copy if you want," she said helpfully.

"No, thanks. It wouldn't be—"

"Kosher? That's okay. You're Christian." She smiled at her little joke. He didn't. "Trust me, it'll be moulage city before you can say 'hit the deck.' So, whaddaya say, Preach? Stay and do the interview?"

"Perhaps later, but on two conditions."

She halted. Her sensuality, healthy or not—he couldn't tell on so short an acquaintance—continued to flow. "Yes?"

"First, I go by 'Chaplain' or 'Lieutenant.' Second, snap up that shirt and keep a nice post-Tailhook body space between us. I don't care if you're a civilian or not. Professionalism is the order of the day. Do you have a problem with that?"

"Give me a break!" she said, obviously offended. She reached for the open snap at her neck, and her fingers tracked down to the next one just a few inches below. "I could go to church in this! Though it certainly wouldn't be *yours*. I've never ever seduced anyone on the job, and if I decided to start, it wouldn't be some self-righteous Arthur Dimmesdale-type, either. That, for your information, was the name of the hypocritical minister in *The Scarlet Letter*. So you can just take your—"

"I get the point, Ms. Marche. And I do recognize the literary reference. Now, if you'll excuse me, I have work to do." He gave Ms. Marche with an "e" his crispest military nod of dismissal. "By the way, the tour is off. You can forget the interview, too." Even if he'd misjudged her, she seemed a tough nut, obviously a seasoned reporter. Probably a tiger in the sack, as well, but he had no intention of finding out for himself. On a hot Hawaiian day years ago, a pair of pert breasts in a white nurse's uniform had cost him dearly.

It'd be a cold day in FHOTC—Fleet Hospital Operations and Training Command—Camp Pendleton's desert hell, if another set of female attributes cost him his Navy uniform, his chaplain's cross and his immortal, admittedly flawed, excuse for a soul. He fingered the cross on his collar as he watched her saunter off, hips swaying rhythmically.

Sweet Lord, have mercy!

AT TRIAGE AND RECEIVING Jo Marche fiddled with the manual film loader on her old backup camera. Mentally she cursed both the uncooperative tab of plastic and herself.

She hadn't come on too strong, had she? She wasn't even *trying* to be sexy, but watching the CO with the *GQ* face and trying to catch up to him had its effect. That man and his body had her motor running, and she supposed the chaplain had inadvertently been the recipient of her overspilling hormones. The CO was bedroom-handsome: an officer with a wow body, snapping baby blues, glossy black hair and a higher rank than Lt. Prim Preacher. He could pose for a recruiting poster or

TV commercial in a second. He had that look—officer, gentleman, woman's dream lover, hero—especially hero. Not just the look, either; McLowery seemed like a good man to her because of the way he handled his troops. Nothing like that priggish chaplain.

Jo did a slow burn. She'd never been big on church, but two open snaps over a basic bra did not equal Tailhook, for heaven's sake! Time to move on.

She pulled out her duty roster. Michael James McLowery. Rank: Capt. Age: 44. Status: Single. *And sexy. Not only that, he's my ticket to the big time. I can't wait to track this cutie down and speak to him instead of just staring at him from afar. Smile pretty for the camera, McLowery.*

No wedding ring on the CO's hand, she recalled.

When a woman had morals and no money…well, business came first, and dating took money. But after their brief meeting to set up an appointment, this man piqued her interest so much it surprised even her. After she wrote her story and business was concluded, maybe she'd check him out on a more personal level. But first her circumstances had to change. She couldn't go on a date and then ask the man back to her car for a nightcap. She had to make a life for herself, a *normal* life. She was thirty-three, a tabloid writer trapped with Elvis and aliens and haunted toilets, and getting older every day. As they said in journalism class, the camera never lies.

Even if the journalist does.

CHAPTER THREE

Naval Fleet Hospital
Camp Pendleton Marine Corps Base
Day 1

Captain Michael James McLowery, Medical Service Corps, CO, Fleet Hospital Training Command, reluctantly locked up his desk. Time to leave the lovely air-conditioning and make the trek to his car and *its* air-conditioning. He hated the heat. Always had, especially since Hawaii, but he could function in it. For the command's sake, Michael hoped this class—officer nurses and doctors, enlisted corpsmen and support personnel—wasn't as slow in the broiling temperatures as the previous group had been. Class wasn't over until every job was finished.

For today, Michael was off the hook. He'd already planned to take the afternoon off to attend the funeral of one of his stepmother's old friends. In long hot polyester dress whites, no less, which were even hotter than the cotton cammies he now wore. How did Sunshine manage to talk him into this one? He spent his whole life trying to stay cool. Damn sun. Damn California. Damn dress whites. The camouflage clothing he wore was hot enough. He could name a hundred guys stationed in the East, from Long Island to Groton to Newport, who

would trade snow and ice for the hell of this relentless
San Diego sun in a second.

Would the Navy give him a berth home in Boston?
Or anywhere on the chilly East Coast? No. God knows
why. At least Sunshine's departed friend had the sense
to belong to an air-conditioned church. He finished with
his computer program, encrypted it with his lockdown
password, then shut down.

"I'm out of here, YN3."

The little Yeoman Third Class with the pixie haircut
and baby face nodded. Mia Gibson was one of many
who'd joined the military to escape a life mapped out
for them by family. He'd heard that as soon as her brothers had finished high school, they'd jumped right onto
the tractors at the family farm—a job they'd been doing
since the age of ten. Farming was a noble profession to
be sure, but not for Mia. She received her high-school
diploma and joined the Navy as soon as she'd turned
seventeen three years earlier. She hadn't been astride a
tractor since.

Michael momentarily turned back to her desk. "My
pager's on if you need me. B or B only."

"Blood or bodies—got it, Captain. Shall I reschedule
your interview with that reporter from Associated
Press?"

"Jo Marche." He surprised himself by remembering
her name. Ordinarily he didn't bother with civilian reporters admitted to Navy exercises. But in this case...
"Please do. I just haven't had time for it. Maybe tomorrow during my lunch."

"You want to eat lunch with her, sir?"

"Affirmative." He didn't have to explain himself to
anyone, especially his Yeoman. "Eleven hundred will
be fine."

"Will do, Captain. Oh, the staff sent flowers to the funeral home. Tell your mother I'm sorry about her friend."

"I will." His smile was warm. "The staff" meant the Chief, but the Yeoman would be the one to pick out the arrangement. She had a pleasant voice and a calm disposition, which made his office a more cheerful place to work than previous duty stations. "Thanks."

Ten seconds later he was as hot and sweaty as the Chief, who met him outside the Admin building. Michael's administrative department head and computer systems coordinator, Chief Valmore Bouchard carried a metal clipboard in one hand, his other swinging freely at his side. Naval salutes weren't required in hospitals or inside buildings except on formal occasions, and the Fleet compound was no exception.

"Leaving, sir?"

"Just about, Chief." Michael took the proffered clipboard, checked the afternoon schedule and passed it back to the smaller man. "How's the class shaping up?"

The question covered three areas: physical (would they pass out?), mental (were they stupid?) and morale (did they take the training seriously?).

"The good news, Captain, is most of them are from Jax or Pensacola."

Michael nodded. That was good news indeed. The two Florida units wouldn't bitch about the heat, or eat dirt fainting. They knew to keep themselves hydrated. In fact, he'd seen one Jacksonville enlisted with his fatigue jacket on. Some of them actually suffered in air conditioning, something Michael could never understand.

"Not too many boneheaded questions in the classrooms, either, sir, other than the usual computer-clueless.'' The Chief snorted, then carefully smoothed his Navy-regulation mustache.

Michael kept silent, knowing that his Chief's ''clueless'' category included people with doctorate degrees in computer science. He also knew that NCIS—Naval Criminal Investigative Services—regularly visited the Chief to test computer lockout safeguards or ask advice. They generally left his office with muttered comments such as ''Good thing that bastard's on our side.''

''You'll handle the clueless just fine, Chief. You whipped me into shape, right?'' No comment, nor did Michael expect one. ''The bad news?''

''We've got a few *Air Farce* prima donnas enrolled.''

Michael overlooked the Chief's sarcastic use of *Farce* for *Force*. ''Flight surgeons?''

''Aye, sir.''

''Those paper-pushers having problems with the heat?'' If so, it was the Chief's problem to solve, not his.

''No, sir. They don't want to pull their fair share.''

''I'll have someone talk with them,'' Michael promised. That *was* his job. The officers were usually the first to scream foul when ordered to lift litters. Traditionally litter-bearing was enlisted work in the Air Force. But Fleet wasn't like military shore hospitals. Fleet was to the Navy what MASH was to the Army. They were fairly identical after the start-up. A Fleet Hospital was initially set down on the beach by ship-based amphibcraft or flown in on cargo jets. MASH was brought on by truck and Army helicopters.

One significant difference existed between Fleet facilities and MASH ones. Incoming supply and personnel runs continually supported MASH. But once a Fleet Hospital was set up, that was it. The hospital became totally self-supporting, so personnel was limited, and as in the MASH units, doctors often had to carry litters. Field-trained Army and Navy doctors might grumble sometimes, but they knew the routine and did their fair share. USAF flight surgeons, who were rarely trained anywhere but permanent hospitals, tended to complain when first confronted with manual labor. They bitched to the Chief, who correctly sent them to the CO. The whole purpose of the Fleet exercise was to bring together a bunch of strangers who could put up and run a war-time-casualty hospital. In the best of circumstances, the unit learned enough in two weeks to avoid being sent back for a second or third session. At worst, the students made the Keystone Cops look capable.

"Have one of my officers give them the standard 'things are different here' talk, would you?" Michael said. "I won't have time."

"Will do, sir. There's one more thing."

Michael didn't like the devilish twitch at the corners of the Chief's mouth.

"They're from Alaska."

Michael's lips compressed over the foul expletive he was dying to say. He'd give his eyeteeth for an Alaska station, but no, the Navy hadn't figured out yet that happy people were productive people.

"Alaska, Chief?" He congratulated himself on his bland tone. The Chief would be all over him if he showed any envy, any weakness.

"Aye, sir. Those snow bunnies have no desert training whatsoever. And it's going to be another bear today, too."

You mean another bitchin' hot afternoon. Not that the Chief would ever say so. His manners were polite, his emotions kept in military-correct check at all times.

This led some fools to assume the Chief was harmless or, worse yet, stupid. Michael never made that mistake. Fleet Hospital was supposedly run by Admin. But Admin was, in effect, the Chief. Treat him and his staff—emphasis on staff—with respect, and he was a benevolent genie in the bottle. Screw with his staff, and you screwed yourself. The Chief had a keen sense of justice, a better sense of honor and a rich wife who made any financial need for promotion nonexistent.

The Chief ran the place like a well-oiled ship's propeller shaft. Which meant Michael could get out of these cammies and take off early without guilt or worry. The Chief always kept his end of Fleet running smoothly. The man was a credit to his uniform. Always would be.

"Make sure our Alaskan students don't end up face-down when they're lifting those litters, Chief."

"Aye, sir. If that's all, feel free to bug out, sir. Oh, and I took the liberty of having someone put your dress whites in the men's locker room. I also had your car started. It should be cool by the time you've changed."

"Thanks, Chief." Unlike when he'd first reported for duty at Fleet, Michael wasn't surprised by the nicety. "That'll save me time." He returned the clipboard. "I'll be back at 0630 tomorrow."

"Aye, sir. My regrets on your loss, sir."

"Thanks, Chief."

No further conversation was required.

SHE WAS WAITING for him by the car, Lieutenant Junior Grade Mellow, Supply Officer for Fleet. Sleek sophisticated Selena Mellow, Michael's cousin. Technically she was his stepcousin once removed, possessing the same blond beauty as her much older first cousin, Sunshine. Michael hadn't grown up with her, but eight years after he'd lost his mother and sister and left for college, Selena had moved into the house of her aunt Sunshine. She hadn't wanted to leave her birthplace when her elderly parents moved to Arizona and retirement.

Michael called her his cousin. He would never call Selena his sister, for Anna alone held that place, but Selena was the closest thing to a sibling he had, and he loved her like family. He didn't see much of her while he was in college, but she made it a point to see him. A "mistake," an only child who'd never been happy about either fact, she treated him as her big brother. Inspired by Michael, she'd even joined the Navy and requested that she be stationed with him.

Loyal and honest, Selena made him laugh. Just the sight of her waiting by his car put a smile on his face. Although she was lower ranking, she didn't bother with military protocol when they were alone, nor did he insist on it.

"Something about a man in uniform," Selena sighed, holding a clipboard with paperwork for him to sign. "God, you look good. If only we weren't related."

He glanced up, amused. "Not as good as you," he said, continuing the banter. "You must drive your fiancé insane with desire." Although he grinned, he meant every word, despite her moulaged face and leg, the camouflaged fatigues with the ripped pant leg, under which he could see a simulated battle wound.

"Who says we've been waiting for the honeymoon?"

Michael held up his hands in mock horror. "Please, loose lips sink ships."

"I can trust you," Selena replied. "Now get in the car before you start smelling like the rest of us sailors. I wish I was going."

He checked his watch. "It's not too late to make the

funeral. Sunshine would rather have us both. Paul will be there, too, I understand.''

Selena beamed at the name of her soon-to-be husband, then the smile faded. ''Yeah, I know, but we couldn't round up enough safe 'volunteers' from the brig or stabilized mental patients for 'wounded.' Even those detached waiting to be shipped out have been—'' she lifted her palms ''—well, shipped out. So I'm a volunteer.''

''They can use other staff.''

''It's not up to me. Besides, I got out of the watch last week when Sunshine wanted me to go to her latest gallery opening, so today is payback. I have to be on my litter near the ambulance in fifteen minutes.''

''Then, cuz, you'd better hit the Porta Potties now. Going by the looks of that leg wound, you'll be bedpanning it for the next forty-eight hours.''

''I didn't think of that.''

''Who'd you tick off in Moulage to get the bum leg?''

''No one. I moulaged myself when I relieved the regular artist for lunch. I made up my own injury from the empty slot on his roster.''

''Well, I'm sorry you can't come. Sunshine will be disappointed.''

''That's the last time I ask my CO to mess with the watch bill,'' she said. ''It's my own fault, but getting last weekend off was worth it. Make my apologies to everyone, would you? Tell Paul I'll call him later if I can.''

''Will do. I'll swing back here after the funeral and look in on you. Maybe I can find a last-minute replacement.''

Selena's grateful smile made him feel like a million dollars. ''No, don't do that. No reason we should both suffer. I have a fiancé to torture now, instead of you.

Time to pass the torch-ure,'' she quipped, winking at her weak pun. The wink looked ludicrous through the made-up bloody face.

"You should be court-martialed for that one," he replied, grinning nonetheless. "I'd better warn Paul about your plans—not to mention your fondness for bad puns."

Her laugh rang out over the compound. "He knows what he's getting into. Here." She shoved the clipboard his way. "Sign this and go."

He scanned it.

"It's just a couple of supply reqs. Oh, and don't forget, the wedding rehearsal is two weeks from next Saturday. You're best man, so make sure you don't schedule any more classes!"

"Already taken care of." He initialed two spots, then signed. "Later, Slick," he said, using his special nickname for her. With no one around, he leaned forward to give her a kiss on the cheek.

"Don't! You'll ruin your uniform." She gave him a little push in the direction of his car. "Go, already. You'll be late."

He returned her wave and hurried toward the waiting car, anticipating its cool comfort.

THE CHURCH IN Solana Beach was a good thirty miles down I-5 south. First Presbyterian catered to the affluent crowd in town and in nearby Del Mar, the horsey set who lived where "the surf meets the turf." The church was made of real granite and marble rather than the usual spray stucco and pressed cheap tile. The cars in the lot were sleek and expensive, as were the people who owned them.

Sunshine, Michael's stepmother, wasn't a member of

the horsey set. But the high-quality Raku pottery she'd been throwing ever since her go-go-boot days made more money annually than a Del Mar favorite during the Futurity Classic. Her Raku was refined and expensive, just like Solana Beach residents. It was also of outstanding artistry and in hot demand by locals, galleries, L.A. movie moguls and top dealers in Tokyo. Sunshine Mellow McLowery happily lived up to her name. She threw her pots every morning and surfed every afternoon with her board purchased years ago in Hawaii. The rest of the day she tended her flowers, fussed over her retired arthritic husband and doled out both love and food to her stepson, Michael, and her younger cousin, Selena.

Those occasions no longer came as often as Sunshine wished. Before he got involved with FHOTC, Michael's last duty station had been in New Orleans, and even though he was now stationed close to home, he preferred to live at the furnished Bachelor Officers' Quarters. Selena lived at the McLowerys', but she spent her free weekends with her fiancé. They usually met at a hotel halfway between her place and his. Since Selena had become engaged, Michael made an effort to stay over a few nights a month because he knew Sunshine missed Selena more than she'd admit. Sunshine wasn't looking forward to the end of Michael's tour at Camp Pendleton. He'd already served more than two-thirds of the usual three-year duty, while Selena would soon resign from the Navy and move north to Silicon Valley, where Paul worked. To all appearances, however, Sunshine gracefully accepted the loss of her ''children,'' and waited for the day she could indulge her grandchildren.

No brothers or sisters came along after the marriage of Lt. Commander Patrick Andrew McLowery to the much younger, sadly infertile, Sunshine Mellow. He'd retired as a Commander, never making Captain due to hard drinking after the deaths of his wife and daughter. He didn't seem to care. Patrick's days of fast cars and hard liquor ended soon after his marriage to Sunshine. He finished his time in the Navy teaching others to fly jets, retired as early as possible and now spent his days running Sunshine's business and nursing his arthritis. He seemed to accept his change of status with, if not wild passion, contentment in his good fortune.

"Trust a damned Irishman to count his wife's pennies," Sunshine often said without rancor.

"Trust a damned hippie not to pay her taxes," was her husband's standard comeback.

Michael smiled to himself as he kicked up the A/C in his Acura to high, slid in a rhythm-and-blues CD and gently maneuvered the car through the daily quagmire of traffic that was Southern California's signature. Sunshine Mellow and the retired jet jockey. What a combination. And whenever he saw them, the scene was always the same.

The two would gently squabble, while Patrick— "Paddy" to Sunshine—made himself busy with paperwork and phone calls and arranging deliveries while she molded her clay. Sunshine never seemed to mind his frequent presence. She was generous with her workshop, her time and, to Patrick, her still-slim body. For that, Michael admired her greatly. Maybe that was why he was so fond of Selena. Both cousins shared their own happiness.

Michael, like all the other men who knew Sunshine, was almost in love with her himself. She'd been half mother, half dream date in his younger years. The adult Michael knew that Sunshine was the only reason Patrick hadn't drunk himself to death, and the only reason Patrick's son was still sane. Sunshine and Patrick were a good combination. Sunshine had hoped Michael and Selena—not actual blood relations—would someday pair off, but had accepted that disappointment with her usual grace.

Michael switched lanes smoothly. He'd hit the funeral service, try to cheer up Sunshine and then get back to Selena and see if he couldn't find relief for her. Maybe he could take her and Paul out for a nice dinner. Surf and turf, maybe, in La Jolla, hopefully with no interruptions. Michael was as protective of his cousin as he was the rest of his family. Paul, a computer tech from Silicon Valley, seemed like a nice guy, nice enough that he didn't mind sharing his soon-to-be wife with the rest of the family. Michael didn't mind returning the favor. Family ranked right up there with duty. Hell, family *was* duty. As soon as the funeral was over, he'd make reservations for four, which would include Sunshine. His father rarely dined out, thanks to his arthritis and the addition of two brand-new sports channels.

As for Michael's twenty-four-hour-a-day responsibility for Fleet Hospital, he wasn't worried. He'd flip his pager from tone to vibrate before the funeral. The only B or B he'd see today would be Sunshine's friend in her rich-bitch customized open casket.

FORTY-SEVEN-YEAR-OLD Commander Coral Puripong, Medical Service Corps, looked over her new command while walking through the canvas-over-concrete tented halls. Fleet Hospital Operations and Training Command, FHOTC, was the last bit of training she needed to be eligible for promotion to Captain. To hell with staying in the cozy Admin section of the tent hospital. All her future plans depended on getting promoted. Everything was budgeted down to the last penny. Nothing must go wrong. She would whip these foolish, lazy, full-bellied Navy personnel at Fleet into a glowing team for her glowing record and glowing new promotion.

Puripong's eyes glittered with anticipation. She had done everything else she'd set out to do in her life. Getting promoted would be the easiest task imaginable.

She glanced up at the sound of booted feet running inside the Fleet Hospital. It was the Black Guard, the pretty woman with the big rifle and carefully pressed starched uniform. Puripong bit back the sharp reprimand on her lips. The guard had that Hard Look in her eyes; the look that meant she knew about bad times and priorities. Especially priorities. If the Black Guard was running with a rifle in her hands, there was an important reason.

"What is it, Sailor?" Puripong snapped out in her best English.

"Ma'am, there's a problem in the Expectant area."

Puripong could barely understand the rushed Southern drawl.

"Slow down, MA2, and start again."

"Yes, ma'am. I just came from the Expectant area. Some photographer there found a body."

Puripong refused to acknowledge the possibility her superstitious Filipina gut was hinting at. "Of course she found a body. Moulaged bodies are *supposed* to be there."

"No, ma'am. I'm talking about a not-breathing, no-heartbeat body, ma'am. There's fresh blood all over a corpse that's ready for six feet under, ma'am. The body's an officer, and the dog tags say Christian. The chaplain's in there sayin' last prayers."

"Last rites," Puripong automatically corrected. *Son*

of a whore in a sailor's bed! A dead body right before promotion review boards! If I screw up, Older Sister will wail loud enough to wake Dead Mother in her grave back home!

"Secure the area!" Puripong snapped the order. "Get me the training command's CO."

"I already secured the area, ma'am. Captain Mc-Lowery's off the compound."

"Where is he?"

"In Solana Beach at a funeral. I had him paged, ma'am."

Damn, damn, damn! He better not shovel goat shit into my *hut!* "Get me the Executive Officer, then!"

"The XO's on leave, but I notified the Officer of the Deck. The OOD said the Captain's on his way. There's a problem, ma'am."

"A problem *besides* a dead body that shouldn't be dead?" Puripong asked with heavy sarcasm.

"The deceased is the Captain's cousin, ma'am. And he doesn't know yet. Someone's got to tell him." The guard's tone said exactly whose responsibility that unpleasant task would be. "Shall I take you to the victim, ma'am?"

Commander Puripong spoke through clenched teeth. "Lead the way."

CHAPTER FOUR

Naval Fleet Hospital, Secured Compound, Expectant Area
Day 1, early afternoon

DANIEL PRESTON stared at the dead woman on the cot, the woman identified as the CO's cousin. Young sailors—kids, really, pretending to be other dying patients—talked and gawked, unsure of what to do. Hell, *he* didn't know what to do! He'd prayed over the dead woman, saying the Protestant prayers appropriate to the religious classification on her dog tags.

The only person who seemed to know what actions to take was the photographer in tight jeans—Jo Marche. She'd roped off the area with a length of fresh film, using it like yellow police tape to keep away the shocked and the curious. She'd quickly taken pictures of the scene, the people present and the body itself without moving or touching anything. In the meantime, he sat there like an idiot, trying to decide how to tell the commanding officer that his cousin was dead.

"Who's in charge here?" Daniel heard Jo Marche ask. "Where're the MPs? Somebody with rank?"

"That would be me," Daniel said. "I've sent for help. I hope you won't mind giving up your film. I doubt you'll be able to keep it."

"I won't mind," she said. To her credit, she spoke in a low hushed voice. "That's the least of my worries. She doesn't look much older than I am. How could anyone do this?"

"I can't answer that. But I will have to tell the CO his cousin is dead."

"She's his cousin?" Compassion flooded her face. "That poor man!" Jo bent over and studied the small bullet hole through the vital heart area. "At least you can say she didn't suffer. It isn't much consolation, but it's something."

To Daniel's surprise, her hand gently brushed back a lock of hair on Selena's cheek, then pulled away as a Filipina officer marched into the room, accompanied by a Master-at-Arms, Second Class, and a Master-at-Arms, Third Class. The officer immediately took charge.

"I want everyone out of this room. Witnesses will muster outside the guard shack." Puripong's eyes took in the cordoned-off area, the photographer and the chaplain.

"MA2, no one is to enter this room until I say otherwise. Touch nothing."

"Yes, ma'am," both MAs chorused as they took their positions, rifles at the ready.

"You two—" she gestured at Daniel and Jo "—follow me. I want your statements and I want them now!"

However, the three weren't able to leave the Expectant area, for Michael McLowery burst through the open canvas door, then stopped, momentarily frozen at the sight of the armed sailors beside Selena's body. He started to approach the bed, but Jo and Daniel quickly grabbed his arms.

"She's...not dead, is she?"

Daniel felt ice-cold prickles descend his spine at the

question—the same question he'd heard years earlier from Michael in Hawaii, over Anna's body. That time, he'd been unable to answer. This time, he couldn't, either, despite Puripong's glare that urged him to do his job. *She* obviously wasn't about to tell him.

"Yes, she is," Jo said quietly. "I'm so sorry."

Michael staggered, then stared at her, his eyes wide, shocked, agonized.

"Dear God, what happened?" he asked.

Daniel managed to find his voice. "She was playing the part of a dying patient. I was told to enter the Expectant area, counsel her and keep her company until she...pretended to die. I came in and found her pretty much as you see her now."

Michael blinked again. "Who? Why?"

"We don't know, sir," Puripong answered. "We haven't gone far with our investigation yet. I've provided the guards with real ammunition and ordered an armed lockdown of the hospital compound. The other patients in this area are outside being questioned. And I've instructed the press woman here—what's your name?"

"Jo Marche. With an 'e,'" Jo answered.

Puripong whipped out her clipboard and located her name on the roster. "Yes. I ordered Ms. Marche here from the Associated Press to act as our medical photographer. The crime scene integrity must be preserved, sir. As I said, all other Expectant patients are outside being questioned by the guards. Once they're finished interviewing witnesses, I've ordered the guards to dust the area for prints. They'll be here soon, but they told me not to expect anything in this heat. As the deceased is your family, you shouldn't be in charge of the investigation, sir, but the XO is out of town. Would you like me to head this up in your place?''

The four of them stood in silence, Jo and Daniel still supporting Michael. Finally he straightened, stood alone and took his gaze off Selena to focus on the others.

''Puripong, isn't it?'' Michael asked.

''Yes, sir.''

''I'm in charge of the investigation. You will take command of inquiries inside the compound—and report directly to me. No one, including yourself, is to leave the compound until a suspect or suspects are apprehended. You, Chaplain, will assist. You, Ms. Marche, will document.''

''Yes, sir,'' Puripong said briskly. ''An autopsy will be required. We'll need the permission of the next of kin. May I prepare the paperwork for your signature, sir?''

Michael nodded, his face a chalky white.

''Chaplain, he's all yours,'' Puripong ordered.

Daniel reached awkwardly for Michael's shoulder. ''Would you like to pray with me and then say goodbye?'' he asked, using words from his counseling textbooks.

''Since she's dead, that would be pointless, now wouldn't it?''

Daniel winced at the harshness in the other man's voice.

''You should still see her,'' Jo said quietly, putting her hand on Michael's shoulder. He didn't brush it off the way he had Daniel's, and Jo continued. ''She didn't suffer. You might want to spend a few minutes with your cousin so you can reassure the rest of her family later. She didn't, you know. She died instantly. And from the peaceful look on her face, she never knew it was coming.

Her loved ones will want to hear that from someone they trust—you.''

Damn! Why didn't I think to say that? Daniel wondered. He felt like hell. Not only had he thought the woman a shallow sexual tease—obviously she wasn't—but she did a better job of ministering than he did. Jealousy and guilt mingled with admiration and relief.

Jo put an arm around Michael's waist. ''Why don't you let me remove her effects for you? Then you can tell your family you were present for that, too. Just stay here, and I'll get them. Preacher, you're my witness. Write down the inventory.''

''Oh, yeah. Right.'' He'd forgotten about that job, too—*his* job—yet this civilian hadn't.

''Okay. One chain with two dog tags,'' Jo said, gently reaching around the dead woman's neck.

''No, just take one to turn in. The other stays with—'' Daniel had been about to say, ''the body.''

''Selena,'' Michael finished for him. ''Selena Mellow.''

''What a pretty name.'' Jo unfastened the silver beads of the chain, removed one tag, handed it to Daniel and refastened the chain around Selena's neck. Next she carefully removed the woman's hair clip, wristwatch and diamond engagement ring.

''She was getting married next month,'' Michael said. ''I was to be best man.''

''I'll bet she was happy about that. Lovely engagement ring. And such an exquisite face,'' Jo said. ''She would've made a beautiful bride. I'll bet she had a gorgeous gown picked out.''

Michael nodded. Daniel winced.

Damn! Why couldn't I have thought to say that, either? I'm supposed to be removing the effects, not some photographer. But she's doing a great job, and there's nothing rehearsed about it. This is who she is—compassionate, not frightened at all, despite the blood. Despite being in the presence of death. While I'm scared stiff.

Jo finger-combed the woman's hair and straightened her bangs, then placed the remaining dog tag back inside the shirt.

"Okay, I guess that's it. I'll sign, the preacher will sign, then you sign. I can stay with your cousin until the autopsy docs show up. You'll need to notify family, I guess. I can help with that, too, if you want, okay?"

Both Michael and Daniel nodded this time and signed the paperwork. Daniel kept the items to file later, as was his duty.

"Sure you don't want to kiss her goodbye?" Jo asked. "I mean, I know it's not a *real* goodbye. But just so you can tell your family you did it for them?"

Daniel noticed Michael focus on Jo as herself, no longer simply part of the surroundings. "Perhaps you're right," the CO said slowly.

He sat down on the bed. Puripong started to say something, then bit her lip. Michael lightly pressed his lips to Selena's still-warm cheek as Daniel opened his prayer book and read aloud the Twenty-third Psalm. *Not very original, but I don't know what else to do. How could I? This is my first death since I became a minister. My first "official" death...*

As Daniel finished reading the words, Michael straightened, his dress uniform still spotless. Jo reached for his arm and walked him over to Daniel.

"You take it from here, Preacher," she said.

But both Daniel and Jo accompanied Michael to the guard shack, the whole compound silent and staring. Daniel started through the gate with Michael until the guard stopped him with crossed rifles. Only McLowery and Jo, the lone civilian, were allowed to pass through.

"Sorry, Chaplain. Everyone's being detained inside the hospital compound until further notice."

"But, Mac, you need me! I can't leave you alone!"

Daniel's use of the nickname just slipped out—although it was against military protocol. McLowery spun around, the use of his childhood name, spoken in such a familiar tone, catching him by surprise. Surprise changed to shock...and then hatred. Even before Daniel saw him mouth the words "Dennis Klemko," he knew.

Michael remembers. How could I ever hope he'd forget?

Naval Fleet Hospital Operations Training Command
Admin Building, McLowery's Office
1400 hours

MICHAEL SAT IN HIS CHAIR, barely hearing the two women in his office. The uniformed Mia Gibson, who had a phone to her ear, was a jarring contrast to Jo Marche, the jeans-clad civilian on the second line. She was talking to the military photo lab—Mia had provided the number—making arrangements to get her photos developed ASAP for the investigation. Mia had Paul, Selena's fiancé, on the phone, just as Sunshine called in to ask if Michael had been delayed.

Michael took both calls himself. He had no choice but to tell Paul by telephone. However, he decided he would inform his mother in person. He briskly told Sunshine he'd been tied up, but would talk to her later back at the house. For the first time since coming to California, Michael felt icy cold, inside and out. He hadn't felt this chilled since Anna and his mother had died.

And what's Dennis Klemko doing here? In uniform? In a chaplain's *uniform? What's with the new name? Did he have anything to do with Selena's death? My God, I have to* work *with that man?*

One hand tightened into a fist while the other reached for Mia Gibson's radio. The young woman blinked as he took it.

"Puripong," he said.

"Puripong here, sir."

"I want a list of everyone in the Expectant room. When you get their personnel files, start your investigation with them—and put Daniel Preston on the top of that list."

"The chaplain, sir?"

"You have a hearing problem, Commander?"

"No, sir. Anything else, sir?"

"Not at present."

Michael saw Mia wince at the violence with which he set down her radio. The photojournalist, to her credit, didn't wince, but her face was unnaturally still. He felt a sudden softening toward her, remembering her kindness to him, just as Chief Bouchard walked in carrying Michael's cammies and a clipboard with paperwork acknowledging a death. Only the CO could fill it out.

I never did make it to the funeral. And I can't leave the compound now—not until this is solved.

"Thanks, Chief. Why don't you take Ms. Marche and get her a drink? She looks a bit shaken. I'll catch up to you after I change."

"Aye, sir. Captain, what the hell happened?"

Michael noted the unmilitary "hell" in the other man's speech. *Even the Chief's shaken. I'm in this alone.*

OUTSIDE THE COMPOUND was the staff's "break area," a net-covered space on the tarmac where sodas and snacks were available, and those sailors addicted to nicotine could pause for a smoke. Jo took the soda Chief Bouchard handed her, wishing it was a scotch and soda, and pretended a calm she was far from feeling.

So much for my plan. Mr. Smart-and-Sexy and his training hospital were supposed to be my ticket out of here. How long before he realizes he has no accurate information on me? And I'm tossed in jail for forgery, trespassing on government property and fraud? Could they charge me with treason? It's still punishable by death—and fake IDs often mean spies or terrorists.

The marines at the rifle ranges over the hills opened fire. Jo jumped and nearly dropped her soda. One of two sailors smoking cigarettes nearby grinned.

"Hey, you'll get used to it. You'll be hearing the heavier artillery later on. Nothin' to worry about."

"The hell it isn't," she muttered. "There's a body in the compound with a bullet hole through it, so don't tell me not to worry."

The two sailors stared at her, then at each other.

"Haven't you heard?" Jo asked. Incredulously she glanced at her watch and saw that only about twenty minutes had passed since the discovery of Selena's death. From the way the men reacted, they obviously hadn't heard.

I'd better keep my big mouth shut, Jo thought as the two reached for their radios and hustled off toward the Admin building. *Time for East St. Louis rules now, not civilized rules.*

What am I going to do? If I hightail it outta here, they'll bring me back. I have nothing to run toward, anyway. But if I can help with this investigation, help catch whoever killed McLowery's cousin, then maybe the man will go easy on me. He's a nice guy—I like him better than the preacher. In fact, I like him more than any man I've met in a long time. Just my luck to meet McLowery at the scene of a family tragedy.

Jo longingly eyed the half-smoked butt still burning in the sand-filled mini oil drum that served as an ashtray. She'd quit years ago, after a three-year high-school addiction, back in the days when she'd copped a tough teen attitude, along with a nagging smoker's cough, like most of the kids at her eastside high school.

I shouldn't. But if I'm going to jail, does it really matter? She picked up the butt, then suddenly, firmly, snuffed it out. *I need to focus on two things: helping Captain McLowery find his cousin's killer—and staying out of jail. The first should take care of the second. But if it doesn't...*

She didn't dare think any further than that.

Naval Fleet Hospital—Morgue
Day 1, night

OUTSIDE THE CANVAS HOSPITAL, the sound of the gas generators filled the air, drowning out most quiet conversation. Inside the hospital, the silence seemed deafening to Michael. The autopsy was in progress and being photographed by Jo Marche. He'd waited outside with Puripong and rat fink Klemko.

Preston, he reminded himself, aghast at his slip into the past and the childhood vocabulary of insults. *Chaplain Preston.* Puripong said the name had checked out. Preston, formerly Klemko, was legit. Michael sent Puripong back to her tasks, leaving him alone with the chaplain. No one save Jo and himself were allowed out of the compound, the murder scene.

"You're free to leave, as well, Klem—that is, Chaplain. Return to your training duties."

"But, sir, perhaps you and I should sit...talk..."

"I neither want nor need your services," Michael said sharply.

"I understand, Captain. However, that young woman in there is not a combat photographer. *She* may need my support. Sir."

Michael felt grudging admiration for the man he would always think of as Klemko. "She handles herself well in difficult circumstances," he said.

Daniel nodded. "She's also not all she appears to be, sir. Her clothes look rather worn and her camera equipment is dated. The gear is all pawn shop specials, judging by the numbers scratched onto the sides. And she's not afraid of death. By her reaction to...the events of today, I'd say she's been in war zones herself."

"Quite observant, Chaplain."

"I may not be much of a minister, sir. But I do have a brain—and I do know that Ms. Marche won't have a personnel file like the rest of us. She and I were the first people on the scene. I know I didn't kill your cousin," Daniel said bluntly. "But I don't know if she did or not. That worries me more than our sudden..."

"Reunion?" Michael finished.

"I didn't plan this, sir. I'm probably the last person in the world you want to see right now. However, I know my duty. To you, to your cousin and to this command. That woman and I are probably the only two people in this compound who dare override or disobey your orders—damn dangerous for two suspects. As I said before, I'm not worried about myself. But a woman who claims to be an AP journalist but can't afford more than threadbare clothes, let alone a decent camera, bears watching.''

"How the hell do you know?''

"I searched her backpack, sir, while she was photographing your cousin. I may not be your favorite person, but I'm not taking the rap for this. I'm no murderer.''

Michael actually managed a smile—a smile that didn't reach his eyes—a silent gesture that loudly contradicted Daniel's words.

"Your sister's death was an accident I set in motion,'' Daniel admitted. "I can't do anything about it. But I can help you get through this, if you'll let me.''

"Not in this lifetime, sailor. Or the next.''

Michael's gaze slid over to Jo, who emerged from the surgery section of the canvas hospital.

"They're finishing up the autopsy,'' she answered their silent question, "but they're done with me. I thought I'd hand-deliver the film to Puripong.''

"No. I'll deliver it myself,'' Michael said. He stood, forcing Daniel to stand, as well. "See the body to the morgue section when they're done, Chaplain. Have the surgeon contact Puripong with the results when she's done. Ms. Marche, you're with me.''

Jo easily kept pace with him, only occasionally watching her step, Michael observed. He knew the placement of all the canvas seams and taped-down running cables; she didn't but seemed graceful nonetheless. Alert and calm.

Not like a murderer at all. She couldn't be, the way she acted around Selena, Michael instinctively felt. As always, he trusted his instincts. Few men with bad instincts lasted long in the military.

"Is Jo Marche your real name?'' he asked.

The woman at his side shook her head. "It's my pseudonym. I don't write under my own name—which is Lori Sepanik, by the way. Too ethnic for the white-bread world of media.''

Klemko was right. One point for him. ''Do you always use pawned camera equipment on the job, Ms. Sepanik? And how long have you worked for the Associated Press?''

''Call me Jo, please. Or Ms. Marche, if you want to be formal. Though under the circumstances…I think we're past polite introductions.''

She swayed on her feet, and Michael caught her arm. ''You okay?''

''No,'' she murmured as he half-walked, half-supported her to a chair inside the manned Ops room.

There were curious looks from sailors.

''Carry on,'' he said. ''Someone get her some water.''

Michael sat her down and pushed her head between her knees. ''Breathe deeply.''

She breathed. Someone approached with bottled water, the lid already removed. Michael shoved it into Jo's hand.

''Here, drink this,'' he ordered. Michael waited until she'd finished the water, and the color was back in her face. ''Feeling better? I imagine you're not used to taking the kind of photos we've requested from you.'' *Unless the fainting is an act to avoid answering my questions.*

''It's not that. Being cross-examined in this heat's what did it. I hate the heat.''

''Really?'' Surprise distracted him from suspicion. ''Everyone loves sunny California.''

''Not me. All I do is sweat. Plus…today…well, never mind about today. This whole place is one oven, isn't it? How can you stand it?''

"I don't care for the sunbelt myself."

"That makes two of us." Jo sat up and pushed her hair away from her face. "To answer your questions—yes, I'm feeling better. Yes, my equipment is from a pawnshop. No, I've never worked for AP before. And even though you haven't asked me yet, no, I did not kill your cousin. Though I'd like to get my hands on whoever did."

Michael gestured for another bottle of water and again handed it to Jo, pleased that she'd answered his questions, after all. "You understand you're a suspect in this murder?"

"I know." She met his gaze straight on, again confirming Michael's gut instinct that she wasn't a killer. "What can I do to prove I'm innocent?"

"I'll take you to Puripong. Give her your film, then answer her questions."

"Sure." Jo started to stand, but Michael shook his head. "Sit down. Not just yet. Are you okay with all this?"

"What do you mean?"

"Everyone here is a trained member of the Navy, and most are in the medical profession. They know how to take care of themselves in extreme conditions."

"Oh." A smile brightened her face. "You mean you're worried about me? Even though I'm a suspect?" Her hand reached out and covered his—an action that shocked him because he found it comforting.

"I'm a survivor. I grew up in the old housing projects of East St. Louis with drug dealers, pimps, hookers and gangs. I didn't like it, but I dealt with it until I got out of there. Same with this. I don't go to pieces—ever—until it's safe to do so. You're the one I'm worried about."

Her hand remained on his. Michael let it stay there only a few seconds more before he remembered he was in uniform, and in command, no less. Shows of affection were not allowed in uniform. He withdrew his hand.

"This has to be hard for you," she said.

He nodded. "It'll be worse if we don't find her killer."

"Why don't you let the chaplain help?"

"No."

Jo's eyes narrowed. "You don't like him? Yet you listened to him when he told you about my pawned equipment—I overheard your conversation. Who is he?"

She's got brains. And a streetwise toughness I might need. Not to mention a very nice body... It was the first time he'd really noticed.

"Our parents were stationed together in Pearl once. We never got along."

"No, it's more than that. You're enemies—or, at least, he's *your* enemy. Why?" she asked bluntly.

She's a little too streetwise for my liking. I've never talked about Klemko to anyone—until now.

"Let's just say he's a childhood ghost."

"Yeah, well, I don't like him, either."

"Why not?"

"I flirted with him a bit and he treated me like an Old Testament whore. I shouldn't have, of course—flirted—but it's not like I was serious."

"Then why do it?" Michael asked.

"I wanted an interview. I wanted a big story for AP. I wanted everything except a murder. You know, you should have family here with you. Isn't there anyone you can call?"

"I already have," Michael said, conscious of the personnel watching his every move. "Let's go. Puripong's waiting. Grab another water on the way. Keep yourself hydrated.''

''I will.'' She grabbed two and passed one to Michael.

''So, you still feel that way?'' he asked.

''What—faint? Nah, I'm okay.''

''Good, but I meant romantically interested in the chaplain.''

''Never was! He's not my type. I was just trying to be cute.''

''Don't. There's no place for it in a murder investigation.''

''I know. Besides, any flirting notions I might've had ended when I saw your cousin.'' She uttered a harsh, vulgar oath directed at the killer.

Somehow, her foul language made him feel better. It was exactly what he wanted to say himself, except he couldn't—not while in uniform.

That would be a Bad Thing.

''Huh? You say something?''

Michael shook his head. *I'm losing it. I've got to go tell Sunshine. But then I'll be back...and I'll find Selena's killer.*

CHAPTER FIVE

Patrick and Sunshine's home, San Diego
Day 2, 8:00 a.m.

THE SMELL OF THE BEACH and frying sausage—tofu sausage, she later discovered—met Jo as she stepped into the breakfast nook. Michael had refused any escorts last night when leaving Camp Pendleton, but he couldn't order Jo around. Nor did he wish to forbid her presence. When she'd climbed into his car with him, he'd found her company more than soothing. He'd found it a necessity. Delayed reaction had hit him in the parking lot and he couldn't insert the shaking key in the ignition slot; Jo had silently traded places with him and driven him home.

All other personnel were to complete the exercise as originally ordered—in the isolation of the camp. Jo had been allowed to exit the compound after turning all her film over to Puripong. Jo's night in the tastefully furnished guest room and lush bed hadn't been restful. She'd had nightmares, but not about death. She'd seen her first overdosed druggie at age five in an alley, and her first gunshot victim at age six, right in her own schoolyard.

No, her nightmares had been about failure. Failing to get her story, since her film had been confiscated. Failing to hide that she'd never worked for AP. Still hiding her forged press pass. Being investigated for a murder she didn't commit. And now she had to sit and eat breakfast cooked by a family member of the deceased. Her nerves were taut with stress. First she'd spent most of the money from her last story on fake ID, then ended up witnessing a crime and photographing the scene. She'd been more or less forced to reveal her true name, which would make it much easier for the military to find out about the ID.

Ordinarily something like this would have sent her scurrying to cover her tracks or even making a quick escape. But she couldn't, nor was her decision hard to make. She vowed to think of Michael's welfare, as well as her own, although that hadn't included staying over-night as a guest of his parents.

I only came along to help him out. She'd seen Michael's type before. He was every brokenhearted parent whose son or daughter died by bullet or knife or drugs in East St. Louis, every child at a loss for words because of the raw violence at school or home.

He doesn't know how to tune it out. He can't, or he wouldn't be carrying old grudges around. If you don't take out the trash or at least hide it away, bad memories will eat you alive. People who hold on to the past never make it for long in the present real world. Not that the military is the real world as far as I'm concerned.

So Jo had insisted on going home with Michael to spend an awkward evening. Michael had left her with his father while he comforted his stepmother, Sunshine, and Selena's fiancé, a civilian named Paul O'Conner. The father hadn't wanted Jo's comfort—or presence, for that matter. He'd made her feel like an intruder.

I am an intruder, but only for Michael's sake. I hope his father isn't joining us for breakfast, she thought, pulling on another worn but clean pair of jeans, a clean shirt and clean underwear, still slightly damp from being washed in the shower the night before. She hoped they'd dry soon in the heat outside. The Thrift Store or Goodwill couldn't carry used underwear, a health law Jo had cursed more than once since most of her clothes were stolen—and she'd given up shoplifting along with the cigarettes back in high school. That forged pass was high quality, and she'd paid dearly for it.

As she was paying now, about to sit down with Patrick Andrew McLowery. Everyone except Paul the fiancé, who'd left last night, had appeared at the table for breakfast. Jo didn't like Patrick. He seemed too sure of himself, too smooth, too charming—especially when he was telling stories the previous night about his youthful self flying jets in 'Nam, even if he was doing it to distract the family from their grief.

If he's not a heavy drinker now, he used to be. I've seen enough of them to know the look. No wonder Sunshine serves him fake eggs and tofu sausage.

Michael's stepmother was another story. Jo had warmed instantly to Sunshine, who treated her like an honored guest. She was gracious and kind, even in crisis, and Jo found herself wishing her own mother had been so giving. But she couldn't enjoy Sunshine's solicitude without guilt.

I should have stayed back at the compound, Jo thought. *I'm not family. Michael's in good hands here, surrounded by all this fancy pottery and stuff. Not only do my clothes clash with the decor, I do, too. I'll have to remember to keep my mouth clean. I sounded like trailer trash yesterday swearing in front of Michael. Still, my intentions were good.*

She sighed once—a poor substitute for a good earthy curse word—slung her denim backpack with her gear and meager wardrobe over her shoulder, then headed for the cooked breakfast Sunshine had insisted she share.

Michael and both parents were waiting as she hurried to the table.

"You're late," Patrick remarked.

"This isn't the military, Patrick," Sunshine rebuked softly as she turned a welcoming face Jo's way. "Let's make some allowances, shall we? Good morning, Jo."

Jo smiled at Sunshine. "Good morning, all."

"Morning." Clad in military cammies, Michael rose from his chair to pull out hers and settle her in before a spread of fresh fruit, eggs—both real and substitute—toast and tofu sausage. "How'd you sleep?"

"The room's great. Thank you for putting me up, Mrs. McLowery. You really didn't have to."

"Please, call me Sunshine," she murmured, pouring everyone coffee. "And it was my pleasure. I'm so grateful Mac wasn't alone yesterday."

Jo didn't know what to say to that, so she reached for her orange juice and took a sip just as Patrick made the sign of the cross and started to say grace out loud. Nervously she set the glass down again.

"You don't pray, Miss Marche?" Patrick asked, lifting his coffee with arthritic fingers when the prayer was concluded.

Sanctimonious old man. Jo decided to match his blunt words with her own. "As a kid I did, but our prayers were usually for more food. There was never enough to pray *over* if I wanted to eat before my brothers beat me to it. I lost the habit."

"So did Mac. My son stopped going to church a long time ago." Patrick shook his head.

"Dad, please," Michael protested. "We have a guest."

"It's okay," Jo said. "Mr. McLowery, I'm not anti-prayer, especially after a day like yesterday. Michael could have used the services of the preacher. But he wouldn't have anything to do with Reverend Preston—"

"That's because the bastard killed my daughter."

Dead silence struck the table.

"What?" Jo said, aware that she'd just triggered some terrible memory, unveiled some painful family history. Michael threw his linen napkin onto his plate of eggs, tipping over his chair with a loud crash in the process. Before Jo's horrified gaze, Patrick and Sunshine also rose.

"Paddy, how could you?" Sunshine asked mournfully. "You promised you'd keep quiet..."

"You told her Klemko's here after I asked you not to? Dammit, Dad!" Michael left the table and slammed out of the kitchen. Sunshine made a move to leave, but her husband cut her off.

"Stay put, Sunshine. I'll go after him," Patrick said, picking up his son's fallen chair before leaving.

Sunshine sat down heavily.

"I didn't mean to upset anyone," Jo said. "Can I get you some water? How about some more juice?"

Sunshine's cheerful face had lost most of its cheer. "It's not your fault," she said, reaching for Patrick's glass of orange juice and taking a sip with fingers that shook. Setting it down again, she said, "This is ancient history, or at least I thought it was." Sunshine rubbed at one temple.

"Would you like me to leave? Or maybe you should go lie down. I could do the dishes for you."

"Resting is the last thing I want. I can't sleep," Sunshine said.

After a few moments Jo asked, "Would you like to talk? I'm a good listener."

"I don't know. It's not my place to say, but under the circumstances—maybe you should know how Mac lost his mother and little sister. And how Dennis Klemko was involved."

Jo listened in horror as the story of Dennis and Michael and Anna McLowery was told. When Sunshine had finished, Jo couldn't help saying, "My God! No wonder he wouldn't have anything to do with the preacher!"

"I thought it was all in the past," Sunshine said again, "but I guess I was wrong."

"I wish you weren't," Jo replied. "Thanks for telling me, Sunshine. I appreciate it."

"I only told you so you can help my son. He's tough on the outside but...we all have our weak spots." Sunshine toyed with her spoon, tapping it against the cup holding now-cold coffee. Then she lifted her head. "I have something to ask you. Mac told me Selena—" her voice wavered "—didn't suffer. That she died peacefully. Never saw it coming. Is that the truth?"

Jo blinked. "I—"

"Don't lie to me. I've been honest, and I want the same from you. I loved Selena like a daughter. Her parents never wanted her—she was born when my aunt was in her forties—but I did. I can't have my own children— never could. That's why my two are so precious to me. I need to know if Mac's lying to me, trying to spare my feelings."

"Oh, no, he's not," Jo insisted. "Not lying, I mean."

Sunshine's eyes narrowed. "Are *you?* Tell me, woman to woman. I need to know. Even if she suffered, I have to know."

Jo reached for Sunshine's hand. "I'm not lying. I took the photos at the crime scene."

"How was she killed?"

"She…" Jo hesitated.

"How?" Sunshine demanded.

"Didn't Michael tell you?"

"No, he said he couldn't release any details until they have a suspect—but I have to know."

"She took a single bullet to the heart. Her face was so peaceful that Michael kissed her goodbye."

"He kissed her goodbye? He didn't tell me that."

Jo squeezed Sunshine's hand. "You ask Michael. He sat next to her and kissed her goodbye on behalf of the whole family. He even watched as her personal effects were removed so he could tell you Selena was treated with respect and dignity."

"Really?" Sunshine asked with a mother's desperation.

"Really. Sunshine, I'm not military. Mac couldn't order me to lie. Even if he did, I wouldn't."

Sunshine's fingers tightened around Jo's. "You swear she didn't suffer?"

"God's truth, she didn't. Puripong was there, and the preacher…well, forget about him, but we all saw the same thing. A quick death. A peaceful face. Just…death, and a still, sad kind of beauty. Nothing else."

Sunshine pulled her hand away to wipe sudden tears from her face. "Why, though? Why would someone kill Selena?"

"I don't know. I wish they hadn't. I'm so sorry."

Sunshine stood up. "Thank you. I…excuse me, but I need to check on…" Her voice trailed off.

"But what about your breakfast? Don't you want to

finish?'' Jo spoke to the walls as a crying Sunshine raced from the room.

Alone, Jo ate her cold eggs and cold toast, then switched her plate for Sunshine's and finished it, as well. She cleared and loaded most of the dirty dishes into the dishwasher. Next she took the leftover dry toast and the cut fruit, wrapped it and stuffed it in her backpack. She couldn't bear to see it thrown out. Finally she loaded the men's plates into the dishwasher.

Just when it seemed that no one would return for her, Michael reappeared, military blue ball cap labelled FHOTC and car keys in hand.

"Let's go," he said. "We have work to do."

Fleet Hospital Compound
Day 2, morning

CHAPLAIN DANIEL PRESTON watched as Jo stepped into the chapel area of the canvas hospital, her camera at her side, just as he started his morning service. By now, almost everyone knew about the death of Selena Mellow, and those who didn't soon became aware of it by listening to his sermon. Daniel watched Jo lift her camera and unobtrusively snap some shots of the gathering from several different angles. Daniel said a few more words, read a final verse from the Good Book, offered a final blessing for the soul of Selena Mellow and sent the assembled worshipers on their way. They hustled back to their duty posts, leaving Jo alone with Dan.

"Good morning, Ms. Marche," Daniel said, closing his Bible and putting it away.

"It's not a good morning at all. For a preacher, you don't pick your words very well. You're new at this, aren't you," Jo said without rancor.

"At what? Praying, or conducting services?"

"Being chaplain to family and friends of the departed. I heard your sermon. All that talk about turning to prayer for comfort. You can't really comfort them, you know. You can only help channel their grief. Once you figure out how to do that, the job's easier. You guide. The sadness is something they have to take care of themselves."

Daniel blinked at her comments. *That's a very astute observation—and something I never realized, despite the seminary.*

"May I ask you a personal question?"

"Ask away, Preacher," she said, fiddling with her camera.

"Do you believe in God?"

Jo shrugged. "I believe He exists. I don't believe He's done much for me or my family, but I guess most people believe that. Like McLowery. Or you."

Daniel almost dropped his Bible at her bluntness. He felt a surge of irritation with her—and with himself.

She had the nerve to grin. "Sorry, Preach."

"And stop calling me that! I'm an ordained minister, a military chaplain. I'm not some tent revivalist from the Bible Belt."

"Well, people call 'em Preacher where I come from. And it seems to me that this canvas—" she gestured above their heads "—is a tent. So technically you're using a tent."

Daniel prayed for patience. As usual, that prayer was ignored. "Tell me, do you respect religion? Or do you always take pictures during religious services?"

"Only during murder investigations. Oh, by the way, while we're airing complaints," she added, "thanks for mentioning my pawned camera equipment to Mc-

Lowery. I'm not a murder suspect yet, however. And next time you want to know something about me, Mr. Minister, why don't you ask first before snooping through my things?''

''Point taken. I apologize.'' Daniel reined in his temper. ''Where's McLowery? In the compound?''

''Not yet. He's over at Admin. Said he needs to talk to his Chief, and then he'll join us, I imagine.'' Jo tilted her head and studied the man before her. ''You didn't kill his cousin, did you?''

He slammed the Bible and prayer book on his podium. ''What the h— What kind of question is *that?*''

''A valid one, considering your history with the man. I had dinner with Michael and his parents. During breakfast your previous name—Dennis Klemko—came up.''

His anger intensified. ''You do know how to be in the wrong place at the wrong time, don't you?''

''No kidding. But at least I can keep quiet. Unlike Michael's father…'' Jo sighed. ''Now you can see why I ask. You didn't kill his cousin, did you?''

''No!''

''I didn't really think so. But since there's an old grudge between you and Michael McLowery, and I'm here under…shall we say, unusual circumstances, we're both prime suspects. Let me tell you, Preacher Man, that cross on your collar won't save you from suspicion.''

''Is there a point to all this?'' Daniel finally asked.

''How about we agree that we're both innocent, team up and try to find the killer ourselves?''

''You aren't a homicide detective, Ms. Marche—if that's even your name. I doubt you're an AP reporter— or any reporter,'' Daniel accused her. ''A wannabe, maybe. I used to be a champion liar, and I can spot a phony a mile off.''

"You aren't a homicide detective, either. And since you're obviously not making the grade when it comes to your ministerial duties, you might as well consider my offer," she retorted.

"My loyalties lie with the U.S. Navy and with God."

"In that order, Preacher? Maybe you shouldn't be taken off the suspect list, after all. I'm outta here."

For a moment Daniel wished he wasn't ordained and could spit out what he thought of her parting shot—before he decided that his energy should be spent on more useful activities—like helping Mac.

JO HURRIED OFF through the maze of canvas and cables, her camera swinging from its strap, her shirt already damp with perspiration underneath her backpack despite the early hour and the hospital's air conditioning.

The preacher's no Billy Graham, but he's right about one thing. How in the world am I supposed to solve a murder? What happens when they find out my press pass is forged?

She headed over to the hospital Admin room, grabbed a bottled water to drink and sat down at the desk closest to a fan blowing cooler air from a plastic vent above.

I hate this heat....

The hot air reminded her of the projects in East St. Louis—the old rattraps that had been declared unfit for human habitation, bulldozed and rebuilt as government-subsidized housing. But before that, the buildings of her youth were hot, sweltering sweatboxes with no window screens or screen doors, no ceiling fans, no A/C. No privacy, either, in the summer, for everyone sat with wooden doors wide open, gasping for air.

Her mother cooked in that sweatbox, while her father—on a small disability pension due to a bad liver from cheap gin—alternated between the drunk tank and running numbers. Her older brother ran numbers, too, until he joined the Army. Same with her younger brother. The baby of the family, Lori spent her days dodging gangs, drunken molesters and drug dealers on the way to school and on the way home—then helping her mother wash laundry in the sink and hang it outside, her frayed clothes in bold view, along with everyone else's rags.

The heat here brought out the memory of those awful smells—urine, dirty diapers, dirty humans and what passed for food in various families. Later on, in her last year of high school, they'd been moved to the new subsidized housing. The old dirty buildings were gone, and screen doors and ceiling fans were part of the new residence assigned to Lori and her parents. But the smells of the poor remained the same. Her dream home—a snug brick house on the chilly coast of Maine—remained a dream. She'd never been there, but she'd read that they didn't have a lot of poor people in Maine. There weren't a lot of people, period. And after living among crowds all her life, that was incredibly appealing. The seacoast photographed gorgeously, too. A nice change from urban blight. One year she'd checked out a coffee-table book on New England from the bookmobile and kept it for a whole three months before her granny found it and made her return it. She'd been foolish to think she could hide something so large for long, and the overdue fines, plus the paddling she'd received, had stopped her long-term borrowing. Still, Maine seemed to have beautiful countryside, no matter the season.

Unlike the foul-smelling Mississippi River in the hot, sultry St. Louis summers. Or the foul-smelling projects in the winter, when the heat provided by steam radiators was set on high to keep the babies and elderly alive, and families spent winters with the doors wide open to keep everyone else from passing out. And letting roaches and rodents creep into the buildings...

Privacy and a cool breeze—that was all she wanted in her life. That, and some money in the bank, just enough to escape from the harshness of her past and present life. She wanted to live in beauty, instead of dreaming about it with her beloved books. She wanted to *see* rugged coastlines and deep woods, instead of gazing at pictures of them, pictures illuminated by a cheap flashlight as she sat in her car.

Look at me now. Crammed into a canvas sweatbox with other sweating people, looking over my shoulder for someone to arrest me—or shoot me. Been there, done that. I've got to find who did this killing. That way I might be able to get Michael McLowery on my side.

Jo finished her first bottle of water and fetched a second.

Michael McLowery. Now there's a man I wouldn't mind waking up with. Nice body, big heart, employed, no police record, doubt he'd hit me. And he needs a woman. But he's not helpless. I really like him. He doesn't collapse in an emergency—or hit the booze like my father. He felt genuine grief for his cousin, too. Despite that, he actually saw me as a person, not a pair of breasts or a nameless face behind my camera.

Jo toyed with the plastic white cap of her half-finished bottle as she reviewed her survival plan.

I've got access to people, but I need to know more about Michael and his background. The preacher isn't willing to help me yet. Time to concentrate on Michael himself. Mac, his family calls him. He won't let this mur-

derer escape. But if I find the killer, Michael will owe me—his gratitude, if nothing else.

If she found Selena's killer, Michael would probably be willing to overlook a forged press pass. *Probably.* Well, it was her best chance at the moment. Maybe, in the end, she'd get a story out of it, too.

Jo strolled through the hospital, unable to find Michael right away. It amazed her how everyone seemed to have a place to be, a job to do and a person to coordinate that job with. Such structure could be either a positive secure experience or a rigid hell. She continued to ponder the point from a journalistic point of view.

It's not like I have any personal experience with structure. My life's been one big improvisation. But I'm getting older. If I survive this investigation, it's time for me to start looking for a little structure myself. No more crappy motels and doing laundry out of my car trunk.

Finally she gave up on the search and asked several people if they knew where Michael McLowery could be located. A corpsman directed Jo outside to the guard shack and suggested asking Puripong.

Puripong—now there's someone I wouldn't want to go up against. I know her type. She grew up in her own version of East St. Louis. I could use an ally here—and a motive for the murder. Maybe one will get me the other.

The guard shack was exactly that—a painted plywood structure with no door, just an open portal—next to the only entrance in the chain-link and barbed-wire fence. Outside, two guards, both males in heavy uniforms, sweated on their guns. Inside, a desk and chair were crammed into the shack, with Puripong wedged behind the desk. Jo could see Michael standing, and the female guard, A. Jackson, in the entry, keeping visitors out.

"May I go in, Guard?" Jo asked, making her voice loud enough to carry to those inside.

"That's MA2, ma'am, and my orders are no interruptions."

Jo deliberately positioned herself where Michael could see her. "Okay, I can wait," Jo said more loudly.

As she'd hoped, Michael spoke. "Let her in, MA2."

"Aye, sir." Jackson slowly, deliberately, let her rifle fall from the rifle-at-the-ready position. She took her time letting Jo pass, which let Jo know the guard was on to her.

Another streetwise woman in the military. Seems the military appreciates cunning. My brothers must feel right at home. Frank's an Army sniper, and Joey's learning all about plastic explosives. Back in East St. Louis they'd be in jail for doing the same thing. Even the preacher knew enough to search my gear. At least the American taxpayers are getting their money's worth with the military. God help anyone who goes against these people. I should've joined when I had the chance. I would've made a good courier. I didn't get raped, mugged, knifed or shot once. Avoiding the enemy's a cinch. Now if I can only avoid jail...

Michael looked up as she entered. "Ms. Marche. Can I help you?"

Jo didn't make the mistake of overlooking another female sailor. She made eye contact with Michael and then with Puripong. "I'd like to catch up on the investigation. Did you figure out a motive yet?"

Michael's face remained impassive, but Puripong's did not. Jo registered the change of emotion. "You did, didn't you. Are we sharing?" she asked.

"Not at this time," Puripong answered.

"So you *do* have a motive," Jo said with a triumphant smile. Her gambit had worked.

Michael threw Puripong a reproving glare. "That's enough, Commander. That information is classified at this time, Ms. Marche. However, since that motive appears to be connected to the military, you are no longer suspect in the murder of Selena Mellow." He swung his gaze back to Puripong. "Commander, I'm warning you to watch your mouth. You just fell for the oldest trick in the book. Keep it up, and I'll be recommending your discharge. Either of you need me, I'll be over in Admin reviewing evidence."

Michael left the shack, his brisk stride barely leaving Jackson enough time to move out of his way.

I'm in trouble now—not with him, but with these two. "Well, that's two women I've ticked off in five minutes. But I can make it up, ladies."

Jackson turned to Jo.

"I apologize for getting by you when you had your orders, MA2," Jo said.

Jackson had no response, nor did Jo expect one. Jackson returned to her guard position, facing outside, and Jo pivoted to face Puripong.

"I won't apologize to you, Commander, because I want to find this killer and I need to know the motive. If you're naive enough to fall for that old routine, then that's your problem. However, to compensate for making you look bad in front of your boss, I'll offer you a piece of information you may find valuable."

Puripong lifted her head.

"I don't know if you realize it, but the chaplain held a memorial service for Selena. You weren't there."

"I was needed elsewhere."

"Then let me tell you this. Wasn't the compound supposed to be secured to prevent anyone from going out—except McLowery and me?''

''It was, and is,'' Puripong confirmed. She gazed down at papers on her desk, affecting a boredom Jo knew she didn't feel.

''And wasn't the compound secured from anyone coming back *in,* except McLowery and me?''

''Again correct.''

''Guess what. Somehow the preacher opened up the memorial service to Admin as well.''

''The chaplain is in charge of morale. If he decided to open up the service to the FHOTC staff, that decision was well within his authority. I assume he cleared it with McLowery.''

''You assume wrong. According to my research, the chaplain of Fleet Hospital reports to the CO of the *hospital.* That's you, not McLowery, correct?''

Jo watched Puripong's head snap up. ''If you'd bothered to read Preston's hand written memo posted on the bulletin board in the hospital Admin, you would've known about the service. And shown up, like I did. It looked bad, you not being there. What's worse is that Preston had people coming in who weren't here at the time of the murder, because I recognized some of them from the main Admin office. Which means the guards let them in. Which also means incriminating evidence could be smuggled out through an accomplice, if there *was* an accomplice. Or perhaps the killer was an outside person all along who came back today to clean up after himself.''

Puripong's curse carried outside the guard shack and brought Jackson about-face instantly, weapon at the ready.

"Back off with the rifle, sweetheart, or your boss here won't get my freebies."

"At ease, sailor," Puripong barked.

Jackson backed up, keeping her eyes on Jo as the other guard continued to watch the gate. Jo took the opportunity to sit boldly on the desk. "Despite the—shall we say, impropriety?—of my actions, I took photos of all the mourners at the service." Jo reached into her backpack, quickly touching the camera inside. "Stick the blame on the preacher for countermanding your orders—he's a brand-new uniform and a reverend, so he's safe—and tell McLowery it was your idea to take these photos. I merely followed your lead."

Jo watched some of Puripong's anger leave her face. "Your assistance is most appreciated, Ms. Marche."

"Naturally I don't expect any favors, but if you could mention to McLowery how helpful I've been, I'd appreciate it."

Puripong said nothing. Instead, she bowed her head and began working on reports. Jackson took over.

"What are you after, Lois Lane?" Jackson asked. "And what are you hiding?"

Jo slid off the desk and looked Jackson in the eye. "I don't have a pot to sit on, GI Jane. I'm tired of writing sleazy articles and getting lousy pay. I started off wanting to do an article on Fleet Hospital, but now I want to write the story of this murder investigation—a *successful* murder investigation—and cash in on it. No one's gonna pay big for an unsolved crime story. As for what I'm hiding…well, we all have a little dirt under the carpet, now don't we? Only, my life's little secrets have nothing to do with a murderer. So I'm helping. All I ask is—remember that. I'm cooperating with McLowery, with you and with your boss Puripong here."

Jo slung her backpack strap over her shoulder. "I've got two brothers in the Army, Commander. Their legal last name is the same as mine—Sepanik. Frank and Joseph Sepanik. They've made a good life for themselves. I want to do the same as a civilian, and I will, if you'll give me half a chance. Even if you won't, I don't miss a trick. I'll work alone if I have to. Now if you'll excuse me, I've got to track down McLowery and pump him for the motive—after I hand him this roll of film."

She stepped outside the dark heat of the shack into the bright heat of the dirt compound, the camera swinging in tandem with her determined steps.

CHAPTER SIX

PURIPONG LIFTED HER HEAD at Jo's departure. "Keep an eye on that one, MA2. She's no fool."

Jackson hesitated, then said, "Permission to speak freely, ma'am?"

"Granted, sailor."

"Miz Marche gave you the film and an out. She also gave you a scapegoat."

"That doesn't excuse the fact that Admin was allowed in on my watch. No one would have dared if the deceased wasn't kin to the CO. I should have seen this coming."

"May I make a suggestion, ma'am?"

Puripong gritted her teeth.

"As long as the dinner's in the pot, you might as well put a spin on the lid."

"Get to the point, sailor!"

"Maybe it *should* be your idea to let those outsiders in. You wanted to see if an accessory showed up—a suspect. That's why you had Marche waiting with the camera. You didn't clear it with the CO, but that's the *only* offense you're guilty of. If the photos help catch a killer, you're in the clear. Either way, it'll buy you some time."

Puripong deliberately hid her admiration. She believed if she let family or staff think they were brilliant, they wouldn't try harder, though Jackson had enough smarts already, it appeared. Why couldn't the military let women run the organization? Women were survivors, and survivors had to think fast on their feet.

"Buying time doesn't get me off the hook with McLowery," Puripong said. "I can't take back my slip of the tongue with the reporter. And as the hospital CO, I'm still responsible for the chaplain's snafu with the memorial service."

"Yes, ma'am. But you were awake all night—and you had half a mind to share the motive with Miz Marche, anyway. She helped you out by going to the memorial service. You were planning to ask his permission when she barged in, weren't you? I could mention that to the CO when I personally requisition more film for your journalist, ma'am. If you want…"

"I am *not* here to tell you your job," Puripong said, the words noncommittal, her expression encouraging. "I am merely listening to my staff at this time."

"No, ma'am. Yes, ma'am. But you know, ma'am, I always thought I'd make a good adjutant to a high-ranking officer. Too bad my marksmanship scores were so high in boot camp. My daddy had bad eyes and no boys to keep poachers away from our chickens, so he was big on teaching us how to shoot. I can hit a bull's-eye, but I can do everything an adjutant does, as well."

Silence. Both had said what they wanted to say. Both knew what the other wanted. Both knew the conversation was over.

"Is that all, MA2?" Puripong barked out.

"Yes, ma'am!"

"Dismissed." Puripong bent her head back toward her paperwork. *If this works out, you may get your wish, Jackson. And I thought the job would be easy.*

Trying to get a promotion in this man's Navy—emphasize *man*—was like trying to find dinner in trash cans back home in the Philippines. She ought to know. She'd done it. Her whole family had. Grandmother, Mother, her two sisters and her baby brother. That was before her pretty Oldest Sister had started whoring for food. Only, she was poor and didn't have money to spend to keep from getting pregnant. So she had to whore for extra food money for the coming baby. Her Youngest Sister wasn't pretty, but she could pick a pocket quicker than her Oldest Sister could turn a trick. Her Drunken Father beat Mother, then ran off, so Mother and Grandmother didn't have to worry about feeding him. Or her Baby Brother, either, because Father had hit him in the head one night. That was the end of Baby Brother. Father had later been put in jail, leaving two extra rice bowls for the family.

That was all that any of them, including Coral Puripong, the Middle Sister, knew of food. One large bowl of rice a day for each of them—if they were lucky. Sometimes it was half a bowl, like if the new Bastard Baby was sick and needed medicine. Or if her Oldest Sister caught something whoring and needed medicine. Or their Burn-in-Hell Landlord decided to up the rent when they complained about having no water in the pipes again.

But two extra bowls of rice! Coral's Grandmother decided one extra bowl would be shared by all until the Bastard Baby was old enough to eat rice. Then Baby Brother's bowl went to him. No one could argue with that. The new baby was a cute little boy, even if he was a whore's child. But Grandmother started a huge fight when she said, ''The second extra bowl will go to my Middle Granddaughter.''

The howls were loud, especially from Coral's Mother and Oldest Sister.

Her Grandmother was firm. "My Middle Grand-daughter isn't pretty enough to whore, nor small enough to steal. But she is smart enough to learn if she has extra food in her belly. I wish to send her to school every day."

The others stared at Grandmother. *No one* went to school every day. Poor Filipinos were concerned with other things, like food and how to get it. Even Coral's Little Sister only went often enough to keep the officials away.

"My Middle Granddaughter is smart enough to learn English. Smart enough to marry an American Sailor." Everyone stared at Coral with more interest. She ducked her head with the timeless insecurity of those without a future. Grandmother had lifted her chin with a bony, callused finger.

"You will get the extra rice bowl. You will eat twice a day—enough for you to stay awake in school. To *learn* in school. To find a Navy Sailor and marry him, so our family will also eat twice a day like you." Grandmother held up Drunken Father's rice bowl. "This is now yours. This obligation is now yours. Do you understand, Middle Granddaughter?"

The faces around her, especially her Mother's, were harsh with envy, hunger, desperation. The smart little brain only Grandmother had realized was there suddenly understood something new. Her family didn't hate her for getting the extra rice ration. They hated her for making them hope against hope that their mockery of a life could be something more—more than just cruel survival.

Coral took the rice bowl from Grandmother's hand

and clasped it to her chest. "I understand, Family. I will not fail."

She hadn't. Every day she ate her first bowl of rice and went off to the Catholic school where the nuns frightened her as much as Grandmother did. Every afternoon she came home, ate her second bowl of rice and spent the rest of the afternoon studying. Every math problem, every English vocabulary word, was to be recited out loud, Grandmother ordered.

"It cost your Oldest Sister extra tricks for your books and school uniform. She wants her money's worth for the Bastard Baby."

The whole family listened to her study. Those on the single bowl of rice didn't learn much, but their hungry bellies and hungrier eyes kept Coral focused, year after year, until she graduated with highest honors, head of the class, a prize student and with a scholarship to college.

Grandmother forced her to turn down the scholarship. "You vowed to take care of us. We have waited long enough. There can be no college for you."

"I will tell the nuns, Grandmother." She did so with a maturity far beyond her years. The shocked nuns listened to her explain about the extra rice bowl. The family needed Coral to marry *now*.

Her Oldest Sister by then had three children at home, and Mother had died of Not Enough Rice. The Oldest Sister took Dead Mother's place at the cooking fire, for she was too ugly to tempt sailors anymore. Coral's Little Sister, now fifteen, was too tall and too pretty to keep picking pockets. She would soon be forced to turn tricks. The Oldest Nephew had a chance to run the White Powder to sailors, a dangerous game. Grandmother now had the Not-Enough-Rice illness and needed expensive pills.

Their Burn-in-Hell Landlord would throw them out into the streets when his Still-Tight-Virgin Daughter married next month. They would all starve.

The nuns had to give the precious college scholarship to someone else.

The whole family watched Coral get on the bus that drove to the Navy base. Rich sailors were looking for Filipina virgins to marry. Rich sailors meant extra rice.

Middle Sister didn't come home for three days. When she walked into her old quarters, Grandmother grabbed her wrist with handcuff strength. The rest of the family crowded close. "Where have you been? Tell me!" Grandmother demanded. "You were supposed to come home before the bars closed!"

Coral reached into her bra and removed money and papers. Grandmother snatched up both, then slapped her in the face.

"Did you break your maidenhead, you brainless bitch? I said to find a husband, not a trick! We raised you for marriage, not whoring!"

Before Grandmother could slap her again, Coral snatched back her money and papers, then, for the first time in her life, pushed her Grandmother away.

"All of you listen," Coral ordered.

Oldest Sister and her three boys clustered together. Coral's Youngest Sister helped a white-faced Grandmother to the bamboo mat.

"I have joined the Navy," Coral announced.

Youngest Sister, afraid of turning tricks and turning ugly like the oldest, flew at her, pummeling. Coral gently pushed her away, just as she'd done with Grandmother.

"Stop it, you foolish girl. Why should I marry a Navy Sailor? He will drink away our money like Drunken Father. He will get me pregnant, go home to America and never come back or send money. His baby will take more rice and we will be worse off than before.''

The three boys moaned. They had known nothing but hunger all their lives. Their mother started crying.

''But if *I* am the Navy Sailor, if I am your Family Provider, all money goes to family. No husband, no babies, no empty rice bowls, no empty bellies! Who do you trust more, this Middle Sister or some Strange Sailor?''

Grandmother gasped in surprise. Coral knelt down on the worn bamboo mat and lifted Grandmother's chin as Grandmother had lifted hers so long ago.

''The Navy took me, Grandmother! The Navy saw the good grades and the good health you and Father's rice helped me get. This money is Navy money! Buy New Uniforms money! They are sending me to America where I will make more! We will have fatter bellies than breeding pigs!''

Oldest Sister stopped crying. Little Sister stopped whimpering. Grandmother lifted wise old eyes, then raised her hand and gently smoothed over the red mark she had left on Coral's cheek.

''I am sorry I doubted you, Middle Granddaughter.''

''I am Family Provider Coral Puripong now, Grandmother.'' Puripong rose to her feet and addressed her Oldest Nephew. ''You, run down to the boat of Elderly Fisherman. His niece just left the Navy. Ask how much to buy her old uniforms. Then come back and tell me. I will slap you if you let that thieving fishmonger cheat us!''

Oldest Sister hugged her first son and shoved him toward the door.

''You, Oldest Sister. Buy rice. Enough so we all have two bowls every day. Fish, too. Your sons cannot make money to support us in our old age if they do not learn. They must go to the Nuns' School. Now send your Second Son to buy Grandmother's pills. Send your youngest to buy a new bamboo mat for her. Make them hurry and stop crying like violated virgins or I will slap you, too.''

Her Oldest Sister smiled. Puripong had never slapped anyone in her life. For a moment the boy's mother looked almost pretty again. Coral counted out money to her, and she in turn doled it out to the boys, who ran to do Puripong's bidding. Puripong turned toward her Youngest Sister.

"You will steal no more. I will not bring you to America if you have a police record.''

"You will take me to America?'' her pretty Youngest Sister whispered.

"Do not interrupt me!'' Puripong yelled. "Listen! You are too old for the nuns, but you can still help the family. You speak English well.''

Her Youngest Sister nodded over and over.

"When the rains come, I shall send you to the beauty school. Then you will get a job on the Sailor Base. You will fix hair and nails of those rich American women. You will listen to them. You will learn all about America from them. Then you will teach our family what you know. You will teach our Nephews English so when I send for the family, all will be ready for America. No one will say we are thieves and whores! No one!''

Youngest Sister fell to her knees and hugged Puripong's ankles.

Puripong pushed her away with one foot—again, very gently. Harshness did not belong in the family; their life was harsh enough already. "Foolish girl! Go make Grandmother comfortable. Get us both a drink and cook us some rice. Then go pack my things. We must find a new place to live before I leave. That will be my job.''

Her Youngest Sister scurried to obey. Puripong knew a moment's regret for the college education she had given up, then shoved it away like a drunken trick. She would attend college later and let the Navy pay. She would go from enlisted to officer, because she was smart and because officers made more money. But that time had not yet arrived. Until then, family was family. She had vowed to feed them as they had fed her. She would never break her word, but she would feed them as captain of her own ship, not as the Kicked-in-Head Wife of someone like her father.

Commander of her own fate that young Middle Sister had become.

U.S. Navy Commander Coral Puripong continued to patrol the halls of her two-week hospital command, her mind alert for anything that might help her career during this murder investigation. She would run both the hospital and the inquiry smoothly, and she would be promoted to Captain. A Filipina captain was rare, but she could do it. Then she would bring the rest of her family to America.

Her Beautician Sister and Pampered Grandmother were already here. Her Oldest Sister and the three Nephews would come next. Her Youngest Nephew would start college in America. The Oldest, Carpenter Nephew, would find a new job, a higher-paying job. Maybe she would let him marry, as Beautician Sister had married a Naval officer now at sea. Beautician Sister would soon move out of the on-base house they shared and into their own base housing when he came back after his deployment. Oldest Sister would tend Coral's house, and Middle Nephew would join the Navy after helping Youngest

Sister move. Of the three nephews, only he was ugly of face, but a hard, uncomplaining worker with determination. He would have a vacation as she had promised, then join the Navy in America. He loved the ocean, had put many fish in their rice bowls and would do well. The Puripongs had often lacked money, but hardly ever brains.

All Puripong's plans depended upon getting promoted. Everything was budgeted down to the last penny. Nothing must go wrong right now, murder or no murder. When this was all over, maybe she would even find herself a man friend. She found safe sex—extremely safe sex—now and then, but had never allowed herself a boyfriend. Boyfriends often wanted wives. Then they wanted boy babies. Or girl babies. Or both, Lord help her! No babies for this woman. She had enough family to support already. A husband was for her retirement— a man in her bed who would make her his Pampered Wife.

If she still had a career left after this mess, a career to retire from. The murder was bad enough; even worse, the victim was her superior's kin.

JO HEADED OUTSIDE into the hot sun, her forehead sweaty. *I hate trying to hustle on someone else's turf. I hate having to hustle, period!*

In truth, she needed to sit down but refused to give in to the urge to rest. This case, thanks to the stress of her foolish romantic notions about Michael McLowery, was taking its toll. Food came first. Jo headed for the mess tent to join the lunch line. After that, she decided, maybe a quick nap to clear her head. Since she'd already met with Michael, she doubted she'd see him anytime soon, so she might as well eat.

Jo was mistaken. Michael joined her in the chow line.

"Don't you get head-of-the-line privileges?" she asked curiously.

"Yes, if I wanted to eat. But I'm here to talk to you," he said, taking her arm and steering her out of line, away from the food.

Jo reluctantly followed him, although her gaze lingered on the serving line. "What do you need to see me about?"

"I've just talked to Jackson and Puripong. I need you and the chaplain, pronto, for a briefing."

"Did you get to eat?" Jo asked, the smell of a hot meal distracting her. "Did they?"

"I can wait. As for the others, that's not my concern. This investigation is."

Jo let Michael lead her to the hospital's thick canvas entrance at the Triage area. The wheelchairs, stretchers and equipment outside all looked like something out of an old *M.A.S.H.* show.

I guess outdoor stuff doesn't change much. Except for the uniforms and the A/C, nothing's really different. Even the ambulances look like old TV vehicles. Only here, this time, the blood is real.

She stepped inside. "Where are we headed?" she asked, almost familiar now with the maze of canvas corridors and rooms.

"To the Expectant area."

DANIEL WAS WAITING for them. Inside the hospital, salutes were not required, but he did rise from the cot where he'd been leafing through his Bible. Michael motioned Jo to a seat, called Daniel to attention and stood before him.

"We've had a possible contamination of the crime

scene and definitely an infiltration of the compound by outside staff. I understand you're partially responsible. You invited Admin regulars to the memorial service— they didn't check with me, and neither did you. Why didn't you go through official channels? That means *me*, Chaplain.''

Michael and Daniel exchanged questions and answers. Jo took the opportunity to draw out the leftover toast— one slice with Sunshine's bite out of it—and the fruit from her backpack, and made herself more comfortable on the cot Daniel had vacated.

The men stared at her for a moment.

''Did you want some?'' she asked politely, and was refused. She shrugged, brushed some backpack lint off the toast and ate her makeshift meal while Daniel received a justly deserved dressing-down for allowing outsiders inside the compound. Jo didn't offer the chaplain her sympathy. Michael bore little resemblance now to the man who'd attracted her. The restraint he'd shown earlier was completely gone.

Glad I'm not in the preacher's shoes. If he hadn't gone through my things and reported on my pawnshop equipment, I might feel sorry for the sneak.

''Fortunately for this investigation, Puripong had Ms. Marche here take photos of your worshipers,'' Michael concluded. ''Do you have anything else to add, Chaplain?''

Jo popped a piece of pineapple into her mouth as Daniel replied, ''My mistake, sir. No excuse, sir.''

Jo sat through a few more comments, ate some more leftovers and then decided she'd had enough of both. ''Now that the proper blame's been assigned, can we get down to motive? And would you both sit down? I'm tired of being fly-level with your pants. What's wrong with zippers, anyway? Aren't those big uniform buttons uncomfortable? Or is that why you stand so much?''

Michael actually stared at her. ''Are you serious?''

''I really want to know,'' Jo said. ''I'm a civilian reporter asking a bona fide question.''

After a pause Michael answered in a brisk teacher-to-student voice. ''Metal zippers could overheat during shelling and burn fabric and skin.''

''Smoking metal zippers…ouch!'' Jo deliberately crossed her legs—not to be sexy, but to break up the tension between the men. ''What's wrong with plastic zippers?''

''Plastic melts—but large plastic buttons are harder to melt,'' Daniel said. ''And they're easier and quicker to replace during lulls in action than zippers.''

''And when you're crawling along the ground, it's harder to pop open a fly that's buttoned than a fly that's zippered. Another reason the buttons are so big,'' Michael added.

''Yeah, but they've gotta hurt when you sit. Talk about a male chastity belt,'' Jo said, uncrossing her legs again. She saw that the men's antagonism had faded. ''Now that I've changed the topic from who screwed up to, uh, personal protection for male soldiers—sailors—may we please get back to more important questions? Let the preacher sit down, too, McLowery, and let's talk.''

Michael's lips thinned. ''At ease, Chaplain. And Ms. Marche, next time save the armchair psychology for the experts.''

The two men joined her on the folding cots in the empty Expectant area as Daniel murmured, ''With all due respect, Captain, it worked. I think the lady's an expert. I'm learning from her.''

"Would both of you quit with the competition and concentrate? I've been cleared of the crime," Jo announced. "It's time to clear the preacher, too, and get back to business. Supposedly there's a military tie-in to Selena's murder—that's what you think, right? And the chaplain wouldn't kill your cousin, either. He's already made an enemy of you once. Why do it again? Why torpedo his own career? It's just not logical."

"Agreed—with reservations," Michael said.

"Then please tell me, who's got a motive?" Jo asked.

"We won't easily find the killer without one," Daniel agreed.

"Killers, plural," Michael announced, grim-faced. "I can't locate the murder weapon anywhere in the compound. I had the place searched twice already—and ballistics so far has ruled out existing compound weapons."

"So there's one person on the inside and another one on the outside who removed the weapon, sir?" Daniel asked.

Michael nodded. "I think so."

"What could these two or more people want? Drugs?" Jo asked.

"Arms and ammo?" Daniel suggested

"Neither. No one's stealing from us. I'll tell you what our search did turn up. Someone's selling fake U.S. citizenship papers to Mexican citizens so they can join the Navy."

"How do you know they're fake?" Daniel asked.

"All active duty military personnel are issued military travel papers, for in-country and out. Civilian passports held by new staff aren't supposed to be used in place of military passports. These, along with birth certificates and other paperwork, are routinely collected and examined. We do that here, as well. One of my staff has a spouse who works with the Border Patrol—he caught the forged one right away and informed the Chief.''

Jo kept silent and deliberately avoided comment on the subject of fake papers.

"Makes sense, Captain," Daniel said slowly. "Once they're in, they get free medical coverage, free board, free food and a paycheck. Not much of one by U.S. standards, but by Mexican standards, a fortune.''

"Wait a minute," Jo said. "Why?''

Michael shrugged. "Without a war draft, our peacetime recruitment levels are down. Americans—this country's Americans—can't be bothered with the low-paying enlisted positions. Those with degrees from college pass up on officer positions. They often make more money in the civilian world.''

"So someone's making money by putting Mexican citizens into our military?" Daniel asked.

"Seems so. San Diego is a border city—a Navy town. Not only do we have the largest concentration of military bases and personnel in the nation, we have the largest in the world. If you wanna blend in with a uniformed crowd, San Diego is the place to do it.''

"Wait a minute and back up. How did you find all this out?" Jo demanded. "I mean, I know that any person born in the Philippines is allowed to join the U.S. military, even though that isn't an American territory. But we don't have a similar agreement with Mexico. So, fine, they have fake papers," she said with a shrug, hoping she seemed nonchalant. "How exactly did you get that information?''

"Yesterday I had our Chief start reviewing everyone assigned to this particular Fleet Hospital class. The paper trail didn't hold up to his computer backtracking for some of our personnel. I just got his report. So far, we have three Mexican citizens passing as U.S. citizens.''

"Someone from Admin would have to be involved,'' Daniel mused.

"Or someone connected with Admin,'' Michael said. "Puripong deliberately let people from Admin attend your service to try to smoke them out, and she requested Jo here to take some photos of them.''

"How clever of her, sir.'' Daniel stared straight at Jo, who stared straight back.

"So for now, you're off the hook, Chaplain,'' Michael continued.

"How does this explain your cousin's death?'' Jo asked.

"I don't know, but it must tie into it somehow…some way,'' Michael said. "Keep your ears and eyes open. Chaplain, I want you to concentrate on the three Mexican sailors—one was in the Expectant area when…the murder took place. Question him first. Maybe he'll feel more inclined to talk to a man of the cloth.''

"What can I do?'' Jo asked, noticing the break in Michael's voice when he spoke of Selena's murder.

He took her arm and helped her to her feet. "We'll talk in private,'' he said.

Camp Pendleton Sports & Snack Bar
62 area—dining room

MICHAEL WATCHED JO dig into her food with a speed that almost, but not quite, bordered on bad manners.

"You didn't have to bring me here,'' she said, cutting a piece from a thick slab of steak, stabbing it with her fork, adding French fries to the tines and circling the whole thing in a puddle of ketchup before popping it into her mouth. "The chow line was fine...really."

"I know." *Hard to realize this woman is poor. But her clothes, the half-eaten leftovers stuffed in her backpack—and the way she looked when I pulled her away from the lunch line.... I've had some rough times, but I've never gone to bed hungry. This woman has.*

"Don't forget to have someone get me some more film," Jo reminded him. "I'm out, and I didn't have that much to start with."

"I won't forget."

Michael had long ago realized that Jo couldn't be from Associated Press. She'd have topnotch equipment and more film than she could carry. Jo was probably using fake ID to get her big story. *And there's no way Puripong came up with that scheme to invite Admin personnel into the compound. That's a Jo Marche scheme to make the best of the chaplain's error, pure and simple.*

Puripong had the wind knocked from her sails by Jo, as well. If it had occurred to anyone to check those mourners, Michael thought, it would be Jo. *I wonder how blind and grief-addled these women think I am? Better to let them believe it, let the whole camp believe it. Someone might get overconfident and slip up.*

He loved Selena dearly, but catching her killer came first. He would grieve for her later, in private, after he made sure that everyone involved was rotting in the brig.

"It's been a while since I've had a steak," Jo said, stabbing more fries and meat with her fork. "Makes this taste especially good."

"Glad you like it." Michael forced himself to take a few bites of his hamburger. *I'll have to check out her credentials....* He sighed. *I'd hate to send her to jail. Some days it's not easy wearing this uniform.*

"Well, what do you think?"

Michael forced himself to pay attention. "I'm sorry?"

"Which one do you think our killer is? A greedy SOB after personal pocket change or some souped-up American patriot following orders? You know, an Oliver North kinda guy who thinks he's doing his duty."

"I haven't fully considered that aspect yet."

Jo dumped more ketchup on her meat and fries, and took a hearty swig of milk. "It might help narrow down the suspects. I'll tell you another thing. There's a woman involved in this."

Michael put down his hamburger. "What makes you say that?"

"Because where I come from, men only kill women for two reasons. One, the woman cheated on him, or two, he doesn't want her to squeal about something he's done. Where I'm from, most men don't like to kill women. But a female killer doesn't mind killing women, and she'd do it in the quickest, easiest way." Jo took another gulp of milk. "You see what I mean?"

"Maybe. I don't know if that applies in the military, but I'll give it some thought," Michael said.

"Good. You see…" Jo pounded on the ketchup bottle again, found it empty and swiped the bottle from the nearest unoccupied table with a graceful stretch of her arm. "When you grow up with psychos, you have to learn how they think to stay safe. I'd bet my last paycheck there's a woman involved in the death of your cousin."

Michael nodded. *I doubt you've had a paycheck for a long time, lady. Though I gotta hand it to you, you aren't out for sympathy—or a handout.* "Anything else you want to tell me?"

Jo shook her head. "No. But woman or not, it's sad about the aliens. My brothers joined the military to escape a dead end. Too bad those Mexicans can't stay and do the same. They have more desire to succeed than some rich guy off the street—like you."

"Issues of security are involved here," Michael said seriously. "And I'm hardly rich," he added in protest.

Jo actually stopped inhaling food at that. "Where I come from, you are. When you arrest those fake sailors at the hospital, I hope you go easy on them. It's not like many U.S. citizens want to take their place."

Michael studied her carefully. "Not even you?"

"I tried. Bum elbow. Can ya believe it?"

"What happens if the journalist gig doesn't work out?"

"I'll waitress in some bar, I guess. Hope for big tips till something better comes around. I don't qualify for unemployment or welfare as a freelance writer. No benefits or anything."

"But you're with AP," he said, raising an eyebrow. "You get a salary."

"Well...not if you're brand-new. This would've been my first job for AP. I should have explained that. And I often travel around and live in different places when I'm researching my stories. Which is why I only have a post-office box in California, instead of a permanent address."

"I see." *I see you cover your tracks quite well.* Michael watched her finish her steak, then gestured to the untouched half of his hamburger. "Want mine?"

"Oh, no. You need to eat it—keep up your strength.

Low blood sugar means the brain can't function at full capacity. You might need that extra energy. Please try.''

For the first time since Selena's death, Michael's smile was genuine. ''You sound like Sunshine.''

''Yeah, well, I'm not your mother. Under better circumstances, I might even show you how different I can be. You're not seeing anyone, are you?''

''Not lately, it seems.''

''Too bad for both of us. My timing's terrible—as usual. You probably want someone classier and more white-collar, anyway,'' she said bluntly.

Michael remembered her kindness during the past few days, the brain she'd put to work trying to help him, and suddenly found himself saying. ''You're wrong. You're a class act.''

''Come on, I'm white trash.''

''You're not trash.''

''Sure I am.''

''You're not. And don't ever say that again.'' Michael didn't realize how forcefully he'd spoken until the stares from other diners finally registered.

''I...okay,'' Jo said, confused. ''I won't.''

They fussed with the remains of their food until they lost the attention of their audience.

''You are a bossy type, aren't you?'' Jo asked. ''Never mind. Eat your hamburger. And for heaven's sake put some ketchup on those fries. It helps cut the grease.''

''That's certainly something I never knew.'' He grinned again, despite his exhaustion and grief. ''And who's bossy now?''

Her eyes twinkled. She went back to finishing the rest of her French fries, while Michael discovered that he could eat a few bites more, after all. *I guess it's all in*

the company you keep. Jo Marche is company I'm start-
ing to get very, very used to.

"You're exhausted. Go home and get some sleep before you get any crankier and scare off all your troops."

"A sailor doesn't scare that easily."

"Whatever. Go home. Go to bed. I'll stay at the camp
tonight. But first, finish your meal."

"Aye, ma'am."

"You mean aye-aye, don't you?"

"One is correct. Two is for Popeye the Sailor."

She actually giggled.

My God, she's gorgeous when she's relaxed and smil-
ing like that. Absolutely gorgeous. And I never really
noticed! Maybe I do need some sack time. But not alone.
Not alone in my bed, not alone in my life.

He continued to eat until he finished his hamburger,
and for the first time since Selena's death felt renewed.
Whether it was because of the food or Jo's company or
both, he wasn't sure.

Was he falling for this woman? If so, his timing was
even lousier than hers.

CHAPTER SEVEN

The McLowery household kitchen, La Jolla
Day 3

"WHERE'S THE PHOTOGRAPHER with the tight jeans?" Patrick asked the next morning at breakfast.

Michael, the only other person at the table, replied. "She spent the night at the compound."

"What, our house isn't good enough for her?"

"I didn't invite her. Drink your coffee, Dad." Michael reached for a paper napkin to place under his own mug. "Where's Sunshine?"

"Arranging the funeral service. I wanted to do it for her, but she insisted on doing it herself. You *are* releasing Selena's body today, aren't you?"

"Yep." Michael turned the pages of the newspaper.

"You should've gone with her, at least."

"I tried. She refused."

"That's Sunshine."

"'That's Sunshine.' Is that all you have to say?" Patrick asked. "How's the investigation coming?"

"Slowly."

"And?"

"And what?"

"Got any more information? When are you going public? When can we print Selena's obituary?"

"No more information, I can't say, and soon, I hope."

"You know, I may not be wearing a uniform, but I'm still your father. Don't answer me like I'm some flunky."

"Dad, I'm tired. Cut me some slack."

Patrick leaned forward in his chair. "You think you're better than me, don't you, son? A better sailor, a better officer, a better *man*."

"Never said that." Michael turned to the sports page and continued to read his paper.

"I'll bet you *think* it. But you know something? A real man would have his own family, his own home, his own kids by now. When am I gonna see some grandchildren?"

"Stop nagging me."

"Your real mother would never have stood for that kind of talk."

Michael refused to answer. His mother and Anna were two things he never spoke about to his father. To Sunshine, yes. His father, never.

"If your mother were here…"

"If Sunshine were here, she'd say mind your own damn business, old man. I can always stay at the BOQ," he reminded his father, referring to the Bachelor Officers' Quarters.

Patrick continued to mutter about the California McLowery line dying out, and how Mac was a disgrace to the family, the family's religion and the family's Irish roots.

Michael tuned him out, continuing to scan the morning paper but unable to concentrate on anything he saw there. *Dad's right about one thing. We need the obit published before the funeral. Usually the chaplain writes it, but not this time. Not this chaplain. Someone else has gotta write it. Sunshine's not up to it. Neither is Dad, for all his tough man act. That leaves…me. I'm not only Selena's cousin, I'm her CO. I guess I've got to write the damn thing myself. Hell.* Suddenly his father's words, the walls, the whole situation, seemed to close in on him. Michael threw the newspaper to the floor and drained his coffee.

"I'm off, Dad. Tell Sunshine I'll call her at lunch."

He left his father still grumbling at the table.

Admin Building, McLowery's office
Camp Pendleton
The same day, 7:30 a.m.

MICHAEL SALUTED TO STAFF outside, then nodded to those inside as he headed for his office. *That damn A/C better be on frigid today,* he thought. The weather report promised more heat, more sun, and Santa Ana winds starting to blow from the eastern desert. No cooling breezes from Camp Pendleton's Pacific border today.

To make matters worse, the *whoom, whoom, whoom* of artillery shelling had started up again. Of course. It was the end of the quarter. Time to use up the last quarter's live ammo with target practice and prepare to receive next quarter's new ammo. You didn't get new unless you used up all the old—which applied to office equipment or weapons of destruction. Ordinarily Michael hardly noticed bursts of noise that didn't have anything to do with his command: rifle practice, artillery shelling over the hill and the frequent helicopter and jet patrols that protected the country's Western coast from foreign trespassers or would-be invaders. The rattling windows and the shaking floor beneath his feet were an irrelevant part of his job environment, something he'd always managed to ignore.

Today Michael found his nerves on edge, bordering on actual rawness. He seemed unable to block out the familiar annoying noises. He felt real relief when he heard Mia, the farm sprite from the Midwest, say, "Ms. Marche's waiting inside for you, sir."

"Thanks, Gibson," he said. Jo would, if nothing else, provide a distraction.

He entered his office and found her sitting in the visitor's chair. He noticed her clean, somewhat wrinkled blouse—obviously hand-washed—the same one she'd worn the day they'd met. Michael didn't care about that. He did appreciate her welcoming smile.

"Hey, you look a little better," she said. "Get some sleep?"

"Some," he replied, tossing his cap on the desk and taking his own seat. "Thanks."

"I'm glad."

She actually sounds as if she is. "So, to what do I owe the pleasure of this visit?"

The smile faded from her face. "Well, it's business, really. But only if you're up to it…"

The *whoom, whoom, whoom* of artillery impacts registered again. Michael forced himself back into his military persona—a persona the woman across from him had briefly made him forget.

"Go ahead."

Jo dropped her eyes to a notepad on her lap. "Two things. I'll start with the easiest one." She took a deep breath. "There's no way I'm gonna be allowed to write up this story, is there? No way I'll get my negatives back, no way I'll even get to write a first draft."

"Correct, ma'am."

Jo bit her lip. "I didn't think so. Would you…would you mind telling me why? Specifically?"

"Specifically, base security has been compromised, which we don't want any potential terrorists to know. Secondly, it's an issue of morale. The rest of Camp Pendleton's troops don't need to know one of us is killing our own. The public doesn't need to know it, and ditto the politicians. That's the SOP—standard operating procedure—and unless I receive orders to the contrary, that's how I must proceed." His military demeanor faded just a bit. "Sorry, Jo."

"Hey, I understand. I kinda figured that part out, anyway. Just wanted confirmation. Well, I'll have to work on something else that isn't military—like my UFO stories."

"I'd love to read some of them."

"You wouldn't. Trust me."

Michael saw her seriousness and remained silent, although he felt more sympathy for her loss of this story than a hardened officer and relative of the victim ought to feel.

"Okay, next order of business," she continued without missing a beat. "I figured that since I won't be writing up any big story here, I could still make myself useful. I, uh, hope you don't mind, but I asked around a bit, and with your staff's help, got together an obit for your cousin."

"An obituary?"

"Yeah. I hope you don't think I'm being presumptuous, but if you're up to answering a few questions and reviewing it, we can whip this puppy off in no time. Spare your family the hassle, you know?"

Michael stared at her. *My God, I've just put an end*

*to her big story and she's doing me a favor? I could fall
for a woman like this....*

"If you want, I could write the eulogy, too. With your
help, I mean. I've never understood how a grieving person is expected to write and read a eulogy. Back home
we shove the job off on the best friend and have the
preacher read it before we testify."

"What do you mean, testify?"

"We each say something good we remember about
the person. Help the mourners relive happier times. I
don't know how your parents feel about me helping,"
Jo said in a rush of words, "but if you want, I'll write
one up—I'm a good writer—and I've got time on my
hands."

Michael continued to stare, the *whoom, whoom,
whoom* of artillery suddenly echoing the beating of his
heart. *It can't be. No one falls in love this quickly,* he
found himself thinking. But the rational part of him, the
part that never lied, knew better.

*I want to spend the rest of my life with this woman—
a woman with a big generous heart. A woman who
hasn't got a cent to her name, lies about her job and
her background, and probably has a forged press pass.
And I'm going to have to turn her in to the MPs for
impersonation, forgery, criminal trespass, illegal entry
of a federal installation and possible spying and/or treason. After she writes my family a eulogy for Selena. God
help me.*

Michael wasn't aware how much time had passed until he saw Jo close her notebook, rise and head for the
door. "I'm sorry. This was a bad idea, huh?"

He jumped to his feet, hurried around his desk and
reached for her wrist, then let his fingers travel to hers
as he gently led her back to her chair. He hoped his

sudden personal revelation wasn't written all over his face. With everything he had to deal with, he couldn't share this yet, no matter how much he wanted to.

"No, it's a good idea. A great idea. You just took me by surprise. I've been worrying about tackling this very job. Dad brought it up this morning."

"Really?"

"Oh, yeah." Reluctantly he released her fingers and returned to his chair, the noise of the mock wars outside suddenly not bothering him as much. "Why don't we tackle both projects right now? The obit and the eulogy. Sunshine will be happy to have them done."

"It shouldn't take long to finish the first," she said quickly. "And I've already jotted down some ideas for the second. Do you want some coffee?" she asked, re-opening her notebook.

He buzzed for Gibson. "Have someone bring us coffee and breakfast from the mess," he ordered.

"You haven't had breakfast yet? You really should eat," Jo said, reverting to the self-confident woman he preferred. "And don't forget ketchup for the eggs and sausage!" she warned. "It cuts—"

"The grease. I know."

She smiled again, one slightly crooked upper incisor peeping out. For the first time in his life, he associated the word "cute" with a dental condition.

Dear Lord, I'm noticing her teeth. I'm getting in deep here. Too deep. What am I gonna do?

What *could* he do, except sit down, finish and review the obituary, then hammer out a eulogy? Hardly the way to begin *any* romance, let alone with a woman he'd be sending to jail. He had no choice. No choice at all. He knew his duty. He was a sworn officer. He'd taken an oath next to the Stars and Stripes. He couldn't disgrace his uniform.

Nor would he. Not even for Jo Marche with an "e" and her beautiful smile.

Fleet Hospital, Main Compound, Typing Room
Day 3, morning

"I CAN'T BELIEVE I'm stuck with a manual typewriter," Chaplain Preston grumbled to no one in particular after the third mistake on a no-mistakes-allowed military form. He lifted his voice. "What's it take to get some whiteout around here?" he asked.

One of the enlisted aides hurried to obey, but not before Preston caught the look of distaste on the man's face.

"Sorry, HM."

The corpsman didn't reply with a "That's okay, sir," to his apology, nor did Preston blame him. In his younger days as Dennis Klemko, he remembered how his father had complained about treatment of the enlisted, by military officers and the media.

"You watch those damn movies, and what do you see? Enlisted acting like idiots. 'Duh, what do we do now, Mr. Roberts? I'm too stupid to figure it out, Mr. Roberts. Even though we run the damn machinery and keep the ship afloat, man all communications equipment and are in charge of sophisticated weaponry, that old ass-kissing, paper-pushing Mr. Roberts has to tell us what to do.' Or Jerry Lewis clowns around, always as an enlisted man. Officers may have college, but let 'em try to fix a broken jet engine, replace a helicopter rotor or pack their own parachutes! Then we'll see who's the stupid one. Hell," he'd say with scorn, "enlisted even get called petty officers. We're not petty! We're the ones who run the damn military! Get rid of the officers, the military still stands. Get rid of the enlisted, and the U.S. of A. can say 'I surrender' to any Commie bastard with a pea-shooter.'' Daniel had heard versions of that harangue many times.

He would've felt more comfortable as enlisted, like his father and grandfather before him. But it wasn't to be. Chaplains were seminary-trained, and a college education rated commissioned officer status, not petty officer status.

My father would have a fit if he saw how I just treated an enlisted over a bottle of whiteout. He's probably rolling over in his grave.

Daniel continued to hunt and peck on the typewriter, his actions interspersed by brush strokes of correction fluid.

''Problems?'' came the distinctly feminine voice.

Daniel dropped the little brush, smearing white on his green cammie pants leg before the brush fell to the dusty canvas floor. ''Dammit to hell!''

''For a preacher man, you sure do swear a lot.'' Jo perched on a corner of his desk, her grin at his clumsiness mirrored by the enlisted who'd originally found him the whiteout.

''Can I help you?'' Daniel asked in a voice he hoped sounded calm.

''Nope. I just came from the Admin building—which is air-conditioned and has a lovely Pentium 3 computer complete with laser printer. My reports are all done. Yours?''

He leaned over to retrieve the brush, cap the bottle and began scraping at his pants with a fingernail. ''Unless you're volunteering to type this...''

''After you went through my undies? And squealed to McLowery? Pul-leeze.''

"Thanks for letting them know about my unauthorized worshipers at the memorial service, lady."

"Tit for tat, Preacher Man. No Tailhook pun intended." At Jo's words, the grin on the enlisted man spread even wider.

Daniel grit his teeth. How could a woman with good looks and better smarts be so annoying? "If you'll excuse me, I have a requisition form to complete—and an obituary to write."

Jo whipped a piece of paper out of her bag. "Here you go—a copy for your records. All done and submitted to the local newspaper via attached file."

Daniel was torn between relief and irritation. Relief won. "Thank heavens! I don't think I could stand using this antiquated piece of junk a moment longer."

"Don't thank me. I did it for McLowery, not you. Did you talk to any of the illegals yet?"

"That's next on my list."

"Next? What's the hold-up, Preacher?"

"I've been…busy with military paperwork. And those people aren't going anywhere," he said defensively.

"Well, your paperwork's caught up now. Come on, let's go find them. You be the dumb cop. I'll play the smart one."

"Don't you mean good cop, bad—" Daniel broke off at the enlisted man's muffled snicker. Ruefully, he followed Jo with as much dignity as he could muster.

Fleet Hospital, Surgical Suite
Escalanta Ortez, Illegal #1

"WHY ARE WE IN HERE?" Escalanta asked nervously. "I'm not sick. Are you?" Her English was heavily accented.

"No, Seaman Ortez. But the surgical suite is one of the few places here with a door, and it provides privacy," Daniel said.

"What's your rank?" Jo asked.

"Seaman, E-3."

There were no chairs in the surgery, so the two uniforms stood. Jo hopped up on the surgery table and made herself comfortable.

"Are you a Catholic padre, Señor?" Escalanta asked.

"No, I'm Protestant."

Escalanta's manner instantly changed. She let loose a little gasp, then crossed her arms. "I have nothing to say to you, Señor. Or to her."

"I haven't asked you anything yet, Seaman," Daniel murmured.

"I did not kill the CO's cousin! I do my job and I do it well."

"Then why are you defending yourself? We haven't even asked about the CO's cousin yet," Jo said in her role as bad cop. "Maybe you have something to hide, after all."

Escalanta flushed at her rebuke. Daniel kept silent.

"We know you're an illegal, Escalanta. You want us to help you?" Jo asked.

"How? By accusing me without evidence?"

"We have evidence that you're not a citizen of the United States." Jo rose to her feet. "You're in trouble, and it's more than violating immigration statutes, Sailor. We're talking a U.S. federal penitentiary for aiding and abetting the murder of an officer of the United States Navy. If we find out spying is involved, you can be shot for treason."

"I am no *traido!*" Escalanta looked at Daniel for assistance.

"Then you'd better find out how to prove it," Daniel insisted. "As chaplain, I can help you."

"As an officer, he can bury you, too. Think about it," Jo warned.

Daniel left the room. *All right, Jo. Let's see what you can get us.*

JO WENT BACK to sitting on the surgery table under Escalanta's watchful eye.

"Can I leave?" she asked.

"No." Jo patted the table. "Wanna sit down?"

"No, ma'am."

"Call me Jo. I'm not an officer."

Escalanta's eyes narrowed. "Then what are you?"

"I work for the CO."

"Work?" Escalanta's eyes traveled up and down every inch of Jo's tight jeans. "I wouldn't call it that," she said.

"Call it what you want. We're close. I've…slept in his house. Yesterday he bought me lunch. And today I ate breakfast with him in his office while I wrote his cousin's obituary."

"Qué?"

"Death notice. Not only that, I'm allowed in and out of here any time I please. If *that* doesn't make you want me for a friend, I don't know what will."

"I'm not interested in talking to the Commander's whore," Escalanta said with a toss of her head.

"I said I *work* for him, not whore for him. Either way, who should you trust? A Protestant chaplain—a brand-new officer—who only cares about his career? Or the

CO's woman, who wants to see her man happy and smiling again?''

Escalanta's eyes narrowed thoughtfully. "You have a point…if you are telling the truth. And if I have done anything wrong, which I have not admitted."

Jo shrugged. "Fine. There are two other illegals here in this compound. You probably know who they are. I do. Tell them what I've told you. Have them check out my story. Then talk it over. If you have any names or details, tell me, and I'll pass them on anonymously."

"I have nothing to say," Escalanta said once again. "I am entitled to a Navy lawyer if I am being charged with a crime."

"You're not a citizen, so you get nothing," Jo snapped. "The only person who can save your hide is me—*if* you tell me who gave you those phony citizenship papers and got you into the Navy. Or tell the chaplain."

"Never!" Escalanta spat. "Protestant padres do not have the secrecy of the confessional. I will tell him nothing."

"I'm a civilian, and I don't *have* to give anyone anything—including names. I'd be most grateful, though, if I could share this information. I'd make sure my good friend, the CO, is grateful, too."

"Do what you want. Am I free to leave?" Escalanta asked.

"Depends. Where are you headed?"

"I am going back to my post. I am loyal to this country."

"You mean, you're loyal to *my* country, don't you? Better watch your words more carefully, *amiga*."

Escalanta left the room, visibly shaken.

Within seconds, Daniel returned. "Well?" he asked.

"Nothing yet, but I rattled her. I've baited the hook and cast it."

"What did you use?" Daniel asked.

"Told her I was the CO's close friend. She assumed I'm McLowery's whore, to use her words."

"Ouch," Daniel said.

"You made the same assumption yourself, Preacher, the first time you gaped at my cleavage. As have others. Might as well use what works—including my looks."

Daniel dropped his gaze before the accusation in hers. "I shouldn't have jumped to conclusions based on appearance. It was a grave error on my part. Please accept my apology."

"What does it matter whether I do or not?" Jo asked. "We're not friends."

"It matters. I've gone through life without Michael's forgiveness, and it's burned inside me all these years. When I went into the seminary, I vowed I'd never cause such hatred in a human being again. I *am* sorry, Sister Jo," he said.

"Well, since you put it that way… We're cool if you skip the 'Sister' part. Though in all honesty, I wouldn't mind being Mac's woman—married or not. And I wouldn't say that to just anyone, Preacher."

"You'd be good for him," Daniel said.

Jo's mood brightened a little. "I think so, too. But we're very different, and I just don't see him making allowances for me. He isn't that type."

Daniel remembered back to Anna's funeral, when Michael had pounded the hell out of him for showing up. He'd carried the scar of his broken nose into adulthood. Despite the years that had passed, Michael still hadn't forgotten or forgiven his transgressions. "No, he isn't. But people do change, and he might change for you."

"Yeah. Just what he needs, a romance on top of a murder investigation."

"He likes you, Jo. What's more, he trusts you. I don't think he trusts many people in this world. Don't underestimate him—or yourself."

Jo tilted her head at him. "You trying to play matchmaker?"

"Me? I've got enough on my hands. I'm new at this job, remember?"

"Well, new or not, say some prayers for him, Preacher. The man's had some hard knocks in life. A shame." Jo slid off the surgical table, her feet slapping the canvas floor. "I'm gonna hit the noon chow line. Join me?"

"No, I'd better talk to those other illegals first. You sure you won't come along?"

"I'll pass for now. I'm hungry. Oh, by the way, McLowery had Puripong put security on them."

"I heard."

"We don't need more deaths." She shook her head. "I don't believe in coincidence. As the cliché has it, where there's smoke, there's fire. There's gotta be a connection."

"Well, clichés generally have a basis in truth," Daniel agreed.

"That's always been *my* experience, Preacher Man. The question is, which truth?"

CHAPTER EIGHT

Fleet Hospital Compound, Chow Line
Day 3, noon

PURIPONG MOVED to the front of the line to get her noon meal. As compound CO, she had the right to move ahead of the enlisted; she'd worked hard for it, and had no compunction about using it. She noticed the press woman already being served. As soon as Jo Marche had filled her tray and sat down, Puripong deliberately joined her. They were alone at one of the tables beneath the green net, which served as both camouflage and shade.

Puripong said silent grace, noticing that Jo didn't bother waiting or praying, just dug right into the fighting-sailor, man-size portions on her plate. The older woman studied the younger. *She's one of the hungry ones—eats like there's no tomorrow. Thank God those days are over for me. Maybe that's why I screwed up earlier. I'm living in the future, thinking about being promoted, retiring, being a Pampered Wife. This woman isn't. She's worried about her next meal, and that keeps the mind alert and wits sharp. I need her on my side.*

"So, Ms. Marche. Anything to report?" Puripong asked, wishing her Oldest Sister was around to cook some decent Filipino food, instead of this bland American beef and potatoes.

"The preacher and I talked to Seaman Escalanta Ortez," Jo said between swallows. Her fork never stopped moving. "She had zilch to say. We did tell her we knew about the other two illegals here. And the preacher will follow up with the men himself. Maybe they'll crack, but I'm not holding my breath. I heard you put protection on those three, right?" Jo squirted some red stuff on her food.

"I did. Jackson saw to it personally." Puripong noticed the packets weren't ketchup. "What are those?"

"Salsa. Adds some zip to the taste. Want some?" Jo shoved some spare packets toward her.

Puripong opened one and added the contents to her meat, took a taste and nodded. "Better. Thank you," she said.

Jo didn't answer. She shoved another chunk of salsa-covered potato into her mouth and chewed.

"I haven't investigated your background yet, Ms. Marche, but I intend to. Is there anything you wish to tell me?"

Jo's fork hesitated.

Oh, yes, she's hiding something. Ms. Empty Stomach actually stopped eating.

Jo's fork started moving again. "Maybe yes, maybe no. But then, considering how ineffectually you operate, I'll keep mum. You might not find anything—*if* there's anything to find."

Puripong scowled less in anger than dismay at the truth of the woman's statement. "I guarantee you, if there's something illegal in your past or present, I'll find it with Jackson's help."

Jo opened more salsa packets. "She's a Master at Arms. My research tells me that's a hired gun, not an investigator. She doesn't have the clearance to get into

Admin's military computers. I suspect you might, but not in this camp. You'd have to get into McLowery's office—and he won't let you out of the compound yet. So until then, ma'am, I'll take my chances.'' Jo dunked her roll in her glass of milk and took a bite, then took a swig from her chocolate milk, as well.

Puripong felt like a little girl again, dealing with her Wise Grandmother, instead of a younger woman. She mentally shook herself. ''Perhaps I should have the CO himself investigate you,'' she said mildly.

Jo smiled even more. ''Why don't you do that? After the rough morning he spent with me writing his cousin's eulogy, I'm sure he'd welcome the distraction. In any case, I'll tell him tonight when he drives me to his mother's house. Maybe I'll spend the night. Again. I haven't decided yet.''

She has her bases covered, I'll say that for her.

''You can spend your time trying to unravel my past—which has nothing to do with the murder—or you can concentrate on the murder itself. I suggest the latter,'' Jo said. ''Oh, and I have another suggestion. You'd better put some security on the preacher. The man's not trained as an investigator—and he might make some enemies questioning the illegals if he slips up.''

''I'd already ordered it,'' Puripong replied truthfully. ''Though I'm not sure how to protect *you*—you keep leaving the compound.''

Jo dunked her roll into the milk again. ''I can take care of myself. Besides, I already have a job. I'm watching out for McLowery.''

Puripong felt a shaft of cold ice slice her gut. ''McLowery?''

''Hey, he's Selena's cousin. Did you forget that? If *she* knew something, maybe the killer figures McLowery does, too. What if he's next on the list? He'd be easy enough to get to. He leaves the compound, regularly. You'd really be up a creek without a paddle then. Maybe even out of a job." Jo stopped eating as Puripong felt herself lose color. "Like I said, I'm a small fish in this murky pond. You'd better get your priorities straight before more bodies start appearing in the Expectant area. Or right at your feet."

Jo scraped the last bit of food from her dish, popped it in her mouth, then rose from the table. "Excuse me, ma'am, but I think I'll get in line for seconds."

Puripong shoved back her own tray and picked up her radio to request a meeting with McLowery. *Time to put someone on McLowery's backside before I end up flat on mine. No one's going to kill the CO on my watch!*

As she rushed through the sun-baked dirt of the compound to the guard shack, Puripong filed the question of Jo Marche's security check into the mental compartment marked "low priority."

MICHAEL WALKED along the compound road, Chief Valmore Bouchard at his side. The two hiked down Christianitos Road, heading west and away from FHOTC. To the right of them lay pure, pristine, original California vegetation—the coastal chaparral ecosystem. To the north, cautious red-tailed hawks and golden eagles circled high above on the updrafts created by hot desert air meeting the cooler marine layers. To the south, the bolder scavengers—turkey vultures, ravens and crows—circled over the artillery and rifle ranges, where man's tools of destruction provided tasty meals of small mammals unfortunate enough to venture into those areas.

Michael needed to talk to the Chief in private. On the west side of the road stood the Hand of Hope. A huge hand made of weather-resistant materials and painted white, it stood just past the bronze plaque marking the site of the first baptism in California. McLowery wasn't a religious man; he hadn't been ever since Anna's death. But he felt the need for a quiet spot where he could talk to the one man in his command he trusted without reservation.

Chief Bouchard seemed the only person around who had no motive. He had no need for money; Michael knew—and so did everyone else—that the Chief had a rich and generous wife. The couple had met in Newport, Rhode Island, she the college-educated daughter of an old-money East Coast family, he a single, uneducated enlisted man from a poor background. Mrs. Chief had ignored the disapproval of her family, married him— trust fund intact—borne him two children, and over the next twenty years proceeded to make a killing in the New York and Los Angeles diamond exchanges. She knew gems, she had wealthy friends who wanted first-class gems, and her bank account kept growing.

Michael had met Mrs. Chief at some of the command's picnic charity fund-raisers. She was a classy lady with average looks but a kind smile and a sharp mind. She took good care of their kids and spent money on a number of charities and on her family. Especially her husband. Hell, his car cost three times more than any of the officers'. Every summer the family sailed to Hawaii and back on their two-masted live-aboard schooner. The Chief's staff knew that when Mrs. Chief called to speak to her husband, she was to be connected immediately or heads would roll.

Only an idiot would ruin a sweet deal like Bouchard had, and Bouchard was no idiot. Rumor had it that Mrs. Chief was busy acquiring controlling stock in a new computer company the Chief had his eye on—something for him to dabble in when the Navy forced him into mandatory retirement for length of service...or when the Chief decided he'd had enough. So far, Bouchard enjoyed keeping the Navy guessing as to his future plans.

With his knowledge of computers, he'd be on top of any suspect list. He had the intelligence, the means and the ability to carry off a covert computerized "paper trail" for establishing false identities. Any operation of this magnitude would demand a high-tech computer mind—but he had no motive. Still, that didn't mean someone else with the same skills and a real motive couldn't pull it off.

Slowing down, then stopping, Michael reached for his canteen and took a big slug. The Chief hadn't bothered with his, in fact, had barely broken a sweat. *The smug bastard. Let's see if he can shake loose some information for me. He's going to do a computer check into the bank accounts of all the mourners at Klemko's service. Let him earn his pay and prove his reputation by helping me find Selena's killer.*

Bouchard listened carefully to his CO's debriefing. Michael finally concluded, "Puripong will furnish you with a list of names."

"I already have it, sir, and took the liberty of starting my own computer checks."

I'm not surprised. "In what order, Chief?"

"Standard military numerical, sir. Social security last four-digit ascending—unless you prefer certain individuals to be bumped to the top of the list."

"I do." Michael ran his fingers over the Hand of Hope, the hand big enough for a person to sit in the palm. "I want you to start with the women."

"Aye, sir."

Michael thought of Jo Marche, Sunshine and Jackson, three women he wouldn't want to go up against. He suspected that even Puripong, on her own turf, would be a formidable foe. What made some women so strong and others like his birth mother or Selena, so vulnerable?

"Any in particular?" Chief Bouchard asked.

"No. Yes." Michael drew a deep breath. "Add Ms. Jo Marche, legal name Lori Sepanik, to the list. Start with her."

Bouchard whipped out his ever-present notepad, green-covered military issue lettered "memo," and said, "Spell it, please."

"S-e-p-a-n-i-k. She says she's got two brothers, same last name, in the Army. The three are out of East St. Louis. Puripong has their first names. Confirm that, as well."

"I'll dig deep, sir."

"You always do." Michael turned toward the clear, unblemished side of the road; he could still hear explosives in the distance. From the corner of his eye he saw the Chief check his watch. "I'm keeping you from your duties."

"I have a few minutes," the Chief said politely.

Michael gazed up at the raptors riding the thermals. "You understand women, Chief?"

Bouchard almost cracked a smile. "I'm still figuring out the one I've got. Here, I treat 'em all as troops in uniform. Makes the job easier."

"This time, pay attention to gender. It may help us catch our killer. We might be dealing with a female." Michael forced himself to face the bombed hills, bullet-torn ranges and bare blackened soil on the other side of the road. "You should probably be getting back," he suggested. "I'll jog over in a few." Since Selena's killing, he'd neglected his military-required daily runs and physical training. He also wanted a few precious moments alone. "If you need me, I'm on radio."

"Aye, sir." Bouchard, who Michael knew never neglected his daily PT, hurried to hitch a ride from one of the rare passing government vehicles.

Even gets a damn jeep ride. Some guys have all the luck, Michael thought. For one petty moment, he allowed himself a smidgen of jealousy, then pushed it away. *But I've got Jo on my side.* He wiped the sweat from his brow, turned away from the Hand of Hope and started jogging back to the heated hell that was the turmoil of FHOTC.

"COMMANDER PURIPONG wants to see you, sir," Mia Gibson said before Michael opened the connecting door between Reception and his air-conditioned office. "Says it's important. Asks to meet with you in the chaplain's office."

"Thank you," Michael replied. He immediately headed toward the compound, through the guarded gate and into the tent. There he saw the chaplain, Jo, Puripong and Jackson. They rose to their feet as he entered. *The gang's all here.* "As you were," he said, tossing his hat on the closest desk and sitting in the nearby folding metal chair. "You wished to see me, Commander Puripong?"

"I did, sir. I'm concerned about your safety."

"Mine?"

"You aren't required to stay on the compound, sir. I can't protect you the way I can protect the chaplain here or the three illegals. Both you and Ms. Marche are vulnerable outside the area."

"I can take care of myself," McLowery replied.

"Despite that, these are not ordinary circumstances." Puripong glanced in Jo's direction. "I must insist that proper security measures be taken when you're off compound."

"I agree," Preston said. "The victim was a family member, sir. Our killer might presume that whatever Selena knew, you were privy to, as well. I strongly suggest you allow MA2 Jackson to accompany you at all times until this case is solved."

"No military members are allowed off the compound once the exercise starts," McLowery said. "Keeping everyone isolated is even more important now that we're dealing with murder suspects."

McLowery watched Puripong and Daniel exchange a look that said, *We knew he'd be difficult, didn't we?*

"Sir, we must insist," Puripong repeated.

McLowery started to rise, until he felt Jo's restraining hand on his arm.

"Listen, Michael, they've got a point," she told him. "Try to see it from their perspective. The preacher here's trying to meet morale needs. Puripong's worried about you getting killed—because it'll screw up her career and Jackson's. They're just trying to cover their asses...and keep yours safe. It's their job. Give 'em a break."

Daniel nodded, Jackson adjusted her weapon, and Puripong's jaw set more tightly.

"I told them I'd try to keep an eye on you, but then I'd have to leave the compound whenever you do," Jo said. "I already did once, since I'm a civilian. If I stuck close, I could guard your back and call for reinforcements if necessary."

"I don't need your protection, either," McLowery stated, despite the surprisingly welcome thought of having Jo Marche's company day and night. Especially at night. What was getting into him? Duty and honor had never been interrupted by thoughts of romance before. Never…

"She doesn't carry a weapon, sir," Puripong ventured to say.

"Not a gun, but she does carry a knife in her pack," Jackson added. "An illegal butterfly with a blade that would shave boar bristles. Tests show there are no bloodstains on it."

Jo lifted her legs, set them on an empty chair and crossed her ankles. "Anyone *else* wanna search my bag?" she drawled.

"A knife is no protection against bullets," Jackson said, directing her argument toward Michael. "I strongly suggest you allow me to guard you, sir."

"Sorry. No one leaves the compound. As for me knowing what Selena might've known—I don't. If I did, I'd have made damn sure *she'd* been protected. Our killer's probably realized that, too."

"How about a guard from outside the compound?" Daniel suggested.

"Can't," McLowery replied. "Thanks to your memorial service, someone most likely smuggled out the murder weapon, remember? Someone from *outside* the compound."

"Which brings us right back where we started, Mac! You can't walk around unprotected. At least get Jo a radio and a cell phone."

Michael felt the old anger rise. "That's Captain to you, Chaplain. Or sir. Don't address me by anything else. As for cell phones, they don't work on base. We deliberately jam the signal in secure areas. Hand radios don't work *off* base, so fitting out Ms. Marche is not going to be possible.''

Those in uniform said nothing to break the awkward silence.

''Come on, Michael,'' said Jo. ''If the preacher hadn't conducted a memorial service, we wouldn't have figured out that the killer had an accessory. As for protection...'' Jo rummaged through her backpack and pulled out an apple. She tossed it to Preston. ''Here, Preacher. Throw this at the cork bulletin board over there.''

''Huh?''

''Just do it,'' she said, reaching for her right ankle.

McLowery watched as Preston did as she asked. A flash of metal whizzed before his eyes, then stabbed at and through the apple, anchoring the fruit and the blade firmly in the cork. Jo stood up, walked casually to the board and removed both. She cleaned off the knife—it wasn't the butterfly, but a switchblade backup—replaced the blade in the leather hilt and put it back inside her sock. The apple she took a bite out of.

''Since MA2 here didn't search well enough to find my second knife—'' Jackson glared at Jo ''—I think I'm the best person for the job—or at least I'm better than nothing. We'll look out for each other, and everyone's happy.''

Michael frowned. ''*Happy* isn't how I'd describe it, Ms. Marche. Where did you learn—''

''Does it matter? From now on, consider us joined at the hip. I'm gonna hit the ladies' room, then I'll be back. Don't let him leave without me, people.''

Michael rose, and Puripong did the same, followed by Jackson and Preston.

''This situation is unsat, sir,'' Puripong protested. ''I think you—''

"The funeral's tomorrow," he said, cutting her off. "I'll have Marche with me and keep a close eye on her. I noticed none of you are worried about *her* safety. Why is that, Puripong?"

"I...as a civilian observer, I didn't think she was my responsibility, but I'll certainly—"

"Never mind. She's mine now," Michael found himself saying.

"Highly unsatisfactory, sir," Jackson echoed.

Michael didn't reply. He stared at the apple juice dripping a slow dark trail from the knife hole in the cork board. That knife sent shivers up and down his spine. All he could remember was the blood draining from the hole in Selena's chest...

...and wonder how he'd ever get through another family funeral.

CHAPTER NINE

Del Mar Presbyterian Church
Selena Mellow's funeral reception
Day 4, noon

JO STOOD TO ONE SIDE of Michael in the large back room where everyone had gathered for the mourners' reception, Sunshine's version of an Irish wake. Michael stayed close to Sunshine and Patrick, while Jo kept an eye on Michael. She felt awkward in this room of wealthy people in tailored garb, especially wearing the borrowed, out-of-style clothes Sunshine had generously lent her.

They fit, but only because they were from long-ago days when Sunshine was slimmer and firmer.

"I'm a pack rat, and I thought they'd come back into fashion again—so I saved them. Take whatever you need, Jo. Take them all if you want and keep them. I'm sure you can find something for the funeral."

Jo had, although the flowered flowing top and billowing maxi-length skirt were a contrast to the tighter blouses and jeans she preferred.

She hadn't packed for a funeral. And these clothes would bring bad memories for the family now. This outfit was going right back into the spare room where she'd slept the night before. Well...except for the underwear, which might be plain, white and dated, but it wasn't as though anyone could see it. She hadn't shopped since her laundry had been swiped from the car....

Jo was peering around Michael to check on Sunshine just as he spoke.

"You okay?" he asked.

"I'm fine. How about you? How's Sunshine holding up?"

Michael sighed.

"She's putting on an act right now," he said, taking her arm and guiding her to the buffet tables. "She'll loosen up later when she's home with Dad."

"Where is he?" Jo asked. "He was here a minute ago."

"He went home. He said his arthritis was bothering him, but I suspect he needed to be alone. He loved Selena, too, although you'd never know it in public."

"But to go home and leave Sunshine here on her own?" Jo said before she could stop herself. "Thank heaven she has you."

"She got me through my mother's and sister's funerals. I'm sure as hell not leaving her in the lurch now."

Jo smiled.

"What?"

"That's the first time I've heard you swear. You need to take that uniform off more often and loosen up. Makes you more human."

Michael returned her smile with a tired one of his own. "I probably should."

"Well, you need any help, you let me know. In learning to relax, I mean," she quickly added. "Not taking off your uniform."

Michael took a plate and filled it with a sample of everything on the table. "I told Sunshine I was going outside for some air. Care to join me?"

"Sure."

"Thanks. I need to get out of here. The only thing worse than funerals is the stupid remarks people make at them."

Michael led the way, plate in hand. In a few moments they were outside in the stiff cooling seabreeze. The grassy bluffs overlooked the ocean, its color the usual opaque bottle-green topped with spindrift from the whitecaps.

Michael took a spot on the ground with little regard for his pin-striped black suit. After a moment, Jo sat beside him. He immediately passed her the plate.

"Aren't you hungry?" she asked.

"I got it for you. Noticed you didn't get anything for yourself."

"Thanks." Jo gratefully inspected the plate. "Don't mind if I do. I figured I'd wait until the family and friends were done at the serving tables."

"Funerals don't dull your appetite?"

"Oh, no. I've been to so many of them I've lost count."

"Whose?"

"All kinds of people. When Dad didn't have food money, Gran would dress us in the best clothes we had and take us to strangers' funerals. Didn't matter what religion it was or if the service was closed or open casket. If there was food, we three kids came and ate," she said, popping a piece of cheese into her mouth. "Gran said that as long as we went to their church and prayed for the dearly departed and family, God wouldn't mind if we helped ourselves at the reception afterward. But we had to be polite and wait until family and friends ate first. I'm a stranger here, so…"

"You aren't a stranger," Michael said. A pause, then,

"I hate funeral receptions. They had a big one after my mother died. I ate a little, but later it came right back up."

"Rough. That's a lousy memory," Jo said. "It'd turn me off food in a second. Lucky for me, I've never been to a family funeral."

"That I find hard to believe."

"What? That everyone in my family's alive?"

"No, that you'd ever be turned off food."

"Hey, I can't let these go to waste. The caterers have to throw everything away, you know. It's the law. The cheese is fantastic. I'll share. You need a little something."

"Jo, this isn't a stranger's funeral for me."

"I know. But Sunshine needs you, and that means you can't let your blood sugar get low." Jo held up a wedge on a toothpick. "You wouldn't dare throw up on your mother's blouse, would you?"

"You and those clothes... I didn't think there was another woman alive besides Sunshine who could wear them and look good." Michael took the cheese into his mouth. "I was wrong."

Jo smiled. She moved the plate onto the grass, and pulled Michael against her. He didn't resist. He lay in her lap as she stroked his head and fed him bits of cheese, deli meat and an assortment of clever little appetizers.

"How's the stomach?" she asked.

"Okay."

"Good. What's this black stuff?" Jo asked.

"Caviar. It's not Russian beluga, but it's pretty good. Ever had any?"

"No—but I know what it is."

"You allergic to fish?"

Jo shook her head. "I ate my share of St. Louis cat-fish."

"I've grown to like caviar. It's an acquired taste."

"Then you eat it." She took a cracker and scooped up some of the roe. He ate the cracker as she prepared a second one for him. "I'll pass. Anything that looks this awful *has* to taste bad."

"It's a matter of what you get used to—and what you expect." Michael sat up, pivoted so they were facing each other and drew her close. He kissed her full on the lips with a gentleness that didn't contradict his mascu-linity one bit. He pulled away, then said, "You either like it or you don't. Come on, give it a try."

Jo shrugged, opened her mouth and popped in the roe-covered cracker.

"Well?" he asked after she swallowed.

"Tasted great," Jo said.

"I knew you'd like it."

"Not the caviar, your kiss. The caviar sucks." She quickly ate a cube of sharp cheddar to clear her palate.

"You're an odd one, Jo Marche. But sweet." Michael released her and returned to his earlier position in her lap, head against her stomach. He threw one arm over his face. "God, I'm tired."

Jo stroked his hair. "Then close your eyes. I don't mind."

"Just for a few minutes." In seconds he was fast asleep.

Jo continued to stroke his hair with one hand as she finished off the food, including the caviar, with the other. She hoped this brief nap would help him through the day. She remained in her sitting position, keeping guard. Somehow, the two of them alone felt comfortable. Felt right.

Fifteen minutes later Sunshine appeared, looking for them.

"Sorry we ducked out," Jo said softly. "But he was beat. I'm going to wake him in a minute."

"Don't. The guests are too upset or too drunk to notice." Sunshine shooed away a fly and joined her on the grass. "You look good in those clothes," she said.

"Mac said the same thing."

Sunshine lifted her head. "Did he, now?"

"Yeah. I think he was just being nice, though. Like getting me some food. Only I made him eat half of it, and then he fell asleep. He was done in."

Sunshine continued to study her. "How's the investigation coming?"

"It's coming, I guess. I'm certainly not a detective, but I think he's making progress." Jo hesitated, then plunged ahead. "I'm worried about Michael. So is Puripong. If the killer thinks Michael knew what Selena knew…" Jo related the events of yesterday's meeting. "That's why I'm hanging so close. I don't mean to intrude. Funerals are for family and friends, but he refuses to have anything to do with an armed guard. I'm all he'd agree to, and only because he said he was guarding *me,* not the other way around."

"So that's why you insisted on having adjoining rooms. I thought maybe you two were—" the older woman paused delicately "—close."

"I wish. But we just met, and under lousy circumstances. Even if things were different, I'm way out of his league. Wrong side of the tracks and all that." *Not to mention that he might be putting me in jail.*

"That's what people used to say about me and Michael's father." Sunshine gathered up the china plate and fork. "But I married him, go-go boots and all."

"Go-go what?"

"Boots. Tight plastic boots for women. Lord, you are so young." She paused. "I should get back inside. Let him sleep. If he complains, and he will, tell him you were following my orders."

"You sound just as military as he does," Jo remarked as Sunshine made no move to leave, but continued to relax, still holding the plate.

"Some of it rubs off. Being a military wife is a way of life. I'm glad it's over for me..." She sighed deeply. "Too bad this reception isn't."

"Stay with me if you want," Jo urged. "You said the guests wouldn't notice, and Michael wouldn't want you alone in there by yourself."

"Maybe I will. Paul—Selena's fiancé—just left." Sunshine dropped the plate back onto the grass, abandoning it to the fly that had hovered in their vicinity. "Michael's lucky to have you."

"He won't want me around when he finds out what I've done."

"Why?"

"I've got a few skeletons in my closet," she said bluntly. "Nothing earth-shattering, but I'm certainly not squeaky-clean. Michael won't bend the rules for me, Sunshine. He's found some of those bones already."

Sunshine, however, remained calm. "Then distract him."

"Yeah, right."

Sunshine leaned closer to her. "Don't underestimate yourself, Jo. My son hasn't let any woman, other than me and to some extent, Selena, get close to him emotionally. Physically, yes, he's had relationships, if you want to call them that. But I'm the only woman in his life now, and well, I won't live forever. He needs someone to watch over his heart. I can't. I suspect you could.''

Despite her misgivings, Jo grinned. ''Matchmaking at a funeral, Sunshine?''

''Why not?'' Sunshine gently touched Michael's cheek. ''You could do a lot worse,'' she said with a pointed glance that Jo immediately understood. ''When you're in my house, if you get a chance to sleep with Michael—or do anything else—I won't mind. And I'll make sure my husband keeps his mouth shut, too.''

Jo remained silent.

''I've offended you.''

''No, you haven't. I do care about your son. But I'm not gonna jump into his bed while he's down,'' Jo said. ''It wouldn't be right.''

''It worked for me. Patrick needed someone. I made sure I was that someone.''

Jo chose her words carefully. ''Taking advantage of the system is one thing.'' *Taking advantage of another human being is something else.* ''What might have worked for you isn't for me.''

''But, Jo—''

''I don't want to talk about it anymore.'' Jo deliberately shook Michael's shoulder. ''Michael, your mother's here.''

With instincts honed by years of military service, Michael woke immediately and sat straight up. ''Sunshine…What time is it?'' He checked his watch. ''Is the reception over?''

''Almost,'' Jo said. ''Why don't you walk your mother back inside?''

Michael rose, let Sunshine brush the dead grass off his suit and took his stepmother's arm. He waited for her, too, but Jo motioned him on.

''Go ahead. I'll be right behind you. I'll bring in the dishes, Sunshine.'' She smiled to show she held no ill will from their conversation.

Maybe that's how some women caught men in the sixties, but sex with a grieving man isn't for me. If she thinks the only way I could get a man like Michael is by throwing myself at him...well, I hope she's wrong. I want him to want me—Lori Sepanik, not a willing body when he needs comfort.

As Jo rose to her feet, plate in hand, she wondered. *Do I have to confess what I've done in order to have a chance with Mac? If I go to jail for fraud, would he wait for me? Is what I'm starting to feel for him worth taking that chance?*

The wind tore at her billowing clothes. She didn't know. She was scared to death—because she was actually considering it.

BACK INSIDE THE RECEPTION area, Michael found Sunshine a seat and became the official host again. *Sunshine's had enough. Time for her to get home and rest.*

He felt surprisingly energized. The nap, the food and Jo herself had given him renewed strength. He showed people to the door, thanked them for coming, had the caterers start clearing and then—the coup de grâce—closed the bar. Michael called cabs or found rides for those who'd had too much to drink, arranged tips for the waiters, waitresses and bartender, then retrieved Sunshine's things. He started the car, cooled it off, walked her and Jo—who had returned—to the car. Before they left, he popped back into the church. He gave the reverend a generous donation and listened to yet another murmured condolence. Finally he collected the guest book, the sympathy cards and the photo of Selena that had sat atop the casket.

All the time he worked, he felt capable, strong, able to function again. The crippling surge of grief had been stanched somehow. The pain was still there, but the agonizing shock of Selena's death wasn't.

The memory of his mother's wake flooded back, and with it the worst part of an overheard conversation.

"They found her stark naked," one of the nurses had whispered. "Just like that picture Michael said the Klemko boy drew."

His mother hadn't disgraced herself, but Michael had. He hadn't been able to eat at a funeral—military or civilian—since.

That was a long time ago. I stopped being a child that night.

He suddenly realized he'd not only been mourning the death of his mother and sister all these years, he'd been mourning the end of his childhood, the proverbial loss of innocence and much, much more. He'd never come to terms with the past—or put aside his anger about everything he'd been cheated of: a happy father, a loving mother, a baby sister. Good friends in Scouting had disappeared, as had school friends, who'd avoided him with the military children's fear of jinxing their own families. So much had changed. He'd never felt happy again, never even realized happiness had stopped being part of his life until now.

Until Jo Marche.

CHAPTER TEN

"I THOUGHT YOU HAD today off," Jo said. "Why are we driving back to the Fleet Hospital Operations and Training Command?"

"Call it FHOTC, pronounced like hot-see."

"You just came from a funeral. Now you're back in uniform. I realize hospitals and the military operate twenty-four hours a day—just like this interstate traffic—but..."

Michael flashed her a quick look, then returned his attention to the road.

"I can see this is a wasted argument. You should've let me drive, though. I'm more rested."

"Looking more like yourself, too," Michael said, taking in her garb of jeans and shirt. "Those clothes of Sunshine's were a real 'blast from the past.' Took me by surprise."

"I'm still wearing her underwear," Jo said. "So I'd better stay dressed if you don't want to be surprised again."

Michael opened his mouth to say something, then closed it again. Despite the funeral, despite the unsolved murder, Jo Marche affected him. She had more sensuality than any woman he'd ever met—and the most off-hand way of expressing it, as well. He felt safe with her, safe enough to eat from her fingers and sleep in her arms. That safety was something new, fresh, desirable, and it sparked thoughts of taking even more liberties, going for more intimacy. Yet not once had she crossed the line of propriety, especially when he wore his uniform.

"Don't worry," he said. "In public, I'm not allowed any displays of affection while I'm in uniform. I can't even hold your hand." All of a sudden he hated the thought of that protocol. "It used to drive Sunshine crazy when she and Dad were first married," he said, understanding for the first time why. "No kisses, no hugs, nothing—except at the end of a war or the traditional greeting when sailors stand Navy into port."

"Pardon?"

"Sorry, I forget you don't know the lingo. When ships go out to sea, the crew stands at the rails of the ship going out for deployment."

"Oh, like in the Navy anthem! 'Stand Navy out to sea...'" Jo sang.

He nodded. "When the ships come in, the process happens in reverse, only everyone in the crew wears dress uniforms. The families get all dressed up, too, and wait with banners and flowers and balloons. When the crew's piped ashore, they're allowed to display affection."

"A lovely tradition. So otherwise, no hugs in military duds. Got it."

"You've got brothers. You never learned about dress and behavior codes from them?"

"They're Army, and they're involved in more clandestine jobs than yours. Army version of Navy Seals."

"Green Berets?"

"Yeah. They aren't colored balloons and confetti guys."

"You keep in touch?"

"Enough. In my family, it's every adult for himself. Mom and Grandma kept us alive and out of jail, so I can't complain.... Though I do miss the boys."

Michael once more glanced away from the road to study her. "In some ways, the military's like one great big family. We look out for our own—usually."

Jo continued to gaze out the window. "Can we stop and look at the ocean?" she asked, startling him with an abrupt but welcome change of subject.

"I'm not allowed to be on civilian land in my cammies. I can only leave my car in them while on base."

"Why?"

"Because cammies have become a popular fashion. By restricting their use to wartime and to military land, we can tell the difference between sailors and civilians."

"Oh. I wanted to walk on the beach...."

Michael heard such disappointment in her voice that he asked, "Haven't you ever seen the ocean?"

"Sure I have. Every time we drive up here."

"I meant, close up."

"No. I wanted to get my feet wet. Maybe put some sand in an envelope and mail it home. My grandmother always wanted to see the Pacific."

"I can stop and sit in the car," Michael offered.

"That's okay. Another time."

"I'll take you to the beach myself." Within the privacy of the car, he reached for her left hand and held it tight. "I promise."

"Really?"

"Hey, a promise is a promise." *And I'd better watch myself or God knows what I'll be promising her next.*

Somehow, that thought appealed more than he would've thought possible.

Her fingers squeezed his, then she loosened her grip. He knew she was graciously allowing him a way to release her hand. He didn't take it. Her hand felt comfortable in his—just like her embrace earlier, on the grass. To most men, it might not seem like much. But for him, right now, it was more than enough.

THE *WHOOM, WHOOM, WHOOM* of artillery met them as they continued the drive to FHOTC in the golden summer light of the setting sun. He noticed Jo flinching at each impact.

"They never target this side of the ridge," he said, wishing he still held her hand. He'd withdrawn his upon approaching the guard shack at the entrance gate. Her physical presence had washed over him and broken through his reserve and his grief like waves upon a crumbling shore. *If only this was over...and I could be with Jo under normal circumstances.* "It's always the opposite side, remember?"

"I know. But it's hard to ignore the sound when you grow up in an inner-city war zone."

"If it was as bad as you say, I'm surprised you didn't get conditioned to the noise."

Jo smiled. "I got conditioned—conditioned to run for cover. You should see me hit the deck, to use your lingo, when the bullets start flying." She faced him, her manner less tense. "Funny, isn't it? You're the one wearing the uniform, yet I'm the one who's been in combat situations. In a real war, I wonder who'd be more prepared."

Michael took his eyes off the road at her words. "I would like to think both of us."

Jo shook her head. "No way. At least not during those first few minutes. I'd react instinctively. Duck and cover. Advance or retreat. I wouldn't even have to think. You would—at least at first. I read that if you managed to survive your first few weeks in Vietnam, you had a good chance of getting home. That the majority of deaths occurred during the very early part of a rookie's tour."

Michael's lips pressed together in a thin line. He didn't like his fighting ability being questioned, especially by a civilian.

"I know I'm right," she went on. "I mean, about what I read. I read a lot. I don't forget much."

Michael slowed the car to a crawl. There was no traffic ahead or on the road behind them. "Is there a point to this?"

"You wouldn't be letting me help if you didn't think me capable. You didn't even argue about letting me play Watson to your Sherlock. Not once did you question my abilities. Why is that, McLowery?"

"Because you're strong. Brave. Smart. And you can throw that knife of yours like someone who knows her life depends on it."

"And?"

"Because I recognize the fighter in you."

Jo nodded. "Exactly. So why won't you recognize the fighter in another man? And use his skills? Like the preacher? Also known as Dennis Klemko."

"Son of a bitch!" Michael jammed on the brakes, slammed the gear into park and exited his car. He left the door open, keys still dangling in the ignition with the engine running. Hot outside air clashed with the cooler air inside, steaming the window glass.

Jo opened her own door to hurry after him. "He's a survivor, too! Anyone can see it. Why won't you?"

Michael continued to stomp through the grass. "Son of a *damn* bitch!"

"He wants to help. He has the skills to help! And he's the only one, the *only* one in this compound besides me, who has no motive!"

"Son of a bitch of a bastard!"

"He and I were witnesses! Only, I was busy with my camera. The personnel pretending to be wounded were flat on their backs. But the preacher was standing," Jo shouted after him. "He wasn't playacting at the time of the murder. If anyone saw *anything,* it's him. Yet you haven't even grilled him like you did me and the others. You wanna carry a grudge, or you wanna find Selena's killer?"

Michael stopped in the grass. The *whoom, whoom, whoom* and harsh cries of birds escaping to the safe side of the ridge filled his ears. He lifted his hands to cover them, but Jo's voice still reached him.

"You can avoid him or work with him. You can't do both. It's one or the other, McLowery. Hate him or use him. Decide!"

Damn you! Michael turned and faced her, fierce anger conflicting with reason and duty. He was prepared to defend himself, to refute her argument—until he saw her face turn white. Despite his anger, compassion kicked in. He rushed over to her, took her upper arms in his hands and studied her expression.

"What?" he asked.

"I…" She swallowed. "I felt the ground move. It's an earthquake, right? We're all gonna fall into the sea!"

"We're not gonna fall anywhere, you idiot," he said.

"Are you making fun of me?"

He saw her fear change into outright terror. "There's no earthquake, Jo," he said in a softer tone of voice.

"It's the concussion from the artillery. It travels through the ground, as well as the air. You didn't notice it in the car."

"You wouldn't...lie to me?"

"No." He drew her trembling body closer and held her tightly. "No earthquake. Just shell concussion." *You're not afraid of me, but a little concussion has you shaking like a rabbit beneath a hawk.*

He continued to hold her close until her trembling stopped. Even then he didn't let her pull away.

"Sorry for being a baby," she said. "And you in uniform, too. Ground concussion, huh?" Jo wiped her sweating forehead. "I am so-o-o stupid."

"How could you know? You don't have earthquakes in the Midwest."

"Just floods and tornadoes." She lifted her head to look over his shoulder and stare at the ridge. "I'll have to do some research. What's with the cannons, anyway?"

"Cannons—actually they're Howitzers—are for more contained destruction. Unlike, say, nuclear weapons."

"I..." She turned even whiter as the ground shook again. "I gotta sit down," she gasped.

He started to guide her back to the car, then bent over and slid his hands under her legs, scooping her into his arms.

"Hey, I'm not that bad," she said, but she grasped his neck tightly.

"I know. If you were, I'd have to throw you over my shoulder, head facing the ground, and carry you by one arm and one leg."

"Like a big wishbone?"

Michael managed a small smile. "That's not exactly

how it's described in the manual. Come on, back in the car.''

When she was inside, he checked her pulse, then put a bottle of water into her hand. ''Drink.''

She took a few sips, then a big gulp. ''So, how do you know when an earthquake's gonna—going to hit?''

''Whenever we haven't had one for a while. Luckily we had a nice temblor last month. Not even three weeks ago.''

''Trembler?''

''*Temblor.* The plate pressure should be okay. No ground stress to worry about.'' He studied her closely. ''I thought you knew all this.''

''No. I've only been in Los Angeles a couple of months. Before that, I was in Vegas, doing some celebrity stories.''

''Two months, huh? So this would be your first quake?''

She nodded. ''How do you tell the difference between the shells and the shaking?'' Jo asked. She winced again, hands around the water bottle, as the *whoom, whoom, whoom* continued, the *pa-chow, pa-chow* of rifles and mortars audible in the pauses between shells.

''Ground concussion is more of a steady vibration that fades. Earthquakes are uneven, and they don't pulsate or fade. It's jerk, jerk, stop. Or one big yanking roll, then a stop, then smaller jerks—the aftershocks. Shells don't cause aftershocks.'' He put on her seat belt and closed her door, then moved around to the driver's side. ''The building windows rattle differently, too.'' He closed his door and fastened his seat belt.

Jo stared at him. ''There's a difference?''

''Yeah. In the sound of the glass moving.''

''How can you tell?''

"I just know. Experience, I guess."

She nodded. "Experience is always good," she said shakily. "Like with the preacher."

Michael didn't hesitate this time. "Point taken, Ms. Marche."

Despite her white face, Jo smiled. "Ask him to tell you about O'Callahan and Capodanno, the two chaplains with the medals." Then her smile vanished. "I'm beginning to see why you hate this place," she whispered.

Michael took the car out of park and gave the standard answer every uniformed used. "It's a paycheck." Then, "Ready? Let's go."

Inner Compound
Chaplain's tent chapel
Day 4, 7:00 p.m.

McLOWERY LEFT JO in the company of a corpsman and the evening-shift cook—one for first aid in case she needed IV hydration, the other to feed her, for he'd learned that Jo Marche didn't pass up food unless she'd been severely shaken. For both their sakes, he hoped she'd eat. But either way, duty called, and since he had to leave her, however reluctantly, she was as safe as he could arrange.

He strode around the hospital, keeping to the dusty topside and making a beeline for the chaplain's tent. Most military religious services, including the daily Masses or the Christian ecumenical services, took place during lunch, which suited Michael's purposes. Preston should be free and they'd have plenty of privacy, as well as shade, during the prolonged summer evening. Because the tent was open air all four sides, he could feel the offshore breeze from the coast. Even the shelling had stopped. He'd already ordered the always-present MA2 Jackson to track down the chaplain and have him report to the tent chapel.

Michael pulled up a chair and grabbed a soda, instead of a bottled water, silently wishing for a beer. He was sick to death of the taste of water.

Daniel arrived a few minutes later. "Reporting as ordered, sir," he said.

"At ease, Chaplain. Have a seat." Michael tossed him a bottled water.

Daniel caught it with ease, but didn't open it. "How was the funeral, sir?"

Michael fought back the sarcastic answer that popped into his brain. "It went well. Thank you, Klem—Chaplain."

Daniel lifted his head. "My God, a civil answer. Jo been browbeating you, or are you simply worn-out?"

Michael heard the compassion in the other man's words and answered honestly. "Both, I guess. She screams a mean sermon. You could take some pointers."

"Tell me about it, sir. I wish I could be more help in a ministerial sense, but I don't begrudge that woman taking my place. Or teaching me how it's done."

The two men stared out toward the west and the setting sun, its orange glow intense against the blue-gray horizon.

"I never got a chance to tell you how sorry I was— am—about Anna," Daniel suddenly said. "I know you don't want to hear it, but I've waited all these years to say it."

"Yeah, well, I'm sorry I kicked you in the face." Michael studied the other man. A white scar marred the bridge of his nose.

"Thanks. I don't suppose I could get your forgiveness, as well?"

Michael thought about that. *I never forgave Anna for dying. I never forgave my mother for checking out on me and Dad. I can't forgive Selena for getting herself killed. Forgiveness is irrelevant, anyway. All that religion bull doesn't mean a thing to me. Not a damn thing. Justice and duty are what count.*

Still, after his talk with Jo, Michael decided that silence was the better part of valor.

"I didn't think so. A shame, Mac. You're hurting yourself more than you're hurting me."

"Yeah, yeah. Tell me about O'Callahan and Capodanno," he said, taking another swig of his soda and promising himself a beer—no, two beers—as soon as he got back to his parents' home.

"Cal and Cap? That's a sudden change of subject, sir. Why do you want a history lesson from me?"

"My reasons are not your concern, Chaplain. And skip the sirs for now. Just don't use my first name."

"Heaven forbid. You know, I never thought you'd be the one to turn cynical. That role I'd saved for myself. Instead…" Daniel smiled, flipped up his collar and rubbed his fingertips over the cross insignia pinned there. The motion seemed to comfort him.

"Cal and Cap," Michael repeated. "I know who they are. I want some details about what they did."

"The long version or the short one?"

"Whatever works."

Daniel relaxed in his chair. "Okay, I'll start at the beginning. The history of the Chaplain Corps goes back to the original Thirteen Colonies. In 1775 the second article of Navy Regulations stated that the Commanders of Colony ships perform divine ship's services twice daily and preach a sermon on Sunday—barring bad weather or battle. Reverend Benjamin Balch was our first official chaplain. He served aboard the Continental Navy's frigate *Boston*.''

"Go on," McLowery prompted.

"By 1802 a chaplain's duties included funeral ceremonies and teaching the crew writing, arithmetic and navigation. Remember that this came at a time when clergymen were among the few educated men, besides the captain and the first mate. Ship's schoolrooms prompted Chaplain George Jones to establish one main teaching center in 1845.''

"The Naval School at Annapolis. That I do know."

"Yep. After that, Naval chaplains were less involved in actual teaching. By 1906 the Chaplain Corps started molding itself into the organization it is today.''

Michael finished his soda. "Cal and Cap," he said.

"Two chaplains have received the Medal of Honor, the highest—"

"Award for military service in this country. I'm well aware of that, Chaplain."

"Lt. Vincent Capodanno, Chaplain of the Third Battalion, Fifth Marines, earned his medal in Vietnam. He left a safe position to join a platoon under severe attack so he could minister to them.''

"He gave sermons during battle?" Michael frowned.

"No, he gave first aid and encouragement to the wounded. A mortar round took off part of his hand, yet he refused medical attention and attempted to reach a wounded corpsman directly in the line of enemy machine-gun fire. He died in the attempt. It was in Quang Tin Province, I believe.''

Michael remembered Jo's remark. *In a real war, I*

wonder who'd be more prepared. The girl from the projects, the officer—or the preacher?

"What about the other chaplain?"

"Chaplain Timothy O'Callahan of the USS *Franklin*—a World War II ship. He was originally the director of the Mathematics Department at Holy Cross College in Worcester."

Michael raised his head.

"That's right. Massachusetts, your home state," Daniel said. "O'Callahan had only been aboard the *Franklin* seventeen days when she sailed into Japanese waters. She was struck by aerial bombs which set off her own munitions. O'Callahan not only ministered to the wounded and dying of all faiths, he organized firefighting crews, jettisoned live ammunition, and hosed down burning ammunition magazines and armed bombs rolling around on the deck."

Another chaplain risking all for his shipmates.

"Even though he was wounded, he and the ship made it back to New York for treatment and repairs."

"He lived through that?" Michael asked incredulously.

"Yes. He later served aboard other ships, and was the first chaplain of the armed services to receive the Medal of Honor."

"Amazing," Michael murmured. He studied the man before him—a childhood enemy with a chaplain's insignia on his collar. *Would I risk my life for this man without hesitation? Would he risk his life for me? Is Jo right? Am I the weak link in this investigation?*

"Is O'Callahan still alive? He'd be in his eighties, wouldn't he?"

"Last I heard, he retired in his hometown of Worcester and went back to teaching math at Holy Cross."

"I'd planned on going to school there until—"

"You were accepted at the Naval Academy."

"You knew about that?" Michael asked.

"Yeah. Tried myself, but no luck. Unlike you, I'm lousy at higher mathematics and science."

The sun now sat halfway below the watermark, the last of its light reflecting peach-gold and mango-red on the ocean surface. Daniel finally opened his water bottle and took a swig. "Why the sudden interest in the history of the Chaplain Corps?"

"Ms. Marche brought it up. Told me to ask you about it."

"Quite a potpourri of information in that lady's head," Daniel said wryly.

"Yeah…" Jo had been making a point about what a chaplain might have to offer—bravery, loyalty, perseverance. A point about looking past personal history and seeing the man as he was today.

"Anything else, sir?"

"Think back to before Selena was killed, Chaplain, and tell me everything you remember. Not just what you told Puripong in your report, but *everything*."

Daniel lifted his head. "I took a wrong turn in the tent. Ended up in Surgery, instead of the Expectant area. I backed out of Surgery—feeling like an idiot. I stopped in Admin—Fleet Hospital Admin—to get directions. Someone there pointed me the right way, and I entered the Expectant area."

"Anything unusual in Admin at the time?"

"No. Well, yes, our female alien was there, but she wasn't the one who gave me directions."

"Who did?"

"I don't know. A male staff member, though."

Michael nodded. "Go on."

"I went past the fake wounded in the Recovery area and entered the Expectant area."

"Where was Ms. Marche?"

"In the Recovery area. Some of the wounded were moaning and posing. One guy was begging Jo to take down his address."

"Not a pickup? You'd think after Tailhook—"

"No, it wasn't that," Daniel replied. "He wanted duplicates of himself as a wounded patient. Wanted to send them to his mother back home."

"His mother?"

"And girlfriend. The kid was young, thought he looked pretty cool. No shirt, bare chest, fake gore, fake stitches and flash burns. Pseudobloody bandage around his head. Like a little boy at Halloween, all dressed up, wanting his buddies to see his costume."

"For the love of—" Michael bit off the rest. "Did Jo oblige him?"

"She took down his address. Was real sweet to him. Almost maternal. If she thought he was an idiot, she didn't let on."

"Is there a point to this story?"

Daniel nodded. "I think this whole moulage thing is why the so-called wounded weren't good witnesses. The novelty of being made up and playing a role distracted them from noticing your cousin's killer. Most of them were just kids."

"Okay," Michael said impatiently. "What then?"

"Well, at first I thought your cousin was pretending unconsciousness. Or maybe she'd fallen asleep, what with the heat and all."

"That's a wrong assumption, sailor," Michael said sharply. "We give the dying the coolest, most comfortable room and all the privacy or company they want in their last hours. Whatever they want, it's theirs. They've earned it.''

''Glad to hear it, sir. I thought you only used extra A/C to boost the odds for the living.''

''And I thought you knew your job, sailor. The dead make the ultimate sacrifice. You may need to repeat this course. Go on.''

''Do you still see things so clearly, Mac? No mitigating circumstances—no mistakes allowed? That's your fatal flaw, and it'll be your undoing yet.''

Michael started abruptly. Jo had said something along those lines to him earlier. He shook his head. ''I said go on, Chaplain.''

''I figured I'd get out my Bible and do a rehearsal in my head before I started role-playing. Anyway, I got my act together, then started talking to Selena. She didn't answer, so I tried waking her up. Only the red wasn't waxy moulage. When I felt warm, real blood all over my hands...'' Daniel broke off.

He's actually upset! Did he seem this devastated when Anna died? I never noticed. I never even looked at him back then, not once. Never considered his feelings. I was caught up in my own nightmare. Yet he must have suffered, too.

Daniel swallowed hard. ''I notified the guard, Jo began taking photos of the crime scene, we notified you. I prayed for the victim and her family, and you know the rest.''

''You prayed for Selena.''

Daniel nodded.

''And her family.''

Another unmilitary nod. Michael overlooked it.

''Then pray that your memory improves, or you're

going to be stuck behind barbed wire long past the training exercise."

Daniel stood up to toss his water bottle in the "plastic only recycle" can outside the tent. "What do you want from me, Captain? A miracle?"

Michael forced patience into his voice. "I want you to go over the events again in your mind. Forget faces. Forget names. Just look for something odd."

"I can't remember anything else!"

A foul, most unmilitary expletive escaped Michael as he lost his patience. "You always had an eye for details, Klemko! I remember how you drew my mother's nurse cap—how the rank insignia and bars were oh, so meticulous, so accurate. How you even had the mole on the left side of her neck in the right place. I remember that perverted drawing, sailor! So don't tell me you can't remember the events of three days ago. When you're born with that kind of observational ability, you automatically take advantage of it. You used it then, you can use it now!"

Daniel's hands clenched into fists. "You..." He actually took a step closer.

Michael rose from his chair to face him. "Don't even think it. I'll gladly see you before a firing squad—but not until you remember who killed my cousin."

Daniel backed down and collapsed onto his chair, suddenly deflating. Pain replaced anger in his expression, and Michael flinched at the look of agony in Daniel's eyes. It reminded him of Sunshine's face at Selena's funeral. Raw. Awful. He felt more than just twinges of guilt.

He sat down again himself, and suddenly Daniel's head jerked up.

"I do remember one thing," Daniel said. "The hats in the hospital's Admin room."

"*Covers,* sailor, covers. What about them?"

"Some had them on their desks, some had them tucked into their belts. But one of the hats—covers—wasn't camouflage, and someone was wearing it." He frowned. "It was a blue FHOTC ball cap. Like yours."

Michael's eyes glittered with comprehension. "Regular staff have to wear those caps. It's the only way we can enter and exit the compound to conduct the exercises. The guards are allowed to pass us and only us—with the exception of Jo Marche," Michael said slowly. "So, were there any staff members wearing ball caps during the service?"

When Daniel looked confused, Michael added, "We have to wear those caps at all times, including church. They aren't available to the trainees—just worn by staff."

"I know—"

Michael exhaled impatiently. "We were your classroom instructors for two weeks before the exercise. Any faces look familiar? Who was wearing the cap?" he demanded. "Man or woman? Male staff members would've taken their caps off for the service. The women have the option of leaving theirs on."

"I'd have to think," Daniel said. "I didn't look closely at any faces the night Selena died, except for the guy giving me directions. He wasn't the one with the staff cover."

"Who had one at the service? Think!"

"I..." Daniel wiped his forehead, then narrowed his eyes. "The person I saw that night was short. That's why I couldn't tell the sex. But I remember..."

Michael held his breath, forced himself to remain silent.

"I remember the height. Jo took photos of the memorial service. I could point him—or her—out," Daniel said with growing confidence. "Yeah, I could."

"If those photos Jo took of the staff members jog your memory, we may have our killer. Get over to Puripong, on the double," Michael ordered. "Have her send for Marche—she's over at the chow hall again—and meet me here. We've got work to do."

Daniel rose and reached inside his waistband for his cammie cover. Michael noticed the man's face was white, almost as white as Jo's had been earlier. The chaplain's hands were trembling, too.

"Belay that," Michael said. "We'll muster back here."

"Sir?"

"Sit down and wait for me. That's an order." Michael hesitated, shoved another bottle of water into Daniel's shaking fingers and rested his hand on the man's shoulder for just an instant. The next words came straight from his heart. "Forgive the browbeating. I only used it to get results. Good work, Chaplain."

He started toward the guard shack, then stopped and pivoted. "Damn good work," he muttered before hurrying away.

CHAPTER ELEVEN

Chaplain's tent chapel
Day 4, 9:15 p.m.

"WHAT THE *HELL* do you mean, we can't get the photos?" Michael said. "*Why* can't we get the photos?"

Puripong hid her nervousness. "They're in the safe, sir—the timed safe. We won't be able to open it until 0600 tomorrow morning."

"Whose idiotic idea was it to lock up the photos in the *timed* safe when we have a perfectly good safe that opens *any damn time I want?*"

Michael's voice rose enough that others inside the compound actually looked their way.

I'm goat dung because it was my idea, Puripong thought. *Why did I ever come to this God-cursed place?*

Jackson turned her head toward Puripong, her lips resolutely closed.

"It was my idea, sir," Puripong admitted. "You said you wanted no one except us to have access to them. You left the compound, sir, so I assumed you would no longer need the photos today," she explained. "To secure the evidence properly, I locked it up in my timed safe. You were at your cousin's funeral. I assumed you would not return today."

Michael launched into a well-deserved dressing-down

on the dangers of assuming anything and how "assume" meant making an "ass" out of "u" and "me."

Puripong waited until the dressing-down was complete. "I take full responsibility, sir."

"As chief of security, I should have checked with you, as well, sir," Jackson said.

Michael started to explode again, then Puripong watched the reporter, who'd arrived here with the CO, reach out and just barely touch Michael's forearm. "We can wait until morning, Captain." The explosion ceased.

Puripong's admiration for Jo Marche—and Jackson—went up. The former knew how to manipulate the man in charge; the other knew how to cover Puripong's ass. *Damned if I'm not going to owe them both before this is over.* However, right now, that seemed the lesser of two evils, considering Michael's temper.

Puripong looked for a way to distract attention from the timed safe. "Captain, Jackson tells me that two of the alien sailors on base are planning to break and run. They've been hoarding food and water. I suggest we place them under armed guard immediately."

Michael paused. His voice sank to a quiet tone. "No. We're going to let them escape. In fact, I'm going to make it easy for them."

"You are?" Jo asked. "Why?"

"Because I want to follow them and see where they take us. First thing tomorrow morning, we open the safe. If all proceeds well, we'll identify Selena's actual killer. Tomorrow evening I'll make sure our two illegals have an opportunity to escape. We put a tail on them, see what we learn. See if our aliens and Selena's death are connected."

"And who will the tail be, sir?" Jackson said. "I'm volunteering."

"I'll let you know. Keep your lips closed, sailors, and your eyes open. Dismissed."

Puripong and Jackson immediately left at a military trot, Michael's eye still on them.

"TWEEDLEDEE AND TWEEDLEDUM," Jo muttered under her breath. "An officer who can't think on her feet and an enlisted who can, but doesn't have the rank to make a difference."

Daniel spoke in an undertone. "I don't know how you got Mac to listen to me, but you did. Thanks."

"Save your thanks," she said. The memory of Daniel Preston rifling through her meager possessions still rankled. "I'm on your bandwagon only to help find the killer." She addressed Michael. "Why are the safes timed?"

"Security reasons. The person working that shift, and only that shift, has access. Troop orders and decoders need to be protected—so do narcotics. Unfortunately, on this exercise, the hospital CO, Puripong, is the head of all shifts, so only she can set the timed code."

"You never told me why we need to see the photos again," Jo said.

Michael tersely explained.

"If you'd have let me keep a spare set of prints, we wouldn't have to wait," she reminded him.

"The prints aren't going anywhere. First thing tomorrow morning, we open the safe. I'll inform the Chief to meet me here—with his entire staff—at 0600 hours."

Chief Valmore Bouchard's home
Midnight

NAKED AND IN BED, Bouchard watched his wife strip before her dresser mirror, a sight he usually enjoyed. His eyes watched her backside, while the mirror reflected her front. But the familiar routine of her undressing, brushing out her hair, removing jewelry and turning off the overhead light was wasted on him tonight.

He was too upset, too sick over the news he'd received before leaving Camp Pendleton. McLowery had found a possible link between the murder and someone on staff—maybe someone right under Bouchard's own command. He'd been briefed about the safe, the photos, the timer, everything. His pride in his command had taken a severe blow.

"So…you going to tell me what's wrong?" his wife asked, leisurely brushing her hair.

"Nothing's wrong."

She made a shushing sound, something he'd learned over the years was her favorite way to express a variety of negative emotions. "Let me guess. They found the killer and you're somehow involved. It's ticked you off big time, and now I have to suffer. You'll toss and turn all night, and I'll have to head for the couch if I want any sleep."

He rolled his eyes—something he did in response to her shushing—without admitting she was right. She erred often on little things, but rarely with big ones.

"I'm right, aren't I," she said with conviction.

"It's only a possible link—we don't know yet if it leads to the actual murderer. The idiot officer playing hospital CO locked the evidence in the timed safe."

She turned around, her slightly—very slightly—drooping breasts swinging with the motion. He couldn't help but notice how much better she looked for her age than he did for his—and they were both the same age. That pleased yet annoyed him.

"You think the killer is one of yours. I can tell by the

way you're acting. Let's see—I know everyone in your office. Who would be stupid enough to murder the CO's cousin?''

Bouchard reached for his reading glasses and the newspaper's crossword puzzle. "I can't get twenty-six down," he said, hoping to change the subject. "What's a four-letter word that means—"

"It wouldn't be any of the senior officers. They have too much to lose. It would have to be someone without a lot of rank...."

"I'm trying to concentrate," he said, knowing she wouldn't drop it. Everyone at work thought him brilliant, yet this woman wasn't unduly impressed by his smarts. She had her own, which was the main reason he'd married her—well, that and the promise of her body. She'd been a gawky, plain, brainy bride. And face it, he was no male model himself, but he'd known she'd be a late bloomer physically. As a Navy lifer, he wanted a high-intelligence, low-maintenance woman for the long haul.

By her thirties she'd ripened beautifully. Now in her early forties she'd peaked into a lush beauty. The plainness and awkwardness had long disappeared, replaced by a style and confidence only time, maturity and experience could grant. Her razor-sharp brain, much like his own, continued to stimulate and challenge, annoy and excite him.

Finally she put down the brush and reached for the thin T-shirt—always one of his older ones—she wore to bed.

"It's gotta be that little farm girl from corn country." She headed toward the bed. "That's my guess. Yours?"

Bouchard's fingers clenched on the newspaper, then he set down the newspaper and his glasses. *I never seriously considered her. Hell, I hadn't wanted her on my staff, but I was told I had to take her. She didn't even know how to use a computer when she came aboard.* Upset, he snapped off his bedroom light too early.

"Hey!" Not yet in bed, Mrs. Chief fumbled around for her bedside light and turned it on. "It *has* to be her. Gibson, isn't it? She's young, dumb, easily influenced, easily intimidated. And here you are, probably thinking she's poor little Miss Helpless. Wouldn't hurt a fly. But fools can be quite effective if no one suspects them and someone else does the brain work."

She slipped into bed, pulled up the covers and reached for the crossword he'd started and tossed aside. "Pen, please."

Bouchard tossed her a pen, not his pencil. "I've been asked to report to the CO tomorrow morning. I'm definitely up shit creek."

"It's your own fault. Men always underestimate women. The smart ones get labeled bitches, the dumb ones you fuss over, and the rest you want to take to bed."

"If you're so smart, tell me why Mia Gibson's a suspect."

Mrs. Chief shushed again and concentrated on the puzzle.

Damned if he'd ask her a second time—but she wouldn't speak unless he conceded her superiority in this instance. Their whole marriage was one big mutually agreed-upon game of intellectual one-upmanship. Neither of them could respect fools, let alone stay married to one. So far, the contest had been pretty much a draw these past twenty years—spiced up by great sex. He'd had his triumphs and she'd had hers. But this—a murder at his command and by one of his fellow sailors—meant high stakes. Personal vanity had to take a back seat.

"Tell me what you think," he wheedled.

"Twenty-six down is *iter*." She smiled. "Couldn't get that, huh?"

"I know what a Roman road is. You can't get fifteen across? *Adit?*"

"I wasn't there yet," she said loftily. "I go corner by corner. And I know what a mine entrance is."

He waited. She outwaited him. He snuggled closer, one hand reaching for her shoulder. She shrugged him off.

"Tell me," he murmured, trying to sound as if it didn't matter one way or the other.

"Call me Queen of the Universe." She completed another section in ink. She always did the damn puzzle in ink. Another thing he loved and hated about her. She never had to erase a word. He rolled his eyes again. She stubbornly continued to work the puzzle. He slipped his hand under her T-shirt. "Queen of *my* universe, maybe." He gently pushed the T-shirt up toward her neck and kissed her soft flesh.

She dropped the superior attitude and grinned. "Whaddaya wanna know, sailor?"

"Why would a woman be involved in a murder?"

"A dumb woman? Because someone—some man—ordered her to. It would definitely be a man who influenced your dumb little Yeoman. Gibson never questions your orders. She wouldn't question some brass, either. A woman, she might. Dumb women don't like other women for bosses. Ask me why."

"Why?"

"Because smart women don't make allowances for dumb women the way smart men do."

Bouchard considered that. "Makes sense."

"Now tell me why a man would have Selena killed."

"Because he's an idiot or a traitor."

Mrs. Chief made the "wrong answer" buzzer noise, sounding like a TV game show. "No. This officer is a zealot. A patriot. He's doing what he thinks is best for his country. Why else would he risk killing a fellow officer?"

"And a harmless one at that," Bouchard added.

"You're missing the point! Selena *wasn't* harmless or she wouldn't be dead. She knew something she wasn't supposed to know."

"There was nothing in Mia Gibson's paper files or in her computer files. I went over all the staff files with a fine-tooth comb—and did the students twice."

"Better do the staff's twice. Especially Selena's."

"Why? Selena couldn't kill *herself.*"

"What kind of logic is that? Her files could reveal a motive for murder. Why not look for the motive first and then the killer?"

"We have the motive. Illegal aliens are being brought in to staff open enlisted billets."

Mrs. Chief rolled *her* eyes. "If that *is* the real motive. Maybe it's a red herring. Better cover your ass, sailor. Someone's going to take the blame for this, and enlisted are easy targets. Review Selena's file. Really review it. Find out *why* she was killed. Then you'll find out *who.*"

With a curse, Bouchard flung back the covers and stomped to his closet.

"I didn't say right now!" Mrs. Chief wailed, sounding like a wounded troop member, instead of an attacking force.

Bouchard cursed again and pulled out his uniform. "You got gas in your car?"

Mrs. Chief sighed and pulled down the T-shirt from her neck to cover her breasts. "Yeah." Then before he could ask—she always wanted him to ask—she said, "Go ahead and take it. Would you stop and get milk and bread on the way home?"

"Yep. And I'll fill up both cars tomorrow." Bouchard quickly dressed, grabbed his cover and keys, then returned to the bed to kiss his wife goodbye.

"Shall I wait up?" she asked, going back to the crossword.

"Don't," he said, knowing she would. She always did.

"I'll leave a light on, just in case."

He stroked her hair and peered over her shoulder. "Twenty-seven down is *ogee*."

"Ogee? What the hell is that?"

"Curved molding. Boats use it."

She scowled. "I hate you." She filled it in. "Drive carefully."

"Later." He kissed the top of her head, and reluctantly left his near-naked wife behind in their warm bed.

Why didn't I dig more into Selena's file? She's not a student, that's why! She's familiar, she's staff—but the others aren't. I've got to stop thinking Navy on this killing. Everyone's the enemy. Damn, I hate working nights. I'm getting too old for this. Lord protect me from Navy officers. Can't even keep each other alive.

He stepped outside and into his wife's car, ready to use sneaky ways to explore Selena's files and maneuver inside the computer mainframe and out through the network. Ways that would be illegal, even impossible...

Except to people like him.

CHAPTER TWELVE

Fleet Compound, Mortar area
Day 5, sunrise

MICHAEL AND JO started sweating as soon as they left his car and headed toward the mortar area.

"Lord, it's hot," Jo complained. "And the sun's not even up yet."

"Be glad you can wear civvies," Michael said. "Try wool socks, garters, leather boots with reinforced soles, military-issue underwear, then cammies. Plus regulation-required starch in the cover. They used to require starch in the rest, too."

"Garters?"

"Around the bottom of the leg cuff. Keeps dirt and bugs out of the pants. Keeps out air, too."

"Well, at least you get paid to sweat. I'm on spec."

Michael stopped his approach to the Admin office. "I thought AP reporters were salaried."

"On an AP story, yeah. Only you're not gonna let me publish this one, you said, so I get nothing."

"Don't you still draw a salary?"

"Hard to say with this case," she said, too quickly.

He didn't like the way the nape of his neck felt at her answer. He already suspected that her credentials weren't legit; her reaction seemed to confirm it. He noticed the Chief's car in the parking lot, still covered with predawn dew.

What's he doing in? Michael wondered. *He's been here all night—but he didn't have the duty.*

"Where are we headed?" Jo asked. "I thought we were going into the hospital to get to the safe."

"It's still locked for another half hour. Time to check on the students."

"Why? What could go wrong when they're sleeping?"

"We don't let them sleep."

"Huh?"

"Remember 'Tokyo Rose' during World War II? Or 'Saigon Sally' during 'Nam? Enemy broadcasts deflate troop morale. We give them a taste of the same thing—all night long, courtesy of loudspeakers, mortars and machine guns."

"You have a script?"

"Nope. Just some personnel who love to wing it with the microphone."

"Talk about karaoke with a twist!"

Michael almost smiled. "You have a novel way of putting things, Ms. Marche." They reached the mortar area, and he mustered his personnel.

Jo sat and watched him from a picnic table. To Michael, the picnic table with its pretty occupant seemed out of place during a war game with standing uniformed. Nonetheless, she brightened the bleak scenery considerably.

"Cancel all ammunition attacks until further notice," Michael ordered. "Gas attacks, as well. I'll reschedule them once I reenter the compound. I'll check back with you after I exit," he said. "Give 'em one last hit for our reporter, then shut down."

"Aye, sir."

Jo watched as the ammunition—what looked like a huge black bullet—was lifted out of a wooden crate, dropped down a mortar tube and launched into the open compound. The explosion seemed terrifyingly real.

"Umm, those *are* blanks, aren't they?" she asked, watching as people within Fleet Hospital grabbed helmets and "hit the deck."

"No, just short loads. About the equivalent of a quarter stick of dynamite, instead of the usual full stick."

"But…couldn't that still hurt someone?"

"That's the point. Keeps them on their toes—or they lose 'em. Come on, back to Admin."

Jo trotted behind him. Michael now wore his "military mode" persona. Speech, movements and walking speed changed radically.

"Do you use real gas for those attacks, too?"

"No, ma'am, just colored smoke. Real-gas training is done under more controlled conditions."

"Then why did you postpone those fake gas attacks?"

"I have my reasons." *I want to give our two illegals a chance to escape. I want to know when they're going and where.* "Come on, let's grab some coffee and chow. By then it'll be time to head into the hospital." Predictably she perked up at the suggestion of a meal, even though he hadn't answered her question.

"I have never seen anyone get so excited about chow hall food, Ms. Marche."

"You have good food. Great food."

"True." The Navy, with its long history of serving a proper "mess" at sea, was generally acknowledged to have the best meals of all the armed forces. "But still…how can you eat in the heat?"

"I'm always hungry. Must be my metabolism."

Michael eyed her lean body. She looked hungry. Acted hungry. Obviously it went through and through, inside and out. *Once I find Selena's killer, once I put that behind me, I'd love to see if I can satisfy this woman's hunger...in every possible sense.* Then his eyes left her curves and took in the black face of his wristwatch.

Twenty-two more minutes, and the safe opens.

FHOTC, Command Admin Building
Chief's office

HIS FRUSTRATION INCREASING, Chief Bouchard checked the chronometer on his computer and damned the Navy once again. *First I get cheated out of sex with the wife and a good night's sleep. Then I don't even get to shower this morning. If I don't find anything soon...*

Bouchard stopped. He'd noticed something. Just a ripple—no, not even a ripple, a speck. The tiniest speck in the conglomerate of commands and language constituting the bulk of Naval Intelligence caught his eye. That speck reminded him of his own little specks—specks that couldn't always be erased when routine paths were broken, rerouted, fouled, disguised and twisted.

Finding that speck was the hard part; trailing it was the easiest thing in the world to him. Once you found the end of the yarn hidden inside the snarl, the rest was so simple. He grinned for the first time in forty-eight hours, leaned back in his hinged chair, flexed his fingers, even took a sip of his stale coffee before checking the time once more. Then he touched his fingers to the keyboard with his usual deft touch.

And Bouchard went exploring.

Hospital Compound, Admin Office
Timed safe

McLowery, Marche, Preston, Puripong and Jackson gathered in the tent's Admin office. Those working the desks—students who had lost the bohemian joy of a pretend exercise days ago—surreptitiously watched the gathering while carefully carrying out their assigned duties.

Jo sat on the closest desk. The students, officers and enlisted of all ages and all levels of experience remained in their seats. The core investigative group stood awkwardly around the safe. Finally the appointed time approached. 0558. 0559. 0600. 0601.

"Open the safe, Commander," McLowery ordered Puripong.

Jackson sprang to attention, shielding Puripong and the safe from prying eyes and attempts at theft, her rifle in her arms. He heard the *snick* as she unlocked her gun safety and hefted it to the ready.

She's good. Never took this exercise as a game for one minute, not even when it was still an exercise, instead of a murder investigation. Mental note—see about getting this one for my command. Where the hell is the Chief? He's late!

Puripong fumbled with the old-style tumbler. The safe didn't open. McLowery glared. Puripong twirled again. This time, the safe opened. He let Puripong remove the photos and pass them to him. McLowery lifted his head to glare at all the nosy "Looky Lous," a term the Navy still used, and watched Fleet student heads bend busily to their tasks again.

McLowery passed the packet to the chaplain.

"Shall I open it here, sir? Or—"

"Here is fine."

Preston opened the package and started flipping through the photos. He stopped about a third of the way down. His finger pointed to a shot of the mourners, leaving a smudge on a barely shown face. However, the color of the hair and, most damagingly, the height of the person in uniform were enough. McLowery grabbed at the one photo.

Mia Gibson?

Immediately McLowery strode to the front gate, the others unsure what to do except follow him. Puripong hastily shoved the remaining photos back into the safe and closed it without setting the timer, a strand of salt-and-pepper hair escaping from her neat bun. Jackson brought up the rear, with Jo and Daniel sandwiched in the middle. Students at the desks gave up pretending to work and watched in narrow-eyed speculation.

At the compound gate McLowery gestured for Jackson to follow and for the rest to stay behind, including Jo. Jackson didn't hesitate for a second, leaving the gated compound area at McLowery's half-trot speed and moving to his side and slightly behind him. McLowery reached for his radio, quickly giving orders to find and detain Mia Gibson.

The Chief's office informed him those orders were unnecessary. As Michael reached the staff Admin building and Mia Gibson's duty location, his radio reported that Chief Bouchard had taken Mia into his personal custody five minutes earlier, and awaited his CO in the Chief's private office.

Son of a computer bastard. How did he know? McLowery hurried into that office.

"Sir," Bouchard said.

"Chief." McLowery gestured Jackson to remain outside the door, then closed it.

The two men stared at the crying girl—she had always resembled a child more than a woman—then at each other. "Explain," McLowery ordered the Chief.

"I rechecked the computer staff files, sir. The Yeoman's records didn't come up clean. I have a printout that confirms a tie-in with your cousin's files—but no strong collaborating evidence tying her to the death."

"Here. Try this." Michael threw the damning photo on the Chief's desk.

Mia shivered. "I didn't *know* the gun was loaded, Captain! I didn't! I was told it was part of the exercise!" She broke down completely, sobbing so hard she fell out of the chair and onto the floor.

Jackson burst into the room at the disruptive sound.

"Detain her," McLowery ordered. "Use my office."

Jackson pointed the gun at the Yeoman. "Get up, sailor."

Mia gulped as her sobbing changed to hiccups. The red-rimmed eyes turned to McLowery for support. He deliberately looked away. The Chief bent down to lift the girl to her feet. Jackson reached for the cuffs at her waist with one hand, the other still holding the weapon.

"Are those really necessary?" Bouchard asked.

Jackson didn't answer, nor did her eyes leave the prisoner. "Hands in back," she ordered Gibson. "Chief, would you assist, please?"

Bouchard took the cuffs and fastened them on Gibson. Then he reached for a tissue and wiped the girl's nose while addressing Jackson. "On your way out, make certain one of my staff accompanies this sailor. Her legal rights are not to be violated, Jackson, understand? Gibson, don't say anything until your defender from JAG shows up. Jackson, radio me when that happens."

"Aye, Chief," Jackson said as Gibson started crying again.

The women left. Bouchard continued to stand at attention. McLowery merely stood. "At ease, Chief. Report."

"Aye, sir. I came in last night to review Selena Mellow's file, looking for any possible motives or connections to others. I found a connection between Selena's file and Mia Gibson's. Gibson was the one who received the orders through a secured computer file for your cousin's mock death. Arrangements were made for Gibson to pick up a firearm loaded with blanks and to be given a time to carry out the 'mock assault.' Only, the gun didn't hold blanks."

"Why the hell didn't you tell me this earlier?" McLowery demanded. "Why didn't Gibson—your own staff—come to you with questions?"

Chief Bouchard stood even straighter. "Gibson didn't think anything was amiss, sir. Orders can come on paper, over the phone, on the computer, or in person. She, uh, rarely questions anything, sir."

"She didn't come forward when she realized she'd actually killed Selena. Why?"

"I don't have the specifics yet, sir—the who, when, where, how. Or the why... You heard me advise her to remain silent until her legal counsel arrives."

"And this sailor who doesn't question anything is a member of your staff?" Michael asked angrily.

"Technically she's a member of yours, sir. Especially since I didn't want to accept her transfer originally because of her lack of Admin experience. I made that point in writing, Captain. You felt she could get the experience here and okayed her transfer. If you wish, I can get a copy of your verification, sir."

Michael's lips thinned. He'd been forced to accept transfers of American citizens who didn't even speak English. He could hardly refuse a young female sailor on the basis of a lack of specific computer expertise. You took what the military sent you from their manpower pool, or you got no one. "That won't be necessary. Go on."

"I didn't find this out in my routine searches because the killer's command came through your terminal, sir."

"*What?*"

"Your system, sir. Not mine. Standard operating procedure calls for me to perform only maintenance on your computers. I do not infiltrate your personal files without express permission. Especially—" Bouchard swung the computer terminal face toward McLowery "—your home network, sir. According to my printouts, *you* gave Mia Gibson the order to kill your cousin, and you did it from your parents' home."

Whoom, whoom, whoom went McLowery's blood pressure. He felt the pressure in his heart, his veins, his throbbing head—and felt like exploding from anger at this new mocking insult to injury. He stared at Bouchard willing him to continue. Bouchard got the message.

"Gibson isn't the fastest horse on the track, sir. She fell for it. But whoever set you up, whoever routed this kill through your system—they're good. Damn good, Captain."

McLowery still couldn't speak. Bouchard turned the monitor back around. "I've already traced the kill order to a personal e-journal of yours. In it you claim to want Selena dead because..." Bouchard cleared his throat. "She was getting married, you lost to the competition, you wanted to marry her yourself.... If you couldn't have her, no one could. Something along those lines."

McLowery's anger increased even more. "My personal journal?"

"Do you or do you not have a personal log, sir?"

"Yes, but I thought it was secure! And I never wrote *anything* like this in it."

"Sir, one keyed entry looks just like another. And nothing is ever secure on computers. Nothing ever will be. Not legitimate entries, not fraudulent entries, either. Not that you'd ever write trash like this in the first place."

McLowery felt his anger level deflate at the Chief's certainty. "My innocence has not been proved yet, Chief. Forward this information to Puripong and Jackson."

"I will, sir. But proof or not, you didn't do it. Nor did I."

McLowery lifted his head. "Oh?"

"No, Captain. I can assure you, if I planned on using a computer to frame someone, I wouldn't leave any traces—and certainly not in your personal log. And with all due respect, sir, you don't have the skills to pull this off." Bouchard gestured toward the monitor with a jerk of his thumb. "There's not a person in this command who would suspect you of this kind of computer expertise. I have the knowledge—that's why I'm in charge of computer security. Secondly, you're medical Admin staff, and you're steeped in medical ethics when it comes to performing your duties. Sneakiness and stealth just aren't part of your Medical Service Corps package."

McLowery stared at the back of the monitor. *Am I so readable? Is that why Selena's death happened so easily? Because I'm predictable?*

"Sir, how did you catch onto Gibson?" the Chief asked.

"Kept my eyes and ears open." *And grilled the chaplain to the point of cruelty.* "You?"

"Just doing my job, sir."

"Who says officers and enlisted can't work together?'' McLowery said. ''Good job, Chief. Keep digging. I need to know who used my terminal.''

''Sorry, sir, I've already tried to find out. But I think I can get you a geographic location—and that may help. Now that I know what I'm looking for, it should make things easier.''

McLowery nodded. ''You been here all night?''

''Yes, sir.''

''Take some extra time during lunch, have a nap. Two hours at least. I need you fresh.''

''Yes, sir.''

''I'll let you get back to work, then. Oh, and next time I order you to muster, I expect you to muster, or give me a hell of a good reason why.''

''If I'd mustered, I would've lost my train of thought, and possibly the evidence I just unearthed.''

Michael noted that no ''sir'' was forthcoming, nor did Bouchard apologize for not mustering under the circumstances, technically violating a direct order. Bouchard was well aware—and so was Michael—that no disciplinary action would be taken, especially since the Chief couldn't be replaced and knew it. He took pride in his job, not his paycheck. Michael had to respect him for that. And frankly, he had his cousin's killer to find. For now, military protocol be damned.

BOUCHARD EXHALED a sigh of relief as McLowery left. *That was close! McLowery almost had my ass. If it wasn't for the wife—damn, will she crow over this. I didn't find a new motive—she was wrong about that— but she was right about going over Selena's and Gibson's files again. My own network sabotaged, right under my nose! Whoever this bastard is, I'll find him and nail him to the wall—for the murder, for messing with my staff, for screwing with my computers…plus sticking me with finding and training a new yeoman.*

Bouchard's temper stayed in check as he stared at the monitor. He never got results when he lost his temper. Some people thought better with adrenaline. He didn't. Chilled veins with razor-sharp pieces of ice worked better for him. Bouchard reviewed what he'd already learned, then reached for the phone to call home and leave a message.

*Roses and dinner for the wife when this is over—and that seafood restaurant she loves that can't grill me a decent steak. As for this bastard—*he gently flexed his fingers above the keyboard—*you may be good, but I'm better. Sooner or later, you're going down.*

MICHAEL HURRIED BACK to the compound, the overhead sun beating onto his starched cover, causing starch mixed with sweat to drip down his forehead. He reassembled his core investigative group in the Expectant area for privacy.

"The gas attack is going to come right around sixteen hundred today—Ms. Marche, that's 4:00 p.m. to you. Puripong, you make sure no one stops our two aliens when they hightail it out of here. And make sure they aren't armed in any way, shape or form. Jackson, you and I are going to follow."

"What about me?" Jo asked indignantly. "Don't you need a photographer?"

"I can't guarantee your safety," McLowery said. "How do I know you're capable of tracking two men across a chaparral desert? This is military reconnaissance. We're not talking paved roads or paths of any kind."

"I can do it, and I'm volunteering."

"Request denied. You'll remain behind."

"I'm also volunteering, sir," Preston said.

"I neither want nor need a chaplain on this mission. I'll expect you and Puripong to keep an eye on our third alien, Escalanta. And see if anyone tries to contact Gibson. Jackson, you're with me. We need to gear up for a long hike. When the gas attack starts, I want us ready."

"Aye, sir. I'll be ready."

"So will I, sir," Preston seconded defiantly.

"Me, too," Jo said. McLowery started to argue, but Jo cut him off. "Come on, Mac, you need me. And the preacher, too. At least give us the chance to keep up. For a couple of rookies, we've done okay so far."

Michael sighed and Jackson politely studied her rifle as Jo and Preston both faced him down. Finally he spoke the words they wanted to hear and he needed to say.

"Permission granted."

Day 5, 1600 hours

THE SOUNDS OF HEAVY artillery over the ridge couldn't quite disguise the lighter *whoosh* of the first "gas" canister hitting the Fleet compound ground. Perfectly shot, it exploded, not near the open area of Triage as usual, but against the far back fence. The greenish-yellow smoke used to simulate gas rose and mingled with the dust thrown up from the concussion. A second canister landed near the first, then a third exploded close to the usual target, the Triage area.

"Why bother with the gas, anyway?" Jo asked. "And why not just wait until dark?"

"These exercises are scripted," Michael replied. "You already know that."

Jo nodded. "It seemed kind of like a movie to me."

"If you want to put it that way, yes. The purpose of this exercise is to teach Fleet Hospital staff different scenarios. First we give them wounded to assist, then we give them wounded with machine-gun fire going on, then grenades in the darkness and so on. We keep escalating the problems, but we do so in a gradual, step-by-step way. Obviously we can't just throw them into a battle situation all at once.''

"So the gas attack is part of the script?''

"Isn't it on the copy we gave you?''

Jo bit her lip. "I have to confess that I haven't referred to the script even once since your cousin's death. In fact, I don't even know where it is…. Anyway, I thought everything you've done since was to draw out suspects—and to keep them isolated on the compound.''

"That's true. I've shuffled things around and made some changes, but I've followed the original exercise as much as possible. I can't shut down training for two weeks just because—'' Michael's voice grew hoarse with emotion. "It doesn't happen in war. It won't be done here.''

Michael watched the compound as men and women in gas masks hustled to do whatever job their position required. Security took the offensive, while medical personnel took a defensive position, lifting and moving triage ''patients'' still outside on stretchers into the relative protection of the canvas, where caretakers put on their own masks and assisted them.

Michael raised infrared scopes to his eyes and watched two men hop the fence and move toward the south set of hills into the main artillery barrages. Michael, who'd attended many races at the Del Mar track with his parents, borrowed the track announcer's phrase.

"And away they go…''

AUGUSTINE AND EYMARD MENDOZA, the two brothers from Mexico, loaded with food and water as planned, easily hopped the fence. Seemingly undetected in the noise and smoke, they headed over the south hills into the main artillery barrages. Live ammunition continued to hit and explode in various areas, but both brothers knew the safe areas and where extra caution was needed. Within minutes they were lost within the native vegetation, what was left of it, of the unpopulated firing ranges of Camp Pendleton and traveled at an easy jog, despite their boots, the heat and packs full of supplies.

Eymard, the shorter yet faster of the two, asked in Spanish as they ran, "How long before we can turn toward the beach route?"

"Maybe by tomorrow morning. If I last that long," his brother panted.

Eymard laughed. "The tobacco will kill you yet, brother. Too bad the Captain can't see you now, breathing like a make-out stud in the bushes with a pretty girl."

Augustine swore, but continued to keep pace with his brother. "Damn him. He drives everywhere in that fancy car of his and sweats whenever he's in the sun. Our grandmother could outrun him."

"But he doesn't smoke. Neither does she. Maybe our grandmother could outrun *you!*"

Augustine gave his younger brother a shove that stopped just short of tripping him. "Shut up and let me breathe," he said, wincing as a loud explosion hit nearby. "Dear God, I should never have left Mexico."

CHAPTER THIRTEEN

Camp Pendleton, Heavy artillery impact zone
Evening

THREE SAILORS AND A CIVILIAN in borrowed cammies jogged through the still-bright sunlight of the California evening. McLowery, the point man, led the way, running rhythmically along the easy-to-follow path made by the brothers between artillery sites. The others in his squad followed, with Preston at the lead. Jo was next, in borrowed cammie shirt so she wouldn't be an easy target, looking distinctly unofficial among them with her worn running shoes, blue denim backpack and unsecured hair. Jackson brought up the rear, her rifle at the ready. McLowery, the only other person armed, wore a handgun at his waist.

"How's everyone doing?" McLowery asked in a normal voice, grateful for the setting sun and the cooling breeze from the west.

"What'd he say?" he heard Jo ask.

"The Skipper wants to know how you're holding up," Jackson repeated.

"I can't hear a thing!" Jo said, continuing her jog.

"You should have used the earplugs earlier," McLowery said, this time a little louder, but not so loud as to alarm the men they were following.

"I did. I still can't hear right," she grumbled.

With military precision, the artillery training had ended exactly at quitting time.

"I could use a break," Preston gasped.

Michael slowed his pace to a jog, then a brisk walk to prevent cramped muscles. The four closed ranks, progressing at a slower walk.

"I warned you to stay behind, Chaplain," McLowery reminded Preston. The chaplain, like all of them, was drenched in sweat. But he seemed to find the run much more of an effort than the others did. Marines were required to run three miles at a fast clip, while ship and sub-bound sailors were required to do a mile and a half. All were regularly tested twice a year on running and swimming speeds—and discharged as unfit for duty if unable to meet the times required. Most fighting sailors ran daily if possible. Obviously Preston wasn't one of those sailors.

"I can still radio a pickup for you."

"No, sir, I'm fine. I just need a drink."

Michael kept a close eye on him. "Don't drink until you've cooled down some. Jo, you okay?"

"My camera keeps digging into my back, but yeah, I'll live." She gazed enviously at Jackson's military pack, padded in the right places and tailored to fit the body.

"How can you run like…" A puffing Preston couldn't even finish the sentence, just gestured toward Jo and her clumsy pack.

"Easy," Jackson said with the first trace of friendliness toward Jo that McLowery had noticed. "She's busy burning all that food off her bony behind. I swear food's all she talks about." McLowery himself had been impressed by Jo's performance. He'd expected her and not

Preston to fall behind first. "She eats like a horse," Jackson added.

"I could run like one, too." Jo grinned. "If I had a decent pack and a sports bra."

"Or if you weren't packing all those MREs," Jackson added.

"If you think I'm gonna eat your dried MREs instead of this…" Jo removed a king-size candy bar from her denim pack and ran it slowly under her nose while sniffing it like a fine cigar. "Oh, yeah, baby. Come to Mama."

"Mama's hollow leg, you mean," Jackson corrected.

"Very funny. And quite untrue, by the way. Here." Jo broke the bar in two, paper included, and threw half to Jackson. "Sweeten up that sour puss of yours."

Jackson deftly caught it with one hand, peeled off the wrapper and popped the whole thing into her mouth so she could return both hands to the rifle.

"Anyone else?" Jo asked.

McLowery, his own mouth wrapped around his canteen spout, waved her away, then said, "Now that the artillery's stopped, our fugitives will be able to move faster. So will we. Let's keep our voices down and our speed up—we won't have the artillery to screen our noise."

"Can't we just follow them in a helicopter?" Preston wondered.

"If we alert them, we won't find out where they're heading," McLowery said.

"Hey, Preacher, you'd better have some sugar yourself or you aren't gonna make it." Jo pulled another candy bar out of her pack and held it in front of his face.

"I can't run on a full stomach. How can you?" Preston groaned.

"It'll take more than a candy bar to unsettle my innards. At home, I'd have to run top speed to the market for cigarettes. Dad would wallop me if I took too long, and I'd run round-trip with a stomach full of mustard-covered sauerkraut and pig's feet. Dad always wanted his smokes after dinner."

Preston hiccuped, bent over double and promptly lost the water he'd just emptied from his canteen. Jackson reached for her radio even before McLowery gave her the nod.

"Chaplain, you're outta here."

"Sir, please—"

"No arguments. You're overtaxed. Jackson, arrange for him to be picked up by jeep. Get me an ETA."

"I'm sorry, Preacher." Jo quickly stuffed the candy bar back into her pack. "I shouldn't have brought up the...well, sorry," she repeated.

Preston wiped his face and straightened. "Actually, I feel better now. Captain, if you call a jeep, the men we're trailing might hear it. So you'd better make up your mind that I'm staying."

Jackson blinked at Preston's insubordination, the radio still unkeyed and frozen inches from her mouth.

"I gave you an order, sailor," McLowery warned. His admiration for Jo's physical prowess took a back seat to Preston's courage. The man wasn't much of an athlete. Unlike the others, he hadn't been molded by years of military training—training that enabled sailors and soldiers to consistently win Olympic gold medals for the United States. The chaplain had obviously had more classroom time than gym time, yet he refused to budge. Worse, his arguments made sense. Still...

"Jo can accompany you. She's nonessential."

"I knew it," Jo said, obviously resigned. "Come on, Preach, I'll walk you back."

"I'm not going," Preston said. "You know why, Captain. I owe you. Tell them."

"Tell your advocate at your court-martial."

Preston reached for his canteen, rinsed out his mouth and spat into the vegetation, then addressed the women. "I caused the death of his little sister when we were both boys."

"Shut up!"

"Then his mother killed herself right after the funeral."

"I said shut up!"

"I joined the Chaplain Corps to make up for it—not that I could bring back the dead," Preston explained to Jackson. "But I can help the living." He swiveled to face McLowery. "If you think I'm leaving the Captain to become family death number four, you're sadly mistaken. The only way I'm leaving you is in a body bag, Mac—"

The mention of a body bag immediately dragged an unwilling McLowery into the past as he remembered baby Anna bundled away in an official black zipped bag. The chaplain's use of Michael's old nickname propelled him back into childhood…when Preston wasn't a fellow officer but Klemko, the enemy. Without thinking—steeped in the fury of that hellish time—McLowery swung. The heel of his clenched hand struck below the other's jaw, just as his boot-camp hand-to-hand drill instructor had taught him. Preston dropped in his tracks, his lip bleeding profusely where his teeth had scored flesh. McLowery stood over him, fists still clenched.

Preston lifted a hand to his mouth, then stared at his bloody fingers. "That's twice I let you take a shot.

Swing a third time, and rank or no rank, I won't turn the other cheek," he warned.

"You keep my personal life out of this mission," McLowery hissed. "Or you'll answer to me." He lowered his hands, adjusted his pack and started jogging forward again.

Jo and Jackson stared at the men, at each other and then at Preston. Jackson helped him to his feet, while Jo pressed one of her bandannas to his mouth. Without a word, Preston brushed it aside. He adjusted his canteen and began jogging again.

"He killed the Captain's sister, and they're working together?" Jackson whispered to Jo.

"Yeah, I know. Thank God I'm a civilian. You people are all insane."

"Just the officers," Jackson corrected in an undertone. "Now get that skinny butt of yours running if you don't wanna be left behind. I can't let those two fools kill each other—not on my watch."

"Or mine," Jo added. She hurried forward to take her place between McLowery and Preston again.

Another hour passed, with the point man and the women easily keeping up. Even Preston seemed to have gained his second wind, while McLowery had no further outbursts of temper. McLowery suddenly held up his fist, the signal to stop and be silent, then reached for his binoculars.

"What's going on?" Jo whispered to Jackson, who shook her head and motioned for silence, her rifle up and at the alert.

McLowery keyed his radio, relaying information to his command—and to his party. "They've made the frontage road and were just picked up by a late-model truck, license-plate number..." He continued to look through his binoculars. "Looks like they're heading toward the I-5. Yeah, definitely Interstate 5 south. Follow them, keep me posted and get us a ride out of here. No, I don't want a jeep. Get me a chopper. Our chaplain here is about ready to drop. Have a corpsman on board to check him out." McLowery signed off and replaced his radio.

Preston immediately sank to the ground to rest. Jackson put the safety back on her rifle and slung its strap over her shoulder.

"Anyone got a first-aid kit?" Jo asked.

Jackson pulled one out and handed it to her. Jo knelt beside the chaplain and proceeded to clean his lip.

"Hitting an unarmed man—one who's carrying a Bible, yet—can't be good for that tote book up in heaven, Captain," Jo said.

"There's no such thing as heaven, only hell," McLowery stated. "But I will apologize, Chaplain. My action was against regulations, could have endangered our mission and was totally uncalled-for under the circumstances. Make sure you file an incident report when you get back to Fleet. I admit culpability. I'll sign and answer for it."

"Yeah. That'd be a good career move," Preston shot back. "Then I can sign the report you fill out on me for insubordination. With our luck, we'd both end up in the brig—as cellmates."

"God forbid," Jackson muttered, then clamped her lips shut.

"Would all of you be quiet until I get this lip cleaned?" Jo asked. "Then you drink some water, Preacher, or you'll be needing a stretcher. You won't need stitches, though. Looks worse than it is."

Their helicopter landed, timed so that the passengers

in the fleeing truck wouldn't notice. A few minutes later, the corpsman on board confirmed Jo's words and applied small butterfly bandages to Preston's lower lip before the rest of the party climbed aboard for the ride back.

Chief Bouchard's office

WHEN THEY LANDED once again at FHOTC, Preston returned with Jackson to the enclosed Fleet compound for medical treatment. Jo headed straight for the ladies' room and the showers, while McLowery entered his office and asked Chief Bouchard to join him.

"What's the latest on the tail?" he asked a few minutes later. "They still have our two men in sight?"

"Yes, sir. The truck left I-5 just a few minutes ago for the beach."

"What area?" McLowery asked impatiently.

"Del Mar and the track, sir."

McLowery silently swore. "So we think the horses are running today?"

"Yes, sir," the Chief said. "We're talking large crowds...and racehorses are trucked back and forth across the border all the time, sir."

Suddenly the men's movements rang warning bells— warning bells for their own safety. McLowery stiffened in his chair. "Have those men taken into custody on the double!"

"Sir?"

"Now, man, now! Get on the horn *now,* or those AWOLs will be dead meat before the day is out." McLowery didn't want two more casualties on his hands.

The Chief picked up the phone and relayed the orders.

He listened to the conversation, then slowly replaced the phone.

"Well?" McLowery said.

The Chief hesitated. "Security says we lost them."

"*Lost* them? They're toe-tagged?"

"No, sir, they ditched us—and did it like pros. We don't know where those two are now."

"Put someone on their truck," McLowery ordered. "Stake it out."

"Already did, Captain. So far, nothing. We're thinking maybe they had a second vehicle waiting."

McLowery slammed his desk with his fist. The Chief jumped—a sure sign of stretched nerves.

"Any further orders, sir?"

McLowery took in the man's red eyes, the wrinkled uniform the Chief had spent the last twenty-four hours wearing, and took pity. "Go home, Chief. We'll start fresh tomorrow."

"Aye, sir. Good night, sir."

It's not. It's not a good night at all. Del Mar is close to Solana Beach. My parents live near the track. My father enjoys the horses. My stepmother does business with wealthy people who visit the track.

The Chief had said his personal computer log was tampered with. Now these two sailors had lost themselves at the track. It was too big a coincidence. Could someone be using his parents as cover? First Selena, then his parents... Why is my family being targeted? Now I need someone to keep an eye on them, as well— someone I can trust.

McLowery tipped his head back on the chair's head-rest, his eyes closed as emotion washed over him. *I need an objective civilian who already has an "in" with my parents. I need Jo. I don't trust anyone but her,* he suddenly realized. *No one…*

Del Mar Race Track, Equine Quarantine Stables

AUGUSTINE AND EYMARD quickly stripped off their cammies, stuffed them in their backpacks and pulled on their civilian clothing.

"If it wasn't for you, that man who picked us up would've killed us," Augustine grumbled from the shadows. "I'm never hitchhiking again."

"Thank God for rush-hour traffic, or we could never have jumped out. That bastard pulled a gun on us. He might've killed us and dumped us in the bushes."

"Good thing you told me to run. How did you know he'd do that?"

Eymard shrugged. "I didn't like the way he looked at us. I've seen that look before. I didn't like it," he repeated.

"Well, we're alive, anyway. But now what?" Augustine asked.

"There's work to be had here at the track."

Augustine nodded slowly.

"People always need good cooks like me," Eymard went on, "and we would eat well. You could clean stables. We wouldn't need references—and we speak English well."

Augustine sighed and switched to English. "Poop brigade, huh? I liked being a sailor better. Still, it beats picking strawberries in the hot sun. Or getting shot in the back."

Eymard shoved his pack in a dusty, spider-ridden corner and threw some clean straw over it. "And *gringos* complain that Mexico is dangerous."

Camp Pendleton, Fleet Compound
McLowery's office
Sunset

PERCHED ON THE EDGE of his desk, Jo listened in horror to Michael's words. Could it possibly be true? His own family might be involved?

"Jo, they weren't personally involved. I said I think someone might be using them like they used Selena. I just don't know why or how," he said in frustration.

"How could you not know?" she asked.

"What do you mean?" Michael leaned back in his chair and swung his booted feet up on his desk.

"How could you not know why? Or for that matter, how could your parents not know how Selena fits in— or why they're being used like this? I mean, back home, the word got out on the streets. Doesn't the military have its own grapevine? I knew when my father or brothers broke the law. They knew when I shoplifted."

"You shoplift?"

Jo flushed. "Not since high school. I'm legit now. And, I might add, beyond the statute of limitations."

"Are you?"

Jo felt a prickle of warning slide down her spine. His tone of voice, the expression on his face—both were red flags, and Jo had never in her life disregarded a red flag. "Legit or beyond the statute of limitations?" she asked cautiously.

"Either."

"I don't steal, period. As for anything else…well, I can't afford a lawyer, so I'll plead the Fifth," she said defiantly. "Unless you want me to lie, Mac. Please don't make me lie to you."

To her relief, Michael smiled, and the red flag seemed

to, if not disappear, become a less angry red. "I wondered if you'd mind doing a little spying for me," he said.

"Spying?"

"Yeah. Like going back to my parents' house to stay—and snoop around."

Jo slid off his desk on the pretext of visiting the water cooler. "Spying and snooping are two different things," she said casually.

"True," he acknowledged. "Snooping is bad manners. Spying means something more serious, so I guess that's what I want from you. Don't worry, though, you shouldn't be in any danger."

"But your parents might be if I muck this up! I don't want to endanger them. I'm not a spy—*or* a snoop."

"You shoplifted," he reminded her. "And they *won't* be in any danger."

"How can you be so sure?"

"Because I've already talked to Sunshine on the phone. I'll talk to my father again later, but Sunshine insists neither of them knows a thing. I believe her. And yet, they're tied to this mystery somehow, just like Selena."

Something's happened. He knows something he's not telling me. "So…I'm just confirming that opinion?"

"Yep. I'm not worried, but it may be argued that I'm not objective when it comes to family."

"While I have no ties to them." *Yet,* she silently reminded herself.

"Exactly. So…you up for it?"

"Depends," she said, stalling.

Michael dropped his feet onto the floor and leaned forward. "You've got physical endurance and one hell of an instinct for self-preservation."

"I don't know...." *Sure, I've had practice lying in the tabloids, but lying to the family of this man and snooping through their home isn't something I'm comfortable doing.* "I could slip up."

"I doubt that. In fact, I'm sure you'll manage just fine."

Jo heard the coldness in his voice, saw the tense set to his muscles and watched his eyes narrow. Before her waited a deadly predator—and Jo knew all about predators, especially when she was the prey. *He knows about my ID,* she thought with dead certainty. *I'm doomed if I don't help him...and maybe even if I do.*

"Okay. If you still want me, I'm in."

"Oh, I want you all right. Come with me. We'll finish this conversation somewhere else."

Tamarak Beach
Sunset

AT JO'S SUGGESTION, she and Michael walked toward the shoreline. Michael had changed into civvies, and she'd stalled by asking for a visit to the beach to collect sand to mail to her grandmother. Before Michael started on the particulars of her new assignment, she needed a soft setting and a soothing atmosphere to plead her case. She'd rather not spy on people she wanted as her in-laws. She also hoped to get back into Michael's good graces. Strangely, or perhaps not so strangely, Jo cared more about his opinion of her than keeping out of jail. Ever the optimist, she decided she'd go for both.

She sat down on the sand, not caring if the dampness soaked through her only spare jeans. Beautiful moments were far too few in the lives of the Sepaniks. Her grandmother had taught her long ago to take advantage, to stockpile these moments and build a protective hoard to help buffer the bad times.

After a few minutes, Michael joined her. Neither said anything. They watched the setting sun as they listened to rushing waves and the harsh cries of gulls feeding along the ebbing tide. Even the unending rush of Southern California traffic couldn't be heard from Interstate 5 behind them. The sun continued to dip behind the horizon, its citrus oranges and yellows reflecting off the water. Only when the last traces faded completely away, signaling the end of sunset, did Jo sigh her contentment.

"We should go before the sand fleas and mosquitoes attack," Michael said, rising to his feet and offering her his hand.

Jo blinked in surprise, the spell broken. "Yeah, I thought it was a beautiful sunset, too, Mac."

Michael said nothing, just continued to hold out his hand as Jo still sat there.

"You're a real jackass at times," she said without rancor. "You beat up a man who's helping you find your cousin's killer, ignore a sunset most people would die to watch and blackmail a reporter who's helping you. You know about my fake ID, don't you."

No answer.

"Yet instead of asking me to go on helping—giving me a chance to come clean—you *threaten* me. As though otherwise I'd simply walk away."

"You don't get that choice, thanks to my background check on you. I wear the uniform, I do the job."

Jo felt a surge of anger mixed with desperation. "That's never been in question, sailor-boy, certainly not by me. And yes, I'm not a saint, but I'm not your enemy, either!"

Again silence. Michael dropped his hand and turned

his gaze to the gulls at the water's edge. Jo got to her feet unaided.

"I guess I am your enemy," she said. "You said earlier you didn't believe in heaven, only hell. My God, Mac, don't you trust *anyone?*"

Michael faced her again. "Should I? My father or stepmother or both have somehow become connected to my cousin's death. The chaplain looking after my supposed soul started the chain of events that killed my sister and mother. And the only inside spy available to me is a former shoplifter with fraudulent ID who can lie to the tabloids—oh yes, I know about your real job— spy with the best of them and almost fool the whole damn United Stated Navy."

"But not you, right? Because you *expect* people to fail you," Jo said with a sudden flash of insight.

"They always do."

"No wonder you don't trust anyone. You poor man." Tears spilled slowly from her eyes.

"For God's sake, forget the pity. I don't want it. Jo, stop that!"

She couldn't. Her tears continued to fall. To her surprise, Michael became even angrier than before. Confused, she reached out for him, but he avoided her grasp and walked down the beach, gulls fleeing at his approach. She knew he wouldn't be gone long, not after that day's hike. Nor did she need much time to make up her mind.

I want this guy in my life, my heart, my bed. I could love him—I do love him! He needs someone he can trust, and that's gonna be me. I don't care if I have to go to jail to get him. I've got nothing to lose except a pawnshop camera and borrowed underwear—but everything to gain.

She crossed her fingers for luck, the way she always had, ever since her youth when she had to run from danger. From her father's drunken anger, or the gangs, or the dealers, or the landlord. She was tired of running…and suspected Michael might be, too. *Time to go for broke.*

Michael returned to where Jo once again sat. She'd composed herself, face placid, exposing none of the steel that had long kept her alive and safe, and even happy at times.

"Ready to brief me about my spy mission?" she asked.

"Not here. In the car."

Jo raised her hand toward him, silently asking for help up. Michael pretended not to see and pivoted away from her. He took a few steps toward the parking lot. Jo refused to move. *Opening gambit, right here, right now.* She continued to sit until he turned and saw she wasn't following. With a curse, he said, "You coming?"

"You going to help me up?"

He backtracked impatiently to pull her to her feet. "Thank you," she said. *Michael, you have no idea who you're up against. I usually get what I want, and what I want is you.*

As THEY DROVE, Jo listened quietly to Michael. He repeated Chief Bouchard's findings and his own suspicions regarding Selena's death.

"If your parents are being framed, and you aren't doing it, then who could get that close to your family? I saw Selena's fiancé at the wake. It couldn't be him. He isn't even military."

"I never said Paul was a suspect. Frankly, he and my

father didn't particularly like one another, but that's no motive for any involvement on his part.''

"Paul works in Silicon Valley, right? Have you had him investigated? Or watched?"

"Both. I don't expect to learn anything from that end. His specialty is hardware, not operating systems. He has no ties to the military except for Selena, and his computer skills are rudimentary at best." Michael shrugged. "Someone far more skilled than Paul made it look as if my parents' home computer, which used to be my personal computer, is the source. That's a connection we—you—have to check out."

"I'm competent around computers, but that's all."

"Your paperwork says otherwise." He raised an eyebrow as he spoke.

"That doesn't mean a thing," she said irritably. "I'm smart enough to hire the right people. Not that it's any of your business." At his sidelong glance, she added, "Oh, all right, maybe it is. To get back to the subject at hand, just what do you expect me to do, go through their trash? Talk into my shoe phone?"

"Stay at the house, offer comfort and listen for the kind of thing that only an objective observer would notice. If anything's wrong, you'll pick up on it."

Jo shifted impatiently, despite her seat belt. "And this is all the training I get on how to be Mata Hari?"

"Wing it."

Jo took a deep breath. Time to take action. "On a few conditions," she said, waiting for his outburst. She wasn't disappointed.

"You're not in any position to be talking about conditions."

"Sure I am. I refuse, you send me to jail, and you get *nada*. Zip. Zero."

"Do you know the maximum penalty for government fraud, especially with the military? Would you like me to list the specific charges for you?"

"I don't give a damn about your list. Now it's your turn to listen to *me*. Keep your eyes on the road and your mouth closed, and maybe this'll work out to everyone's satisfaction." Jo reached forward and shut off the radio. "Number one. I always wanted to help you find Selena's killer. I must confess to feeling hurt that you thought you had to blackmail me into helping. All you had to do was ask. Ask me *first*, then threaten if I refuse. But you didn't give me that chance. Frankly, you don't give *anyone* the chance to do right by you—but that's a problem for your shrink, not me."

"I don't have—"

"Don't interrupt, please, and if you don't have one, you should. Number two, if you want to make yourself miserable living in the past, fine. Only don't spread it around when it comes to Preston. He's obviously trying to better himself and to make up for what happened to your sister. And let's face it, you were just kids at the time."

"*Now* are you done?" Michael asked tightly.

"No. Number three. I don't care if you send me to jail, because I haven't got a cent to my name. I've lost my feature story and my photos. You'll probably find out any skeletons I have in my closet, if you haven't already. That means I either get to dance at the strip joints and let horny losers stuff their money into my panties to earn a living—or you lock me up. As far as I'm concerned, jail's easier to stomach."

She ignored Michael's blanching at her blunt words and continued. "So save the threats for someone who has something to lose. You're so busy hosting your own pity party that you don't even notice the people who'd trade places with you in a Yankee minute!''

Jo exhaled audibly and turned toward the car window. She'd never fallen into anyone's bed without being in love, and she'd never gambled on a man for anything *but* love. This time, she intended to lay it all on the line—her career, her freedom, her future for one very special man. A mixed-up man at times, but she knew she'd never find anyone as good for her as Michael McLowery, even when he made her furious—like now. Her big gamble was coming up—so big she almost couldn't find the breath to go on. Then, from somewhere deep inside, she did.

"So here's my deal. I'll help you spy, snoop, whatever, as long as I get to do so as your woman. A spy needs a good cover story. Here's mine. Grief threw us together. I get to eat and sleep at your folks' while I keep my ears open. You give me girlfriend status. We even…share the same bedroom.''

Michael stared at her longer than safe driving permitted before his attention snapped back to the road. "Do you get fiancée status, a roll in the hay and a diamond ring, too?''

Jo flinched at the harshness in his words, and harshness seeped into her reply. ''Your holier-than-thou stuck-up kind never buys diamonds for white trash like me—and right now I don't have a problem with that. In fact, I consider myself lucky. But you owe me for the insult. So I want to act as your port in the storm. When the storm is over, we 'break up' and go our separate ways. You go off to play Navy, me off to jail.''

Michael took his eyes off the highway again to gauge her seriousness. ''Why aren't you asking me to cut you a deal?''

"Why ask when I already know your answer? I do believe you'd send your own parents to jail for jaywalking, then congratulate yourself on being a good citizen and soldier."

"Sailor."

She paid no attention to his remark. "When I'm in your home, you treat me with respect. Like I'm the kind of woman you waited your whole life to find. You've spit on my integrity, Captain. It's payback time."

"I refuse to be blackmailed."

"Yet you didn't mind doing the same to me. If you want my help, you'll let my story stand." *And maybe, just maybe, if I act like your woman, our relationship might head in that direction…lead to love…lead to marriage. I've got nothing to lose and everything to gain. It's a pretty old-fashioned ploy, but what's a woman in love to do?* "I'm not even asking for sex—though I won't refuse if you offer nicely. It'll give me something to remember while I'm showering with all those female prisoners. If sharing a bedroom with me is too much to ask…then you don't care about catching Selena's killer, after all. You don't care about a damn thing except yourself."

"You have no right—"

"If I knew who her killer was, I'd get out of this car and out of your life so fast your head would spin. Until then, shut up. Just…shut the hell up." Jo immediately reached forward and with trembling fingers turned the jazz station back on at full volume. "And that's all I have to say on the subject."

CHAPTER FOURTEEN

Patrick and Sunshine McLowery's home, guest room
8:00 p.m.

MICHAEL GENTLY SET Jo's backpack on the floor. "You want the right or left side of the bed?" he asked.

Jo didn't answer. She hadn't said a word to him in the car from the moment she'd turned the radio back on, and since his parents weren't home, the silence had continued, much to Michael's dismay—and fear. Sometime in the past week he'd come to rely on Jo's presence in his life. He'd even thought about the possibility of having her in his future. Her words earlier had chilled him to the bone. Had he been taking advantage of her strength without giving anything in return? Had she turned her back on him the way he'd turned his back on Dennis Klemko/Daniel Preston?

The idea of Jo feeling the same cold hatred for him that he'd felt for Preston shook him badly. He'd become so complacent in his independence and his lack of ties to others that the loss of one woman's good opinion of him should mean nothing. Less than nothing. Yet it burned through his chest and settled in his gut as a premonition of what a failure he truly was in personal relationships. "How about if I leave you the side nearest the window?'' he asked Jo in his kindest voice. "It has a nice view of the ocean. You liked it the last time you stayed, right?''

Jo didn't bother admiring the view again, but she did finally speak. "You don't really live here, do you?'' she asked. "The room is nice, but it's not exactly…you. Or is it?''

"I usually live in the BOQ—furnished Bachelor Officers' Quarters.''

"Why not get your own place?''

Michael shrugged. "Why bother? I get transferred every three years. I only stay here from time to time to please Sunshine.''

"I know you can't have overnight company at the BOQ. Where do you go with your women to be intimate?'' Jo asked curiously. "I mean, you *do* have relationships, don't you?''

His spirits rose just a little. If she truly despised him, she wouldn't be asking about his sexual history. "When I have time for them. Which isn't often.''

Jo sat on the bed and crossed her legs, then stared at the bed itself. "You don't do it right here, do you? In your parents' house?''

"Lord give me patience.'' Michael opened a drawer, removed some clean clothes and headed for the door. "I'll be downstairs showering,'' he announced. "I suggest you do the same. Use the bathroom up here.''

"In your car?'' Jo asked, continuing with her theme.

"No!''

"Where? The beach? That would be romantic, don't you think?''

Michael swore and left, slamming the door behind him.

Jo did as he suggested, appearing dressed and down-stairs a full five minutes before Michael emerged, clean and freshly shaven.

"You're still wearing the same jeans," he said.

"That's because I only have two pairs with me. These are the cleaner of the two. I would've packed more if someone hadn't ripped off my laundry."

"There's a washer and dryer in the garage. Feel free to use them."

"Thanks, maybe later. Is there anything to eat around here?"

"We can go out. Or I can fix you something," he offered, trying to make up for the earlier tension.

"I meant just for a snack. I thought we could take advantage of the empty house and snoop around. Where are your parents, anyway?"

"Probably out for a late meal themselves. Here." Michael grabbed an apple and a banana from the kitchen and tossed them to her. "This should hold you for a while."

"Thanks." Jo immediately rubbed the apple on her shirt and took a bite. "You have a basement?"

"No basements on the beach."

"Attic?"

"Not to speak of. How about a dusty spare room?"

"The one where Sunshine keeps her old clothes?"

"Yeah. We can start there. This way." Michael led her upstairs and showed her inside. "I doubt we'll find much. Nothing but junk."

"How can you say that?" Jo gestured to the clothes in open boxes on the floor, the chunky jewelry carelessly strewn on dresser tops, the piles of faded curtains and throws on the bed. "My God, this is a treasure trove in here!" she said reverently. "Everything's in such good shape. I'd have to pick through the thrift stores for weeks

to find stuff that's such fine quality. Even the shoes—"
she held up a pair of sandals "—are like new. Barely a
scuff on them."

"Take them if you want. Sunshine won't care."

"Oh, look!" She pulled out an old leather box, sat
down on the sagging mattress and opened the lid. "Old
photos. Come see." She picked up a handful. "Is this
you?" she asked, holding up a black-and-white baby
photo.

"No, that's Anna, my sister."

"She's a real cutie. I adore my brothers, but I always
wished I had a sister—someone I could talk to and do
girl things with. I don't have any photographs except for
the school pictures of my brothers. We couldn't afford
a camera, and I always wanted one."

Michael carefully returned the photo of baby Anna to
the box. "Put those away, please. They won't help us
find what we're looking for."

"How do you know?" Jo asked as she put the photos
back and replaced the lid. "You should go through them
later. Maybe something will point us in the right direction."

Jo slid the box toward him, then crossed to the closet
and opened the door. "What's this?"

Michael gathered the box under his arm and followed
Jo to the closet. "My mother's wedding dress."

"Which mother?"

"Sunshine. Selena was going to wear it."

"Oh." Jo gently fingered the lace beneath the plastic.
"It's so sad to see it hanging here."

"My first mother was buried in her wedding dress, I
was told."

"I'll bet she was a beautiful woman. Your poor

mother,'' she added softly. "Losing her little girl like that.''

"I wouldn't know. The ceremony was closed casket because Mom committed suicide.'' Then he said abruptly, "At Anna's funeral, she snatched my sister out of her open coffin. God, what a zoo that day was....'' He couldn't believe he'd spoken the words out loud. He'd never really talked about his sister's death or his mother's before, but talking to Jo seemed easy, almost comforting.

Jo pulled him down on the bed. She seemed to know that he *needed* to remember and asked him questions about the funeral, both funerals.

After a few minutes, Jo stood up to rummage in the closet again. "Look, an old tuxedo!"

"From my prom.''

"And this Scout uniform?''

"The one I wore during the ceremonies when I made Eagle Scout.''

Jo touched it just as carefully as she had the wedding dress. "A whole roomful of memories. You are so lucky. My family never had the space for mementos or the money. We never even had clothing we didn't wear to death. That's one reason I became a writer, you know.''

Michael shook his head, confused.

"So I'd have a way to write down and keep all my memories. And keep something that was all mine—my words, my stories, my hopes and hates, my dreams and schemes.'' She grinned. "Especially the schemes. I used to have a box full of diaries.''

"Used to?''

"Uh-huh. A pipe froze and burst one winter and ruined my diaries. I cried and cried over them until Dad popped me a good one in the mouth. I still get sad when I think about it.''

Michael fumed at the thought of a young girl being hit in the mouth and for a moment wished he could pop her father right back in exchange. ''You could write your autobiography later on.''

Jo actually laughed. ''Who'd pay me for that? It's not like I've led a very interesting life—and the few parts that *are* interesting are too incriminating to put in writing. Dad would've got a longer sentence than the one he's serving now. It's probably a good thing those diaries were ruined.'' She closed the closet doors. ''Well, no secret codes here. No books, either. You weren't a big reader, huh?''

''Not until college. I liked the outdoors too much. Still do, usually, other than during summer.''

''You need to go to Maine. That's what I want to do. I hear the summers there are nice and mild. My grandmother's a big reader. So's my mom. They always took me to the bookmobile. Someday, if I ever get my own house, I'm going to have them live with me. I'll build us all a huge library. I want lots and lots of books. Did you ever read *Little Women*?''

He shook his head. ''The title doesn't appeal to young boys.''

''Someday, you'll have to read it. It's one of my favorites.'' She went over to the dusty old drawers and ran her fingers over the wood. ''This is exotic hardwood—really valuable stuff. What is it?''

''Teak with monkeypod accents—from Hawaii. The furniture here was my boyhood set.''

''The wood feels like silk. A shame to shut it away up here where no one can enjoy it.''

''Sunshine's holding on to it for when I get married.

If I get married. She thinks her future grandchild might enjoy having it.''

Jo opened the top drawer. "Look at this! Army soldiers and an old dump truck. Were these yours?''

"Yeah. I didn't even know these were here." Michael picked up the truck and spun the dusty, worn wheels as Jo fussed with the green figures. "I was crazy about this truck.''

"It's an old Tonka—an antique. You could probably sell it to a collector if you don't have children. You want kids?''

"I don't know. I wouldn't know how to make them happy, since I wasn't a happy kid myself. I always thought Selena would give Sunshine babies to fuss over." Michael gently laid the truck—and the memories associated with it—back in the drawer. "She keeps everything," he said.

"She kept everything of *yours*," Jo corrected. "You're a lucky guy to have two mothers who loved you.''

"My first didn't love me enough, or she would have stayed alive.''

Jo smiled and sorted through the different Army men. "You're wrong. She did love you, or she wouldn't have taken such pains to kill herself so far away from her family.''

"How do you know that?" Michael asked sharply.

"Sunshine told me a little. And your mom probably did all your laundry and cooked tons of food in advance so you'd eat, too.''

Michael blinked. "Chicken potpie and cherry Jell-O with bananas.''

She raised her eyebrows. "That's what she cooked?''

"Yeah. My favorite meal as a kid. She made it for us that night before she left. I...I never realized it before."

"See? People can love other people but still hate life. You know what I mean? She found life intolerable, despite her great love for you." Glancing at Michael, she said, "This is such an interesting room. You're so lucky." Jo replaced the toy soldiers and closed the drawer. "I should go downstairs to throw out this peel and my apple core," she said, picking up the trash wrapped in a napkin on the dresser.

"Go ahead. I'll be right behind you." Michael took just a moment to look around the room he rarely, if ever, entered. The past pulled hard at him. He was back in the yard playing with his toys, watching the gray government car pull up. For once he didn't fight the memories. He let them come of their own accord.

Jo was right about two things. He let the past affect him far too much—and yet he hardly ever examined his assumptions about it. She was right about his second mother, too. Sunshine, a true artist, never threw anything remotely reusable away. If there was any connection between his parents and Selena's death, besides the computer, any connection between his family and a killer trying to divert suspicion, this house could hold the answer.

Michael only hoped he could hang on to his sanity long enough to find out.

McLowery house, guest bedroom
Midnight

MICHAEL FINALLY RUSTLED UP enough courage to come upstairs to bed. He'd stalled long enough. First he'd found an old pajama set of Sunshine's from the spare room for Jo to wear, then busied himself fixing dinner while Jo did her meager laundry. He couldn't decide which was more shocking, her appetite or the sad shape of her clothes. He used better cloth to wash his car. He remembered old movies his father had taken in 'Nam of the war orphans—clad in rags and scarfing his father's candy as though there might literally be no tomorrow. Jo reminded him of them, and suddenly he understood her pride. Why she wanted to be treated like someone special—like his beloved.

Once he understood her, he didn't find it so hard to accept her terms. Before he could tell her that, his parents returned to find him in the kitchen and Jo in old pajamas eating her third helping of dessert. The pajamas were covered with fat Vs, looking like either incomplete triangles or chubby boomerangs. She'd scooted upstairs, leaving Michael to "explain" her presence—and his— in the guest room.

Patrick sighed, muttered something about sin and safe sex, and went straight to bed. Sunshine lingered for coffee and to help him clean up the kitchen.

"I like Jo. I hope you're not stringing her along," she said. "Someone could get hurt."

"Trust me, she knows the score."

Sunshine dumped out the coffee grounds at the sink. "I'm not talking about her. I'm talking about you. Jo's the first woman I've seen you with since you were stationed here. She could break your heart—or make you a happy man, if you gave her the chance. You're not getting any younger, Michael."

"Now you sound like Dad. I'm not in any rush to settle down."

"You should be. You need a woman in your life...and not just for, shall we say, romance. You need a woman's influence, a woman's practicality. Selena's gone, and I'm not as young as I used to be, either. What's going to happen to you when I die?''

Michael's dishrag stopped midswipe. ''Aren't you being a bit morbid?''

''I just came from my niece's wake, so no, I'm not. Death is a reality. Your father didn't love me the way he did his first wife, but he had enough sense to realize he needed someone. Some men do well as loners. You don't, Mac. You never will.''

''So I should take on a woman I barely know and…what? Hope for the best?''

''At least give it a serious try. Give Jo a chance. She cares about people. She cares about *you*. There could be more if you'd meet her halfway.''

Michael resumed wiping the table. ''We're sharing the same room, Sunshine. I think that's close enough.''

His stepmother shook her head. ''You don't know much about people, Michael, and even less about women, especially women like Jo—or me.''

''You're comparing yourself to her?''

Sunshine finished rinsing out the coffee filter and refilled it for the morning. ''I grew up in a culture where bodies came cheap, especially women's bodies. Sometimes sex was merely a form of entertainment, sometimes it was traded for a meal or a place to crash. 'Free' love wasn't, let me tell you. It isn't so different for poor women today. They often have to use their bodies for survival. That makes a woman's heart even more valuable. Women like Jo know what really counts in life, Michael. She could teach you that.''

Michael suddenly remembered how Jo had talked about dancing at strip clubs if she lost her job—and how jail might be a better place. He remembered that neither option upset her too much. She accepted both with surprisingly little resistance—yet had fought him tooth and nail when he'd insulted her character. He became aware of Sunshine watching him.

"Maybe you *do* understand." She smiled and kissed him on the cheek. "I'm tired. Good night, Mikey."

"Good night, Sunshine."

She left Michael to finish the dishes or not, as he pleased. Michael did finish them, then finally headed upstairs, but not before rummaging around in the cupboard and grabbing a few candy bars and a bag of chips, plus a soda from the refrigerator, just in case his new roommate wanted anything.

Jo was resting under the covers, but sat straight up and turned on the bedside lamp as soon as he entered the room.

"Sorry. I didn't mean to wake you."

"That's okay. I was just resting." She shoved her hair out of her eyes and groaned. "Now I'm hungry."

Michael dumped his calorie stash in her lap. "Help yourself."

"Really?" Her smile brightened above the silly triangle print of the outdated pajamas. She began with the soda and chips.

"No candy?" He noticed she'd switched off the room's air conditioning and had opened the windows, letting in the smell and sound of the Pacific. The sound felt comforting, soothing—like Jo herself. Sunshine's words rang in his head, and then his only thoughts were of the woman before him. She filled his senses, his head, his heart, his soul. Despite the absurd pajamas and the fact that she was cramming potato chips into her mouth, she became the most erotic Venus he could have wished for, dreamed for and wanted. Definitely wanted. He was

hit with a wave of desire so hard his knees almost buckled.

"Have to eat my veggies first, then dessert." She
grinned, reaching into the potato chip bag. "Your parents in bed?"

"Yep." He sat down on the chair and removed his
running shoes and socks. "Hope those crumbs don't end
up on my side," he said, his voice just a bit unsteady.

"They won't end up on either," she said before popping not one, not two, but three large chips into her
mouth at once. Still chewing, she asked, "Whatcha
wearing to bed?"

"T-shirt and boxer shorts—at least while you're
around."

Jo swallowed and dug for more chips. "You don't
have to wear a shirt if you don't want. Won't bother
me."

"You sure?"

"I'm used to it." She opened the soda and took a
slug. "Whenever Dad was working, I always had to
share a bedroom with my two brothers. They didn't wear
shirts, either."

"You didn't have your own room?"

"If Dad got busted, I'd sleep with Mom and
Grandma." Jo finished off the potato chips and opened
one of the candy bars. "You want some?" she asked.

"No, thanks." Michael removed his slacks and shirt,
and folded them with military precision. "Where did
your grandmother usually sleep?"

"On the couch. I was jealous, because that was the
only place I could read late at night. Which is exactly
why she liked it. So I used to pretend to get sick."

"Pardon?"

"Whenever one of us got sick, we'd have to stay on

the couch so we wouldn't pass on our germs," Jo explained. "I'd leave a light on all night and read until dawn. Or else my grandmother found me asleep and turned off the light for me. I knew the bookmobile schedule by heart—guarded my library card like gold. No matter what, Grandma or Mom always took me. The adventures I had, the places I traveled in those books, lying on that ratty old couch..." She sighed happily at the memory. "This is a great room for reading. Soft sheets and no relatives whining about the lights being on. Wish I had a book right now."

"Tomorrow you can rummage through Sunshine's books in the spare room. For now, there's just me." Michael sat on the edge of the bed, then swung his feet up. "Though I can't see you holding a book with both hands clutching food," he said as she swallowed the last bite of her chocolate bar.

Jo giggled. "Yeah, right, like we had any extra food back in those days. Well, maybe on Thanksgiving and Super Bowl. The locals bet heavy on the football games, which meant Dad had extra money, so we did get treats. But if I dared to eat something in the same room with my brothers, they'd gang up on me and steal things like this." She held up the remaining unwrapped candy bar. "I never ate candy around my brothers. My momma didn't raise no dummy."

"How can you laugh about it?" Michael couldn't understand her good cheer.

"Why not? You can bottle up all your resentment and make yourself sick. Or you can get drunk or stoned. Or you can laugh...or cry. You can't change anything." She unwrapped the second bar. "Might as well enjoy what you can, laugh at how life screws with you, and hope and pray for moments like these." She patted the bed. "Soft clean sheets and chocolate. A good-looking guy. A beach view." Jo gestured toward the curtains. "Life's little moments can be life's best moments. Without them, what's the point of getting up in the morning?"

He watched as she took a big bite of chocolate. "Maybe you're right."

"Of course I am." Jo smiled and held out the candy bar. "It's got caramel," she tempted. "No coconut."

"I hate coconut," he admitted.

"Then come on, share the wealth."

"Okay." He carefully lifted the candy bar out of her fingers and set it on the end table. Then he leaned forward, cupped his fingers around the back of her neck and pulled her close to kiss her. Her chocolate-flavored lips met his, and he kissed her gently. Her arms slid around his shoulders, his hands encircled her waist, and they kissed a second time, and a third. By then they were both prone on the bed, their clothes rumpled, and one of the pillows had fallen to the floor.

"You're a good kisser," Jo said, tapping his nose with her forefinger. "Are you as good a lover?"

He stopped and toyed with her hair. He fiercely wished he could take off the whole silly outfit and explore the curves beneath more intimately, skin to skin.

"You're supposed to say, 'Wanna find out?'" she prompted.

Reality set in. "Damn."

"Damn?"

"I can't count how many instructional talks I've given the troops on safe sex, but I've never covered being prepared in my own mother's guest room."

Jo's pliant body fell away from his. "Look, if you

don't want to do it or you're too tired from the hike today, just say so. You don't have to lie.''

''I'm not lying. I'm prepared on my own turf.''

''Yeah, right. The back seat of your car?''

''Come on, Jo, I'm hardly going to stock my mother's bathroom. Perhaps you…?''

''I can't afford it. Hell, I don't even have a place to store it, Mac. That's if I slept around, which I don't.''

The quiet sounds of the waves filled the room.

''Damn. I'm sorry,'' he said.

''I am, too. It felt right to me.'' She sighed, then reached for the candy bar and finished it. ''I'm still hungry.''

Michael gathered Jo into his arms. He lay back down and held her body against his. After a moment she relaxed, and he pulled the sheet over them both. He kissed her hair.

''That feels good. You're an officer and gentleman, after all.'' Jo whispered. ''Too bad for me. The gentleman part, that is.''

They rested, the sound of the waves coming through the open window. He felt her relax more completely. His own body relaxed, as well, from the strain of the past week, the run through the artillery. Exhaustion finally banished his sexual tension. He actually felt he could sleep well for the first time in ages. He'd just closed his eyes when she spoke again.

''Mac?''

''Yeah?''

She remained in his arms, but lifted her head to look at him, her eyes dark in the moonlight. ''Do you think they have bedbugs in prison?''

''I don't know,'' he said honestly. ''At least you won't be wearing triangle-covered pajamas.''

"I thought they were boomerangs. I kinda like 'em."

"They look good on you. Jo," Michael found himself saying, "if you end up in prison, it won't be because of me. I can't promise anything more. Wish I could."

Her eyes opened wide. "I didn't ask. I don't beg, either."

"I know. Now lie down again before you get a stiff neck."

He inhaled her sweet, chocolate-flavored breath as she kissed him on the side of the nose, all she could reach with his arms still around her, her back against his chest.

"You know, a girl could fall in love with a little encouragement—especially when she's halfway there already."

"What?"

"You heard me. Good night, McLowery."

Maybe she's right about those little moments, he thought as he hugged her. *Maybe I can get through this yet.*

CHAPTER FIFTEEN

Solana Beach,
Day 6, morning

MICHAEL ROSE EARLY without the aid of an alarm clock. Years of military work hours kicked in, even on his days off. He knew the same held true for his father. Leaving Jo sleeping in a tangle of sheets, he drove Patrick down to the beach for his morning walk.

"We haven't done this for a while," Patrick said, his cane in one hand, the other hand shoved in the pocket of his slacks. "I'm surprised you came with your old man when there's a woman in your bed."

"I cleared Jo's visit with Sunshine," Michael muttered. "She doesn't mind."

"No, that damned hippie wife of mine wouldn't. I guess I don't, either."

"Better watch out, Dad. You'll get struck by lightning." Michael grinned, then grabbed for his father's elbow as he slipped.

"Getting soft in my old age, I guess. Damn doctors. Use it or lose it, they say. Walk on the sand. It's easy on the joints. Idiots." Patrick shook free of his son and readjusted his grip on the cane. "They haven't learned a thing in the past hundred years. It used to be go to Arizona to take the cure. Now it's move to California for the sand. If it wasn't for Sunshine's nagging, I'd never see another doctor again.''

"Better than cancer," Michael said, repeating Sunshine's stock answer to Patrick's complaints.

"Lord almighty, you sound just like her. Sometimes I almost forget you're not her flesh-and-blood son."

The two men walked in silence for a good fifteen minutes until Patrick stopped and sat on a rock. "This is where I take a break," he said.

Michael nodded and leaned against another piece of rock, sharper and not a comfortable seat. They looked out at the ocean, the heavy marine layer still just off-shore.

"So, how's the investigation coming?" Patrick asked. "You've cross-examined me and Sunshine to death about the computers. I assume someone wanted you to look guilty."

"Something like that. But Sunshine's computer didn't yield a clue when I checked it over last night."

"Yeah, I heard you in her office," Patrick said.

"But I'm no expert," Michael went on. "I'm going to take it to work tomorrow and let my chief take a look at it."

"You think he'll find anything? Or can't you tell me?"

"I don't know, and no, I'd tell you if I knew. I've got our actual killer—but I don't think she's the only one. She isn't the type and hasn't got the brains. Someone was giving her orders. She hasn't told us who—not yet, anyway."

"Damn. Any other suspects so far? Any more leads?"
Michael shrugged.

"That good, huh? Well, keep at it. I'm glad you found out Gibson pulled the trigger. Selena was a good kid—

reminded me of Sunshine at her age. Your stepmother still cries at the drop of a hat, and I'm almost as bad. Seems like we McLowerys are always burying our women.'' Patrick surreptitiously wiped his eyes. ''That's two daughters I've lost.''

Michael nodded, and the men walked in silence for a while.

''Dad?''

''Hmm?''

''If you had it to do over again, would you have joined the military?''

''You don't understand, son. It was different in my day. Before Vietnam came along, being a sailor was an honest occupation, something to be proud of. The Korean War was a 'good' war, just like World War II. Whenever war broke out, we joined up. It's what men did—and were expected to do—in those days. I did what was expected of me, found out I was good at my job and decided to stay.''

''You didn't answer my question,'' Michael said, still watching the waves. ''Are you glad you stayed?''

''I'm surprised you have to ask. Hell, yes, I'm glad. I loved it. Fast cars, fast jets, fast women—hot damn, we had fun. Of course, a woman who kissed on the first date was considered fast in my day, but we didn't care. They were exciting times…and more innocent times, too. I was lucky enough to make it into the elite club of officers who ruled the skies during the day and bought drinks for women in the bars at night. I miss it. Still miss it. Unlike you.''

Michael lifted his head. ''What do you mean?''

''You've never really enjoyed your job, have you, son? Never smiled going off to work. Never hung around with buddies. Never bought drinks for beautiful women and bragged to them about your exploits in uniform, let alone kissed one just for the pure joy of living. The Navy isn't even a paycheck to you. It's just something to fill the day.'' He shook his head. ''I've got damn good memories of people and places I've loved. What do you have?''

''Pride in the uniform. Satisfaction from a job well-done.''

''That's it? That's not enough!''

''It's kept me grounded through the years.''

Patrick swore. ''I never thought I'd agree with Sunshine, but you need a hard kick in the ass. Life's more than that. I'm glad your mother isn't alive to see you today.''

''How could she be?'' Michael's tight smile didn't reach his eyes. ''She was a coward, while you were so intent on keeping the status quo you remarried before she was cold in the ground.''

Patrick rose from his rocky seat, one fist clenched, the other gripped tightly around his cane. ''My wife was no coward, and I married so you'd have a mother.''

''Don't bullshit me, Dad. You married so you'd have a woman in your bed, hot meals on the table and a built-in baby-sitter. I've never told you how to live. Allow me the same courtesy, and save the sermons.''

''As if you'd listen. You're too damn stubborn.'' Patrick's anger faded. ''There's that much of me in you, at least, even if you do have more book smarts than I ever did. Too bad those smarts never convinced you to enjoy life. You're my pride and joy, Michael James. I'd like to see you happy.''

Michael watched as his father checked the time on the black, military-style watch he'd never given up wearing, even after retirement.

"Your mother should have the coffee on by now. Better go wake your chippy and tell her to get dressed."

Michael nodded and offered his arm to his father. Patrick took it.

"So, she a good kisser?" Patrick asked.

"That's a personal question."

"Here's another. Will I ever have grandchildren?"

Michael refused to answer.

"May the Irish saints preserve us, you haven't touched her? She obviously likes you."

"So she likes me. I don't want to take advantage of her," Michael said, defending himself. "It was Jo's idea to share a room, not mine. And trust me—nothing happened."

Patrick suddenly looked every one of his years and then some. He didn't even have the strength to shake off his son's arm. "I said you were my pride and joy. You're also my biggest failure."

Side by side they returned to the car without speaking another word.

McLowery household, garage
10:30 a.m.

"SO NOW WHAT DO we do?" Jo asked as Michael finished going through the last of the storage boxes in the garage. They'd spent the time after breakfast searching for any possible clues. Patrick and Sunshine had headed off to a La Jolla art gallery to deliver more Raku selections; she preferred to deliver her works personally whenever possible.

"We could go back to the spare room and search again, I suppose," Jo suggested. "We didn't really dig."

"I think that's a dead end. Sunshine's computer is in my car. I don't know what else we need."

"I think we need a snack first," Jo said. "And not any more fruit, either. I need some good, all-American junk food."

"You ate all the candy bars," Michael reminded her, shutting the last box and setting it back on the shelf. "But there's ice cream and Sara Lee cake in the freezer. Will that do?"

Jo smiled and tossed him a bottle of unchilled water from the nearby open case. Michael caught it, unscrewed the top and offered it to her first. She shook her head, so he drank it empty, tossed it into the garage recycle bin and walked her back to the kitchen.

Minutes later they sat side by side at the kitchen table, a single plate filled with cheesecake and ice cream in front of her.

"I don't know where else to look for a connection between this place and Selena's death," Michael said.

"You've gotta try the obvious places now. Like your parents' desk. And their medicine cabinets. Sunshine's purse, too."

"I am *not* rifling through my mother's purse!"

"I didn't say *rifle*. Just ask her permission first. Same with the desk. Tell your parents you can't leave any stones unturned when it comes to finding Selena's killer."

"Gibson was Selena's killer."

"You know what I mean." Jo stopped eating long enough to study him. "If you don't want to find out that they were involved, just say so. I'll understand."

"Understand what?"

"That you're just going through the motions. Selena was your cousin, after all."

"You've got a hell of a lot of nerve!"

Jo seemed surprised at his reaction. "What? You said you wouldn't send *me* to prison. I'm guilty as sin, and you couldn't possibly care for a stranger more than you do your own family. So if you want to settle for Gibson going to jail as the one who pulled the trigger and forget about who ordered her to do that...well, I don't approve, but I understand about protecting family, whether they're guilty or not. Besides, even if I didn't, you're the one with the clout, not me." Jo took another bite of cheesecake. "Do you have milk to spare?" she asked.

"No," he said quietly. "No, I don't."

"Darn. Cheesecake goes best with milk. I thought I saw some in there last night. Sunshine must have used it up."

Michael shook his head. "I meant, no, I don't care about them the way I care about you."

"You...what?" Her fork hovered in midair.

"I care for you more than I do my parents. Much, much more." He didn't know what else to say. He stood up, retrieved the milk and a clean glass, and set both down before her. She didn't say a word, and the fork still hovered, so he poured.

"That ice cream's going to melt if you don't finish." He felt awkward taking the milk back to the refrigerator.

Jo dropped the fork. It clattered twice on the plate, then stuck to the remaining cheesecake as she rushed to him in front of the open refrigerator door and threw her arms around his waist, her food-covered lips lightly soiling the back of his shirt, her nose pressed into his spine. It seemed the most unromantic gesture any woman had ever made to him, and yet it felt better than any gesture—even the most sexually intimate—he'd ever experienced before.

He slowly pivoted in her arms until her face pressed against his heart. He kissed her hair, her ear, her cheek, and still she held fast. He stood there, taking in her nearness, letting her choose the timing, the stance, the words.

Finally she pulled away from him, her eyes bright, her lips curved upward. "You'd better close the refrigerator door," she whispered.

He kicked at it and managed to connect. "Come on, Mata Hari. Finish your snack, and let's rifle through my father's desk."

Del Mar Racetrack, "Employees Only" stable area 10:30 a.m.

DANIEL BREATHED IN the smells of lathered horses, much-used paddocks, sweating men and fried food. It mingled with the dubious aroma of large, unemptied Dumpsters and the noxious fumes from heavy traffic on Interstate 5 just outside the track's massive parking lots. Unlike the public areas, there were no lovely ocean waves here, no quaintly tiled and frescoed buildings, no colored brick walkways around lush green turf.

Only the sight and smells of men working the lowest jobs in order to survive. If it wasn't for the cross under his T-shirt and the pocket-size Bible he always carried in his jeans, he could easily have been mistaken for one of those men. There was a time in his life when Daniel *had* been one of those men, although his reasons for working were less than honorable. Back then, he'd merely wanted money for booze. He showed up for work when he had to, drank himself sick with the few dollars he earned and started all over again when whatever woman he slept with got sick of his drunken, self-pitying ways and kicked him back out onto the street.

He thought he'd come a long way from places like this. Here grown men shoveled horse manure into huge piles to dry in the sun. They used rubber scrapers to wipe off lathered sweat from horses after their workouts, cleaned hooves and feet, wrapped or unwrapped insured, expensively shod equine legs. They performed these tasks over and over again. Many of the workers didn't speak English. English wasn't needed for cleaning up after horses. And not speaking English meant the workers had to be satisfied with earning absolutely the lowest wages around. Despite that, the track could be a good place for family men willing to work hard for a future; it was definitely a haven for pursued men who needed a place to hide.

Daniel's familiarity and ease in settings like this allowed him to stroll through the "Staff Only" walkways unchallenged, looking for the two men from Fleet. Occasionally he stopped and made a few friendly inquiries in the street Spanish he'd picked up on his travels. He'd bet the men were still in the area, probably working food service or barn brigade. Yes, the uniformed military police had searched for the missing pair, but they'd been too obvious. Daniel had a much better chance in casual clothes. If he found the sailors, he had a twofold mission planned. He wanted to help them out, and he wanted information from them in return.

I want to know who ordered Selena's death. Michael needs to know—perhaps then he'll listen to me. He's as lost a soul now as he was at his sister's funeral.

The sun continued to climb, burning off the marine layer and signaling the end of the cool-morning workouts. Horses and trainers reappeared at the stables, where groomers arrived for the equine handoff and owners showed up to question the trainers. Daniel deliberately headed for the staff food court, knowing the owners and groomers would have had an earlier lunch, while the riders and trainers would eat during this lull. Daniel followed the general crowd, hoping the missing Navy cook would be working at the food court.

What else can he do? Food service—one of the jobs always open to the unskilled, the unfortunate and those without references. Men had to eat, and new men in a place such as this had no allies. As in prisons, dubious carnivals or any low-wage industry, old-timers were suspicious of newcomers. Daniel was more than just confident. He knew how desperate men thought as much as anyone could know. Today he came not just as a minister, but as a hunter.

The mouthwatering smell of *refritos,* salsa, frying meat and tortillas reached Daniel's nostrils, along with the sharper smell of hot coffee and cold beer. The lines of workers were thick at the serving areas, but the line moved quickly, with precision. Military precision, Daniel noticed. Seconds later he saw the two men from Fleet. One, the shorter, did indeed wear a cook's uniform and see-through plastic food-service gloves. He busily fried *carne asada* while the other rapidly ladled out the meal with a sailor's efficiency and boredom.

Daniel casually joined the line for the taller man. If he remembered correctly from the chase in the artillery field, the taller man, Seaman Mendoza, didn't run as well as the shorter cook, Mendoza. Nor did Daniel want to risk any physical confrontation among hot meat, scalding grease and deadly frying pans. There *would* be a fight, of that he was certain. No man who worked places like this would passively accept questioning, maybe arrest. There'd be a fight, and Daniel felt his adrenaline pump, his muscles tense, when there were only four men left in front of him, then three, then...

The tall sailor looked up to ladle food for the one man left between Daniel and the table. He looked down again, then up. His eyes met Daniel's, dropped again to the ladle, then lifted once more as recognition flitted across his face.

Before the man could even drop his ladle, Daniel launched himself across the food table with the practiced ease of a man who'd cleared bars and tables in numerous brawls. His head sailed into the other man's soiled apron, catching him directly in the stomach. Daniel knocked the wind out of him, rendering him momentarily helpless. He immediately sat on the disabled man's chest.

A few men jumped out of the way as the cook's attention was diverted from the frying meat to the commotion. Immediately the shorter brother came to the taller brother's aid, a long sharp knife in his hand. Most of the lunch line backed up, while those farther back surged forward, trying to see the cause of the disturbance. Daniel reached for his ankle and the military holster with the loaded pistol strapped inside. In seconds, the old barroom brawler had the safety flicked off the gun, pointing it straight at the face of the knife-wielding man.

Eymard froze, his hand, still clutching the knife, slowly rising in the age-old gesture of surrender. Daniel stood. With the gun aimed, he jerked his chin in command. Immediately Eymard obeyed the silent order and dropped the knife.

"You and your buddy, move away from the table," Daniel ordered. "Over toward that empty holding pen."

Again the man obeyed, helping his gasping but otherwise uninjured brother to his feet. The two headed away from the food, Daniel behind them, gun still drawn. As the three entered the more isolated holding pen, the others slowly fell back in line. Another cook watched the frying meat, while the men simply ladled their own food, ignoring the trouble that clearly wasn't as important to them as eating before another long afternoon of hot grueling work.

"Nailed by a padre," the taller brother, Augustine, said in Spanish to Eymard. "Promise me you won't tell the family."

"As if I'd betray my own brother," Eymard replied angrily, his anger obviously directed at life in general.

"I speak Spanish," Daniel replied in their language. "Down on your knees, hands behind your heads."

"Gonna read us our rights, Padre? Or pray for us before you shoot us?" Eymard jeered, his cook's apron puddled in the dirt before him.

Daniel's tight smile put neither prisoner at ease. "I'm not a padre, I'm a chaplain. And I'm not a cop."

"Then why are you here?" Augustine asked.

"Why are *you* here?" Daniel countered.

Augustine shrugged. "We're brothers. I'm the oldest, and our Navy names, rank and serial numbers are all you're getting."

Daniel thought for a minute before answering. "I don't care who you really are. I do care about Michael McLowery. He's *my* brother."

Eymard and Augustine Mendoza took Daniel's words at face value. They swore at their bad luck, for they were men from a country where family bonds and family loyalty equaled a man's honor.

"We're going to jail for sure now, brother."

"No, I told you, I'm not here to put you in jail,"

Daniel said. "Tell me what you know about Selena Mellow's murder."

The kneeling men, hands clasped behind their heads, glanced at each other.

"Sit down," Daniel said. No reaction. "At ease!" he barked out. The two immediately sat on their rears, feet flat on the ground, hands on their knees. Daniel continued to stand and let his gun arm straighten, let the barrel point at the ground. He flicked on the safety.

"Tell me how you were recruited into the U.S. Navy. I want names, descriptions, locations, contacts. Tell me the truth—remember, I'm a man who can spot a lie— and I let you go."

"Brother, did you hear?" Eymard asked in rapid-fire Spanish.

"Don't believe him! He's a sailor—he *has* to turn us in."

"He's a Protestant padre. He has to tell the truth, doesn't he?"

"Shut up and let me think!" Augustine snapped.

"Skip it. Your thinking led me right to you," Daniel said harshly. "Tell me what you know, and we both get what we want. Don't talk, and I'll turn you over to my brother, the CO. He's not as patient as I am."

Eymard blinked. "What do we do, Augustine?"

"Talk. It's not like we have a choice." Augustine sighed.

"There's always a choice, gentlemen. Once you learn that, the world is yours. Shall we pray first?"

"Later," Eymard said, switching back to English. "If you don't mind, we'd like to keep our jobs here. Work, then talk. You pray by yourself in the meantime. We'll bring you grub."

Daniel nodded. "I'll be waiting. Try to run, and I'll catch you."

Augustine threw him a begrudging glance of admiration. "I know. Come on, brother."

Eymard rose and dusted off his dirt-stained apron with torn filthy gloves. "How you like your meat, Chaplain?"

"Served with fresh gloves."

Eymard smiled for the first time in weeks. "Done. If you're lucky, I may even shoo the flies away."

"Then hustle your butts, sailors. I don't have all day."

CHAPTER SIXTEEN

Del Mar Racetrack
Midafternoon

DANIEL SAT IN HIS CAR, windows down, sun beating everywhere. He busily scribbled down the information he'd received from the brothers. They claimed they knew no name for the person they'd spoken to on the phone, the person with an unidentifiable, sexless voice who'd recruited them into the Navy. But the places and incidents described might lead someone with book smarts to get the name—and to figure out the connection to Selena's death, whatever it was. *Someone like McLowery.*

Strange how a man could be so intelligent with facts but so clueless with people. In some ways, Daniel himself was just the opposite. He was no Rhodes scholar, would certainly never be a published theologian—but since the childhood tragedy in Hawaii, he'd learned how far he could push people and when to back away from trouble. He might not always have made the right choice, but he recognized when he needed help, whether he asked for it or not. That and common sense had kept him alive. He knew people, even if he didn't always know how to talk to them. Others were both intelligent and sensible—like Jo Marche, he suspected. Then there was the best category to be in: smart, sensible and lucky.

But luck didn't exist in his world, or in the world of the two men he'd just left at the track. Just the cold hard facts.

He hoped they'd stay at Del Mar and at least make enough money to get home, wherever in Mexico their home was. Daniel would stand by his word and not turn them in. Wearing a uniform didn't cancel out his duties as a minister, and national security wasn't at stake over two luckless brothers, not with the few bits of information he'd received from them.

Daniel paused, tapping the cheap pen against the lined Navy-issue tablet. He'd exchanged the two brothers' freedom for the information. Despite the computer link the Chief had discovered, this new information pointed away from Michael—and his family. Daniel decided to go see Michael as soon as possible to brief him. Michael would have to start the investigation all over again—*still* without a major piece of this puzzle.

A motive.

The McLowery home
9:30 p.m.

DANIEL REACHED for the doorbell, hesitated and dropped his hand, then reached upward again and pressed. The double notes of the chimes sounded. Daniel shifted, uncomfortable despite the casual clothes and sneakers he wore. The only concession he made to his profession was his ever-present chain with the gold cross mounted against a Navy anchor, presented to him on his ordination. He felt for it, rubbed his fingers over it, then tucked it back inside his shirt. Perhaps he should've worn his uniform....

Michael himself opened the door. "What are *you* doing here?"

Daniel overlooked the other man's hostility. "I need to speak to you. Sir."

"Ever heard of a pager? Or a phone? If my father had answered the door—" Michael broke off and stepped outside onto the porch, closing the door behind him. "What do you want?"

"Someplace we can talk in private."

"Here's fine."

"You'll want to be sitting for this one," Daniel said. "And without an audience. Including Jo Marche."

To Daniel's relief, Michael didn't argue. He gestured toward the rocks along the beach in the distance. "Good enough?"

"Lead the way."

A few minutes later, Michael leaned against a large rock, his arms crossed defensively. Daniel didn't bother with a rock—or with any preamble. He came right to the point.

"I managed to track down the two sailors at the track. They told me something you need to hear."

Michael straightened. "They're in custody?"

"Maybe…if your men are still watching the track. I don't carry handcuffs. I'm a chaplain, remember?" Daniel didn't elaborate, nor did he allow Michael to interrupt. "They claim Selena wasn't the intended target. That her death was an accident."

Daniel gave him a moment to take in the news. Kindness and brusqueness mixed together as he dropped military protocol. "It gets worse."

He again waited for his words to sink in—for the listener to prepare himself. "We've been going about this investigation all wrong. You automatically assumed Selena was the target."

Michael immediately defended himself. "I didn't assume she was a target as much as I think the Navy is. Selena wore a uniform. She was killed to cover up the recruitment of illegals as military personnel.''

"I'm aware of that, just as I'm aware that someone's trying to pin the blame on you with the Chief's computer findings. Still—"

"Will you get to the point, Chaplain?"

Daniel took a deep breath. "We've been looking for a motive for Selena's killing. We need to investigate the person Selena replaced as a mock patient for the Fleet exercise. As I said, I learned today that she wasn't the true target."

Michael's eyes narrowed.

"I understand that you borrow ambulatory and stable patients from alcohol rehab, the psych wards and good-behavior prisoners from the camp prison," Daniel went on. "Selena switched places with someone slated to have major leg wounds. That tells us two things. The real target was not regular staff, and the real target was a man. One of the Mexican brothers was in charge of supplying support staff with water and drinks before the hospital exercise went live and the compound went into lockdown. Claimed the makeup artist was old Navy, a real traditionalist who refused to give women any fake wounds that would make them need to use a bedpan. Said it was okay for male soldiers to unbutton their flies during the exercise, but no lady would be dropping her drawers on his watch. And unless a woman outranking him said otherwise, the female moulaged patients would be fake ambulatory or fake dead."

Michael's face paled as comprehension dawned. "Selena had her leg moulaged—a wound that would neces-sitate 'surgery' and bedpan use during the drill. I even remarked on that—told her to get out of the exercise.

But she'd taken time off earlier in the month, so she got stuck playing patient when ordinarily…'' His words trailed off. ''I remember now. She told me…. She relieved the makeup artist, did her own moulage. She went by the roster and gave herself the same wound as the person she was replacing. My God,'' he whispered. ''That's it!''

''You see what I'm driving at? She wasn't—couldn't have been—the original target. Since this was a drill, men and women recovering from surgery would either go to the ambulatory section of the hospital near the Porta Potties or the bedridden section farther away from them. Both sexes room together in a Fleet hospital,'' Daniel emphasized. ''Our spit-and-polish makeup man made certain all patients designated as bedridden were men. And we had no women sent over from prison or any of the wards. I checked the roster.''

''Women in the military rarely end up in alcohol rehab or the brig.'' Michael's voice didn't hold its usual military snappiness.

''Fleet students are rarely used as patients, correct? Because then they can't learn the drill. So if there aren't enough students, staff from FHOTC fills in.''

''Like Selena.''

''Which is why our two runaways said they don't think Selena was the target, but I think her bed definitely was.''

''She wasn't a random hit?''

''Can't be. The Expectant area is on the farthest side of the hospital from the main gate. Why would someone risk a longer escape route than necessary? No, the target was a certain person who was supposed to be in a certain place.''

"But wasn't. I need to find out who she substituted for."

"I already did. He's not going anywhere, Mac. He's in the brig. I suggest we get over there first thing tomorrow."

"Why wait?" Michael jerked his head toward the house. "I'll change. You have a set of khakis or cammies with you?"

"In the car, like any good sailor. But I already have the information you want. The prisoner Selena subbed for is Darrell Wilcox. He's due to be released from pri— the brig in two days. You can't talk to him without a lawyer present, and Legal's closed right now."

Michael took a few brisk steps away from the outcropping, then stopped at Daniel's words. "Assuming our runaway aliens aren't lying to cover their butts. And you're right about the name of our would-be target."

Daniel shrugged, a gesture never allowed in uniform. "I just came back from the brig. I checked out the records to confirm my theory."

"They let you? After hours, no less?"

"I have access around the clock, and I don't need Legal. Don't forget, Mac, I'm a chaplain."

A long pause ensued, filled only by the ocean waves, advancing and retreating. Michael's next words took Daniel totally by surprise.

"A damn good one, I see. Thank you…Chaplain, for your assistance."

Daniel heard the respect in Michael's use of his title. He could have taken pride in his triumph then, but didn't. "Don't thank me for doing my job. Just let me continue to do it. You can't solve this on your own. Don't shut me out. Don't shut Jo out. You need us both."

Daniel didn't expect an answer and he didn't get one.

"I'll meet you at the brig whenever you're ready, sir. Will 0700 be early enough? Shall I expect Ms. Marche?"

After a few seconds Michael responded. "Aye, Chaplain. Do you...do you think this will lead to our killer?" His voice revealed uncharacteristic hesitation.

"I do." Daniel waited, hoping Michael would ask for comfort, for prayer, even continued company. He waited in vain.

"Good night, Chaplain."

Daniel nodded. "Good night, Captain. Tell Jo I said hi."

MICHAEL HEARD the former Dennis Klemko's car drive away. Suddenly the old name didn't fit anymore. The bullying nasty liar had disappeared, replaced by a man worth admiring. Chaplain Daniel Preston had changed in ways he envied. Preston had grown older—*grown up*—while Michael felt as vulnerable, as powerless as a child at his sister's or his mother's funeral.

Could Daniel be right? Was Selena just another victim of the vagaries of life? Like his sister Anna, whose freak death had triggered his mother's bizarre suicide? If Selena had indeed been killed in place of the real target, could he bear that knowledge without going berserk?

Bad enough thinking Selena had a definite enemy. How could he handle the news that she'd simply been in the wrong place at the wrong time—if indeed that was true. Had Anna simply been in the wrong place at the wrong time, too? Had he made an enemy of Dennis—another child—because he himself couldn't handle life's blows without Sunshine holding his hand? Was she still holding his hand?

Had he grown up at all? Or was he still a little boy playing grown-up in a grown-up's uniform, a boy-man whose emotional instability had crippled Selena's investigation? Michael sank to his knees, his face in his hands as his innate honesty answered that question.

The years of his life played out before him. Years without a steady woman in his life. Years without true joy or happiness—nothing but duty. His uniform—was it his only identity? He suddenly felt like nothing more than a kid playing with green plastic Army men in the yard. He'd cheated himself, his family, his friends. Most of all, as a child he'd accused another child of murder— and that child had eventually grown up. Although *he* hadn't.

Until a dead-broke photographer with battered equipment and a former drunken womanizer had shown him how to live in the real world. How to make the decisions demanded of grown-ups.

His father's words burned in his heart. *"You're my pride and joy. You're also my biggest failure."*

His father had lost a wife and a daughter, yet continued on. Jo wore borrowed underwear and wrote trash to stay out of strip joints, yet joked about growing up in poverty-stricken East St. Louis. The maternal yet infertile Sunshine had raised a motherless child and loved him as her own. He remembered something she'd once said to him as a boy.

"True adults do what has to be done with a smile. That smile is the difference between adults and children, no matter what their age. Life isn't fair, Mikey. Life will never be fair, because then it wouldn't be life. If you can someday accept this, yet still stretch and reach for the stars, nothing will hold you back."

Michael lifted his face from his hands and rocked

back off his knees to sit on the cool damp sand. His emotions were too deep for tears. His body felt limp, shocked. He couldn't return to the house—not yet. But his resolve fired and gathered strength. He would find Selena's killer, regardless of personal cost. He closed his eyes and tried to put his tortured mind—and that tortured child inside him—to rest, at least long enough to do his job. Perhaps someday he could put that child to rest for good—and smile, as well.

He didn't know how long he'd been sitting there when he heard, "You okay?" Michael opened his eyes and found Jo standing above him.

"I saw the preacher drive off. You didn't come back."

"Just needed some air."

"I was worried. So was Sunshine. She started to come after you, but I told her to stay put."

"I'm okay."

"Are you?" Jo lowered herself next to him on the sand. "Or are you just saying that?"

"Better than I was. Truly." He saw some of her tension melt.

"That's good. You've been a zombie since the funeral."

He murmured a "Yeah." He actually meant he felt stronger than he had in a very long time, but he didn't feel the urge to correct her. He'd been correcting everyone except himself, a definite mistake.

"The preacher give you a pep talk?"

Michael managed a smile. "Something like that. He has a way with sermons."

"Uh-oh. Fire and brimstone?"

"Not the man's style, but I got the message. Seems I've been wallowing in self-pity."

Jo gasped. "He actually said that?"

"No. I filled in the blanks. He gave me a lot to think about."

"Oh. Well, I'll get going, then. I don't wanna disturb you."

"You could never do that." Michael reached for her wrist and gently held her in place. "Stay."

"As long as you want." The joy in her smile chased away much of the night's dampness and made him wish he could say out loud the words in his heart.

Be careful. I just might hold you to that. Sadly, he didn't have that right, not yet. He grasped her other wrist and pulled her closer. "What would you rather be called? Jo or Lori?" He saw her hesitate. Saw the vulnerability on her face.

"I don't mind the Lori part of my birth name, but I get tired of all the misspellings with Sepanik. And the stupid Polish jokes. My cultural heritage isn't Polish, anyway. I'm bona fide U.S. of A. white trash."

"Never trash. So you'd rather be Jo Marche?" Their knees touched, and he dropped her wrists to encircle her waist.

"No. I'm not ashamed of who I am. Or where I come from."

"Then who do you want to be?"

"I guess…" He watched the play of emotions on her face as he drew her even closer. "I guess I think of myself as Lori-Jo. Like Billy-Bob. Or Peggy-Sue. Jo is my goal, the writer I want to be. I'm not there yet, so I'm still part Lori—Lori-Jo Marche-Sepanik. Does that make any sense?"

Michael nodded once.

"Why ask?" she asked.

"Because, Ms. Lori-Jo Marche-Sepanik, I'd like to know exactly who I'm kissing."

He pulled her onto his lap and gently kissed her nose, her forehead, her cheek before claiming her lips. Jo didn't resist. She surged against him, alive and passionate, a study in contradictions. Strong yet vulnerable. Bold yet approachable. Hard-edged realist yet sensual romantic.

"Lori-Jo," he whispered. "I like that," he said before kissing her again.

Then they were down in the sand, body to body, her soft curves blissfully molding against his military-conditioned muscles. Their kisses seemed like heaven. He couldn't get enough of her, and she immediately flowed into his arms, her generosity showering him with comfort and passion and caring and love, all at once. The combination was so tempting Michael had to pull back—but not too far back. He rolled away from her, sat up, then gathered her onto his lap. He tenderly brushed the sand from her hair before buttoning an open gap on her blouse, the white lace of her hand-me-down bra peeking through.

She reached for his face, her palm warm against his cheek, her sigh filled with frustration and tenderness. "I wish you'd stop starting things you can't finish. My grandmother told me there's a word for boys like you."

"An officer and a gentleman?"

"Actually it's something along the lines of a male tease, but it's Polish and doesn't translate well. Doesn't matter. I have a surprise for you."

He lifted an eyebrow, confused.

"Guess what I found in the bathroom cabinet that wasn't there before? Courtesy of Sunshine, I think. Not that I asked for them," she quickly added. "But the wrapper's new, and I checked the expiration date. The box is right off the drugstore shelves. So if you want to go back to the house—''

''No.''

Pain flickered across her face. He quickly hurried to erase it. ''Lori-Jo, listen to me. I don't mean no to *you,* I mean no, I can't right now. Chaplain Preston stopped by with more than just a sermon. He brought new information.''

By the time Michael finished relating Daniel's theory and his plan to revisit the brig in the morning, Jo's hurt feelings and sexual arousal had disappeared.

''No wonder you're not in the mood! I hope you can sleep, at least. You need your rest.''

He felt guilty accepting her kindness, but remained silent. He wouldn't hurt her more by telling her the real reason he'd refused her generously offered emotional and physical love—and Sunshine's blatant purchase. Her initiative in accepting motives for his withdrawal cut to the quick, glaringly exposing how inadequate he was to handle life…to handle love. He'd shut down years ago.

Sunshine's propped me up since my mother's death. If I take Jo into my life, it'll be as a lover, a wife, a soul mate, not as another leaning post. I need to know I can face the truth about this case and myself…can stand on my own two feet emotionally. Jo deserves that. Until I know if I can, no commitment—because there's no having sex with this woman. It would be making love and making her mine forever.

He would never have thought it possible, but the stakes in this case had just rocketed higher. He now battled for more than honor and country, for more than duty, more than justice for Selena.

For the first time in his life, he battled for his soul,

and a chance at real happiness. Most frightening of all, he had no idea how the battle would end. He'd never been more terrified. This officer and gentleman finally understood the meaning of that trite old saying.

Michael James McLowery was scared to death.

CHAPTER SEVENTEEN

Camp Pendleton Brig
Day 7, 0700 hours

SILENCE REIGNED inside the brig, unlike the noisy atmosphere of public jails. Prisoners in bright orange jumpsuits with stenciled green numbers across the back worked on tasks with the same focus and precision as their colleagues on the base. Inside, floors were mopped and waxed, breakfast trays removed and cleaned. The few windows in the reception area showed outside work details for supervised minimum-security prisoners. The grounds were raked and watered, while various military vehicles were washed by men in orange, monitored by the MPs assigned to guard them.

In the visitor-reception area, Michael couldn't help but wince at Jo's pleased reaction. "What a nice place! Much better than jails back home where I used to visit Dad." Her voice dropped to a whisper. "I don't suppose they'd take civilians? In case I get...you know..."

Michael shook his head to answer her question and warn her off. He continued to stand in the spotless reception area while waiting for Chaplain Preston to return. Despite being assigned temporary duty to Camp Pendleton as a student of Fleet, Daniel had obviously been busy. Michael noticed his familiarity with both brig procedure and staff. They accommodated Daniel with more than the usual military efficiency. They were cheerful, social, even pleasant. The chaplain did seem to have a way of fitting in with people; he could make himself at home with the good and the bad, the familiar and the unfamiliar. Unlike McLowery.

Michael felt ill at ease in the jail. The inmates stood against everything he defined as duty. Liars, cheats and thieves mixed with brawlers, drunks and insubordinates. He wondered how Daniel could so easily avoid differentiating between the humanity of the military's trained war makers—legal killers all—and those who killed a single man in a fit of anger or chemical-induced insanity. The line between the ''good guys'' and the ''bad guys'' was a bold black for Michael, yet Daniel had been able to get information from two escaped aliens he saw as allies, not the enemy. Daniel didn't judge. He accepted people as they were. Michael knew he wouldn't have been as tolerant, or as successful.

However, a good leader knew how to use his troops— and with Jo and Daniel flanking him, he had a better-than-average chance of discovering information leading to the arrest of Selena's killer. The arrival of their brig escort interrupted his thoughts.

''If you'd follow me, sir. Ma'am.''

Michael, Jo and Daniel were led to a secure room with no windows where Darrell Wilcox and his lawyer were seated and waiting. The guard unlocked the room and let them in, closed the door and stood outside at attention. Introductions were made. Michael learned that Lieutenant Gillette was the name of the female lawyer, and Darrell's rank was Third-Class Petty Officer. Gillette confirmed the Third Class's permission to have Jo present.

"There aren't many lookers in this place, sir, that's for sure," Darrell volunteered. "Well...morning, ma'am. I'd shake hands, but..." His chin jerked downward.

His hands were chained to a waist belt, the usual procedure for military prisoners. Handcuffs on men trained in hand-to-hand combat were little protection for their guards. Michael noticed Jo's barely perceptible recoil. Darrell's words were polite, but their tone and his darting glance weren't. Despite the jacket she wore—early mornings were damp—Darrell spoke to Jo's bustline, not her face. Michael could see that Jo didn't like the man.

Neither did he.

"I've already briefed the Third Class and his counsel," Daniel said. "He's agreed to answer any questions that won't incriminate him."

"I did the crime, served the time and I'm outta here tomorrow, sir. Don't wanna screw up my release. But ask away, sir."

"I'd like to look at your case file first." Michael reined in his temper as Darrell checked out Jo's thighs in her tight jeans.

"My client's records aren't available to you without his permission."

Daniel spoke up. "Those records concern his robbery convictions, Captain. I've explained to the Third Class and his counsel that you might detain him here regarding his alleged involvement in the murder of an officer. Cooperation, Third Class, is to your benefit." Daniel's smile and tone were a vision of pastoral caring, but Michael saw that the emotion didn't begin to touch his eyes, which were icy cold.

Michael decided that Chaplain Daniel Preston could be just as powerful an opponent as an ally.

"Against my counsel's advice, I told the chaplain here to help himself. You too, sir. Read all you want," the prisoner said.

The lawyer pushed over the file, a release form with Darrell's signature and hers on top. Michael read, signed and reached for the file. He didn't like what he saw inside.

Record of juvenile petty theft. Problem working with women. Past count of sexual harassment, but dropped. Past theft of car radios on military property. Present conviction, multiple counts—planning the breaking and entering into military-base housing by three-member civilian crime ring for theft of electronic items, especially computers. Illegal resale of said electronics as legitimate sale items on government property. Assault on military dependents.

Michael then read that the sailor had decided to turn in his associates and provide all details of who, what, where and why in return for a light sentence and dishonorable discharge. He felt distaste rise in his throat. Not only had the man broken the law, he'd betrayed his buddies. Michael would hate to be in battle with this man watching his back. He flipped through the pages listing names, addresses and details, stopping when one item caught his attention.

One of Darrell's civilian thieves hadn't been able to participate in a planned burglary. Darrell himself had stepped in to fill the role—and inadvertently caught two women at home alone. He'd assaulted both of them, but their cries brought help from able-bodied sailors living next door, and the subsequent arrest of the gang. The military housing unit where Darrell's luck ran out was listed under the name...

Michael's head jerked up. His gaze met Daniel's. Jo

leaned over and stared at the typed name above Michael's forefinger.

Puripong.

Parking lot, Camp Pendleton Brig
0900 hours

JO HELD TIGHTLY to Michael's left arm, despite his uniform and being in public. Daniel walked close beside him, on his right. Michael's fury registered in his rock-hard forearm, the tight set to his jaw and the murderous expression on his face. Worse yet was his frightening total silence. She hung on to his arm for dear life, afraid that if she let go he'd do something stupid, crazy, violent—even though bars and bricks separated him from Darrell, and distance separated him from Puripong. As a woman whose own life had often depended on being able to spot murderous intentions, she knew Michael teetered dangerously on the fence separating civilized from primitive. She somehow had to disarm him using the most powerful weapon she had—words.

"If you beat the tar out of Darrell or Puripong now, we won't learn the murderer's motive. And you do want to know why, don't you?" Jo blurted.

Both men stopped and stared at her, the chaplain as shocked as Michael at her sudden question.

"Well, don't you, McLowery? Don't you think Sunshine wants to know? And Selena's fiancé? And Gibson and her family? We've got to find the connection between Darrell, Selena and Puripong."

"That bitch has gotta be involved!" Michael ground out.

"She probably is," Jo agreed. "But as a journalist, I

want to know the details before you draw and quarter her.''

''Keelhaul. That's the Navy term,'' he muttered irritably.

''Whatever! Just let me get my story before you play vigilante, okay? Wouldn't you know, I'm out of film, too. Where's the PX? Can I go in?''

''BX—Base Exchange.''

Jo shook off Michael's arm. ''Stop correcting me! Whenever you fly off the handle, the rest of us have to put up with it. But I get your lingo wrong and I get a damn lecture! We already have a preacher here, so why don't you just forget the sermons? And while you're at it, stop acting like a little kid.''

Michael stared at her, jerked out of his anger. Before her eyes, he changed from a stranger to the man she loved—and had purposely hurt. Pain replaced his rage. Michael shook himself free of Jo, pulled his car keys from his pocket and proceeded to unlock his door.

''I didn't mean it,'' Jo tried to call after him. Her legs shook so hard her knees buckled. Michael, inside the car and staring at the steering wheel, didn't see, but Daniel did. He caught Jo before she sank to her knees on the spongy black asphalt, which was heated and leaking tar under the blazing California sun.

''Thank you, Lord,'' she whispered.

''Amen,'' Daniel seconded, pulling her against him to hold her up.

''I didn't want to hurt him,'' Jo whispered. ''I just wanted to shake him out of that mood. He was scaring the hell out of me.''

''You were amazing. Absolutely A-1 amazing. I didn't have a clue how to reach him. Thought he'd gone off the deep end for sure. You got him back for me, Sister Jo. For us.''

Jo drew a deep shuddering breath. ''Yeah, well, it's not over yet—and I told you before not to call me Sister. I don't do churches.''

''Neither does Mac,'' Daniel said.

''I'm beginning to think he doesn't even do sex, let alone marriage. I'll never figure that guy out.''

''Wrong. You know him inside and out. Certainly well enough to be his wife. You'll get married, and in my church, if I have the last word—and I'll call you Sister Jo then, and every Sunday after when you show up. Kids included.''

''Ha! That'll be the day.'' Jo smiled, and felt some of the man's spiritual strength flow into her own battered soul. ''Hey, you just did for me what I did for Mac—except you distracted me with pie-in-the-sky dreams instead of insults, you sneaky Bible toter.''

Daniel smiled, and this time the smile did reach his eyes. ''I'm learning.''

Jo managed to straighten up and stand, although Daniel's strong hands remained steady on her forearms. ''Thanks.''

''You're welcome. You okay now?''

''I'm fine—adrenaline letdown, that's all. I vote we let you and the MPs question Puripong. I want Michael McLowery in my bed, if the idiot will ever take off his uniform, but I can't seduce him if he's in the slammer for murder.''

''I agree. We don't need Puripong and Mac in the same room. It's going to be hard to keep him away from her, though.''

Jo allowed Daniel to release her and guide her to the car. ''Why? Doesn't she live out of state?''

"Nope. She lives right here on base."

"I thought she was a student...on temporary duty. I'm wrong?"

"She *is* a student, but her permanent station is the Camp Pendleton Hospital. Her family lives in military family housing here."

"Hell." Jo flicked a quick glance at the car. "Let's not tell him."

"He's got the rank and the authority for an official inquiry. He'll insist on being there. And he's got the right, you know."

Jo exhaled slowly through parted lips. "I guess we can tag-team him again if he starts going funny on us. You know where this housing is?"

"No. Michael should. We may as well get it over with, Sister Jo."

"I suppose, but for God's sake, don't let him drive. He'll kill us all."

Daniel dropped his ministerial demeanor. "No one else is dying here, lady. Not one single damned person."

Jo recognized the steel behind those words and felt very glad that her man had Chaplain Daniel Preston on his side.

Base Housing, Complex Three, Officers' area
1230 hours

MICHAEL SAT IN THE BACK SEAT of the chaplain's government car. He'd allowed Daniel to drive, Jo beside him. She'd offered to sit in back so he could give directions from the front, but Michael had refused. Then she'd wanted to sit in the back with him, but he'd refused that, as well. As he sat in the chaplain's car, he watched the spouses—mostly female, some males—the children and their friends stop and watch the chaplain's car progress.

Nervous civilian parents peered out of windows. Military children on summer vacation, some wise beyond their years, dropped their toys or stopped their skateboards as the car drove slowly through the housing areas. Only when it went past their homes did the spectators' nervousness disappear with relief that they weren't *the ones.*

The ones about to get the bad news. Michael saw the irony of the situation. Once, he was the child watching the government car slowly drive through the officers' housing area; he was the child who checked for the chaplain's insignia collar and then raced inside to his father. Now he was in that feared car—the Death Car.

"Chaplain, we should call first, let these people know Puripong isn't dead," Michael said, his voice an order.

"Way ahead of you, sir. I called earlier from the brig," Daniel replied.

Michael settled back against the seat, the kind of seat that reminded him of Anna and reminded him of other times when other military families had lost a loved one. Sailors didn't need a war to die. Their training, their weapons, their way of life could and did kill. How many of these children would have parents around to see their grandchildren? Outside, he saw a little girl and boy playing with Styrofoam gliders. Toy gliders—were they still around? They used to be the favorite toy of pilots' kids. Only his were made out of balsa wood back then. The balsa was so thin, it always shattered after one or two crash landings.

Crash landings and death—the worst fear of every pilot's kid. He remembered an air show he'd attended as a young boy. The show had featured the local base's best precision-flying team. Michael had seen his first crash at that performance. There were mechanical problems with the plane. Suddenly the cheering spectators with their Brownie cameras and eight-millimeter Bolex movie cameras stopped talking, stopped filming. Even the children knew something was wrong; they'd grown up with the sounds of runways and bustling hangars and flight towers and plane engines. After a while, no one registered normal plane sounds—the brain filtered them out. But this time, the abnormal sound of a plane engine gone wrong froze children and adults alike. Michael's popcorn fell to the ground as his eyes lifted heavenward to see the pilot battle a wild, bucking Brahma bull of a craft.

The pilots on the ground mentally estimated the failsafe eject time. The plane descended as the pilot bravely wrestled to find a crash area that wouldn't threaten the crowd. The plane flew lower and lower as uniforms and civilians mouthed, "Come on, come on," and "Eject, eject."

Michael himself thought, *Come on! Jump and yell "Geronimo!"*

Geronimo was the legendary Apache warrior whose holy men had accurately prophesied that no bullet, no arrow, no blade would ever touch him—and whose name was reverently invoked by modern warriors who coveted his legendary invulnerability to all the weapons of war.

The plane came ever closer to the ground. Women's hands reached for their children's. Men's hands clenched into fists. Michael remembered that neither parent had touched him. He'd continued to watch, shocked at how low the plane was. Then the cockpit flew off. A collective gasp from the crowd registered the pilot's tumbling body. Less than a hundred feet from the ground, close enough for all to see, he pulled the ripcord on his parachute.

Seconds later the plane crashed in a big ball of fire. Babies cried, tiny backs arched in protest at the sudden noise. Mothers held them tightly, but the explosion, not their children, had their attention. The silent crowd stared at the pilot to see if the half-inflated parachute would fill. Michael counted to himself, just like his father had taught him, just like he did when he played pilot.

ONE one thousand, TWO two thousand... The parachute blossomed open. The crowd gasped again. The pilot was so close to the ground they could see his head and his knees jerk, hear the *crack* of the silk snapping wide open as it met the resistance of the air.

THREE three thousand... The wind blew the pilot toward the fireball of jet-fueled inferno. *FOUR four thousand.* The man had beaten the odds to save the lives of others, and now this wind. The pilot didn't have enough room to maneuver. *FIVE five thousand...*

The crowd watched. The fire trucks didn't even move from their position as the pilot sank into the orange flames and disappeared completely from view. No one said a thing, no one in that vast crowd moved. Michael felt sick inside. "Daddy," he finally dared to whisper, "Is he dead?"

His father didn't reply—and Michael had his answer. Patrick had reached for the hand of his son and his wife, and as one, the crowd silently walked away from the airstrip and to their cars in the parking lot. Except for the tears on people's faces, he could almost have pretended that nothing had happened.

Now, THE ADULT MICHAEL watched the faces outside, feeling deep compassion for those families, the brave spouses and children, who never knew when, or even if, their loved ones would return home from "work." He wondered how they handled the stress or the tragedies in their young lives.

Did the children he now watched grow up before their time when tragedy touched their lives? Or did they simply shut down, as he had after Anna's funeral? Michael gathered his resolve. No more hiding. Time to emerge from behind the invisible walls he'd built all those years ago.

The car slowed and stopped outside the residence of Commander Coral Puripong and her family.

CHAPTER EIGHTEEN

Living room of Puripong home
Base Housing

THE INSIDE LIVING AREA was spotlessly clean and taste-fully decorated. It was as unique and individual inside as its standard government exterior was faceless and uniform.

Jo sat in a wicker chair across from two of Commander Puripong's relations, the grandmother and Puripong's married younger sister. The grandmother looked out of place in this luxury, for her ravaged face and scarred, callused hands told of a hard life. Jo noted that the sister was a good deal younger than Puripong and a good deal prettier—not that Jo judged anyone by physical looks alone. The grandmother with her battered face and body had the canny smarts of a survivor, Jo quickly realized. The pretty sister with the immaculately done hair and nails definitely followed the grandmother's lead.

Jo leaned back in her wicker chair, watching the silent interplay between the two Puripong women, and wondered if Michael and Daniel knew they wouldn't get any information unless the grandmother allowed it. The grandmother acted as if she couldn't speak English and constantly interrupted the conversation for long, lengthy translations from the granddaughter. The granddaughter spoke English well, but she acted less intelligent than Jo suspected she was.

Jo figured both acts were ruses to protect Puripong, so much so that when she asked to use the bathroom, she'd missed nothing while she was gone. The two Filipinas took more than an hour to give out less information on the robbery than Jo had learned from Darrell himself. Michael's frustration matched Daniel's, Jo saw. The other two women had patient cunning, a trait Jo knew no offspring from any well-fed, white-collar family like Michael's could ever understand—or breach. Finally the men threw in the proverbial towel and rose to their feet.

"If you think of anything else, you can reach me at this number," Michael said, leaving his military business card. Daniel did the same. Michael reached for Jo's hand to help her up, but Jo shook her head.

"Wait for me out in the car, please," she said.

"But..." Michael hesitated.

"Trust me," she said.

"Let's wait in the car, sir," Daniel suggested. "Don't get up, ladies. We'll show ourselves out."

The two women exchanged quick nervous looks as the men left. Jo sat back in her chair and settled down comfortably. They waited. Jo waited, too, gathering her thoughts. Women had a different timetable than men when it came to conversation. Women who'd grown up with hard times knew when to remain silent and when to strike. It wasn't until the two women again exchanged nervous glances that Jo spoke.

"What did Darrell do to you? And why did Commander Puripong arrange to have him killed?"

The younger started translating to the older, but Jo held up her hand. "Please, don't insult my intelligence."

She jerked her head toward the front door. "I'm not military, but I think I know what happened," Jo said, trusting her instincts. "The men outside think Puripong wanted Darrell dead. The Captain's family member, Selena Mellow, had to work because she'd taken a weekend off earlier in the month. Unfortunately for her, she took the bed—and the fake wound—assigned to Darrell. He remained in jail, unneeded here at Fleet, while Selena ended up dead at your granddaughter's hand. Commander Puripong will be arrested. I—we—want to know why she did it."

Jo sat back and waited again. The grandmother spoke up in accented but perfectly adequate English. "Who are you, Miss?"

"The Captain's future wife," Jo said boldly. "I can help you if you'll let me. I want you to tell me why this happened."

Now the granddaughter lapsed into her native tongue, but the grandmother sharply cut her off in the same language.

"I admit nothing, but I would like to hear your theory," the older woman said.

"The incident report says Darrell and his crooks broke into your home at a time they thought no one was here. The other two took your computer and big-screen TV while Darrell stood guard. When they left, he decided to help himself to something more." She stared pointedly at the granddaughter, who looked about the same age as Jo herself, but with a timeless beauty Jo envied.

The granddaughter's face remained a blank mask, as did the grandmother's.

"I met our thief in the brig today. His eyes were all over me—like a pimp checking out new meat. I know the type. I've met those creeps before. My guess as to what happened? I think you—'' Jo addressed the younger woman ''—were raped, and for whatever reason, Coral decided to take care of the matter herself, without the police. So you didn't report the rape. Only Selena wanted off work early, and everything went wrong. Coral Puripong's unknowing accessory, one of the Fleet staff, accidentally killed the wrong person. I may as well admit that I took a peek into your bedrooms after using the bathroom.'' Jo turned to the grandmother. ''You should have taken down the nursery, Mrs. Puripong. Because I saw baby clothes with price tags on them, purchased months ago—yet I don't see a pregnant woman around. It makes me suspect...'' Jo shrugged. ''Maybe you should tell me what happened, instead of listening to my guesses.''

The grandmother sighed heavily, then spoke to her granddaughter in English. ''Please make rice and tea for me. Perhaps our guest will join me.''

''But—''

''Obey me,'' the grandmother said quietly.

Without another protest, the beautiful woman glided out of the room.

''Now there are just the two of us,'' Grandmother Puripong said. ''I will speak to you without a witness, woman to woman. I will also deny anything you repeat if I need to protect my family.''

Jo nodded. ''I understand.''

''I believe you do.'' The old woman slowly exhaled and reached for a pack of cigarettes. ''Do you mind? I am an old woman. So few pleasures for me these days.''

Jo picked up the coffee-table lighter, a large silver piece with markings from some far-off Oriental port, and flicked on the flame.

''My Middle Granddaughter has looked after us since

she was seventeen. She is the clever one in our family," Grandmother Puripong remarked after a few deep drags. "Let me tell you about her."

Jo sat and listened as the woman told of the old days back in the Philippines. The grandmother smoked two, three more cigarettes, and Jo continued to listen. The granddaughter returned with chopsticks, rice and tea. Jo—with no chopstick experience—politely accepted only the tea. The grandmother eagerly partook of both while talking.

"I am always hungry. My whole life I have been hungry," she said. "My doctor tells me I am too thin, and he blames these." The grandmother stubbed out yet another butt and sipped at her tea. "You understand he's wrong."

Jo nodded.

"Let me tell you why I stopped smoking once—unless an old lady's stories bore you."

Jo sipped her tea. "If they did, I would never let it show. My own grandmother would have tanned my hide."

"Your elders raised you well." She lit another cigarette. "So I will tell you what you wish to know. Then you will tell me what I should do for my Middle Granddaughter."

OUT IN THE CAR, the engine and the air conditioner running, Michael tapped his knee with his forefinger. "What's taking her so long?"

"She's a woman. I don't pretend to understand them," Daniel said from his spot in the driver's seat. "But Jo seems to know what she's doing. We've got to wait. If anyone can get us that motive, she's the one."

Suddenly aware of Daniel's piercing gaze, Michael

stopped tapping his knee. "I've got a question to ask you."

"Yes?"

"Why did you draw that picture of my mother?"

"Finally. After all this time. I wondered if you'd ever get around to asking."

"Well?"

Daniel looked out the window as he began his response. "I always liked to draw, Michael. I was, and still am, damn good at it. As a kid, I would have killed for drawing lessons. Instead, I got stuck with Scouts. I hated it."

"You did?"

"Yeah. All that talk about duty and honesty. I got enough of that from my father. Then when he was killed in Vietnam, I had to hear more of it. Duty. Honor. Bull to me. Pure, unadulterated bull to a fatherless child. My father chose the military as a way of life. He shoved it down my throat every minute of every day. I had to say yes sir, no sir, no excuse, sir. I did it at home, I did it in Scouts, too, but all I wanted to do was draw. However, to my father, drawing—art—was for sissies. Poor man, he actually thought a set of watercolors would turn me into a homosexual—only that isn't the word he used. As if uniforms and guns would make his boy a real man."

Daniel turned and faced him. "So I was forced to listen to all the duty and honor speeches. Then Dad was killed in 'Nam, fighting a war that wasn't even our business."

"But your father wasn't a politician. He died following orders," Michael said. "Doesn't that count for something?"

"Not to me then, not to me now. My father was killed by friendly fire."

Michael blinked.

"Oh, yeah. I wasn't supposed to know, but I was a sneaky little bastard—had to be, if I wanted to keep up my sketching when Dad was around. When I found out his death was accidental, I hated the military even more. The ironic thing is, I ended up doing what Dad wanted most for me. Joining the Navy and wearing the uniform." Daniel lifted his hand and rubbed the cross on his collar gently, reverently. "But I decided to come up with my own definition of honor and duty."

Michael remained silent, noting a look of peace and maturity on the other man's face that became him well. Daniel dropped his hand.

"But I'm getting ahead of myself, not answering your question. Back in Hawaii I wanted something all my own, a hobby that didn't have any connection to Dad or the military. And I liked art in school. Man, I lived for art class. So I drew pictures. Sheets and sheets of pictures. Earlier that week I'd checked out this anatomy book from the base library. The author said a strong knowledge of the human body was necessary for every good artist. Your mother was my first figure."

To Michael, Daniel's words held the ring of truth. "You were practicing...." Michael broke off, unable to finish.

"Anatomy. Yeah. I was a rotten little brat back then, but I wasn't sexually knowledgeable enough to get a cheap thrill from a naked woman. Hormones had nothing to do with the death of your sister. Anna died because I lied to protect the one part of me that kept me sane. Made me happy. I lied about you because I didn't want my father to find out I'd been drawing, instead of being a good little duty-and-honor Scout. I lied, Mac," Daniel said, meeting Michael's gaze head-on. "That was my crime."

"All these years, I thought…"

"…I'd been responsible for the death of your sister, and you're right. I set those events in motion with a single lie. Lying is easier for those without courage. I lied when I agreed with my father that art lessons were for sissies. I lied every time I put on a Scout uniform. And I lied when I told your mother you drew the picture. Lying was easier," Daniel repeated. "I finally quit when I gave up hookers, six-packs for breakfast and hating you."

Michael blinked. "You hated me? Why?"

"*Think*, Mac! I thought I was a murderer! Being what my father called the art sissy was bad enough. Being the baby-killer was living hell! No one else knew, but I felt it all the same. When my father was killed, I was more relieved than anything—he'd never know how my drawing had caused such grief. He'd never throw I-told-you-so in my face. And then I felt even more guilt for being glad he died. You ruined my life—or so I thought."

"My God," Michael whispered.

"Exactly. When I finally faced the fact that I alone was responsible for triggering your sister's accident by choosing to lie, I finally, *finally* grew up. I thought if I could help others through their dark times, I could redeem myself. I can identify with less-than-model citizens. I was one myself for years. Mac, I can never undo your sister's death or your mother's. But my father, despite his faults, swore an oath to God and country, and died by that oath. Who was I to do any less? I might have been a disgrace to my Scout uniform, but not this one. Never this one."

Michael spoke. "Strange. I felt the same way. That's how I ended up in the military. Except that I took my mother's place in the hospital, not my father's in jets."

"We are our parents' sons," Daniel said with a wry grimace.

"You're much more than that."

"What are you talking about?"

"Don't shoulder all the blame, Daniel. You're innocent. I yelled for my father because I was afraid. When he hit the brakes and spun the car to assist me, that's when Anna was thrown. I always blamed myself. Out loud I blamed you, but inside I knew it was *my* fault all along. Mine, not yours."

Daniel's eyes opened wide. Suddenly Michael understood that the former Dennis Klemko's pain had been as tortured as his own.

"You may have set events in motion with your lie," Michael went on, "but I finished the job because I was afraid, too. Afraid of facing my mother, afraid of the troop catching up to me, afraid of my father dying in 'Nam. He served two tours there. Two years in that hellhole. I worried Mom would get sent, too. I spent the whole war—my whole childhood—afraid. So don't blame yourself, Chaplain. We were children of war, children of fear. Victims of fear." Michael said the words with conviction for the first time in his life and reached for Daniel's shoulder with his hand. "So was Anna. Her death was an accident."

"I could have prevented it," Daniel insisted in a hoarse voice.

"No one could've prevented it. Not you, not me, not anyone. We were kids back then. We deserved pity and—to use one of your religious words—absolution. It was an accident. A tragedy, yes, but still an accident.

We didn't have parents who could explain that. So I'm doing it for them. For us.''

The two men stared at each other, years of hate and guilt falling away until Daniel lowered his wet eyes. He clasped Michael's hand, squeezing it with gratitude and relief.

Michael squeezed back. Then aware of his uniform and embarrassed at this physical and emotional intimacy with a male, withdrew his hand and pointedly checked his wristwatch. ''Where is that woman?'' he muttered. ''What's she's doing in there, anyway?''

Jo STOOD IN THE NURSERY with Grandmother Puripong.

''This was to be my great-grandchild's room. We wanted it ready for when my granddaughter's husband came back from sea. We were all going to surprise him.''

Jo felt tears prick her eyes. The beautiful young woman washing up the teacups and rice bowls in the kitchen hadn't been raped, although that had been Darrell's intention. She and her grandmother had beaten Darrell off, then the neighbors had arrived—but not before Darrell had delivered a vicious kick to the pregnant woman's belly. Later that night, long after the MPs had left, she'd suffered a miscarriage.

''So the killer of my great-grandchild is allowed to bargain for his freedom by testifying against the others, who are merely thieves. Your country sets killers free. This my Middle Granddaughter could not allow.''

Grandmother Puripong slowly pivoted and returned to her chair in the living room. Jo did the same.

''It doesn't sound right to me,'' Jo protested. ''Surely the judge saw the hospital records....''

Grandmother Puripong shook her head. ''They do not

know he is a killer. There are no records. Neither of us went to the Navy hospital.''

''Why not?''

''The pregnancy was more than five months along, and my Youngest Granddaughter felt a military doctor was too dangerous. My Middle Granddaughter had already decided to take matters into her own hands,'' she said simply. ''We knew a hospital record of the miscarriage would link her to Darrell's death, so we went to a civilian doctor, instead.''

Dear Lord. Jo's heart went out to the younger Puripong. ''Even without records, you could've told the authorities and gotten Darrell the sentence he deserved.''

''We could have talked to them, yes. But would Darrell truly get punished? Your country is no different from ours. Women are still at the mercy of men. Your government refuses to pass a law saying women are equal. Women are passed over in favor of men for promotions in the military and in the civilian world. Men make more money than women, and as a result women still depend on men. You know this to be true. You yourself wish to help me by using your influence with a man.''

''Nonetheless, you can't let this rest, Mrs. Puripong.''

''It is not my decision to make, nor has it ever been. My Middle Granddaughter is our family head. All major decisions are hers to make. The consequences are hers to bear, as well.''

''But...'' Jo could have wept at the loss of life, the loss of career, the loss of dreams and hopes for the whole Puripong family.

The old woman reached for her cigarettes with bony fingers. ''I had planned to stop, but with no baby coming...'' She lit up, dragged and exhaled on a long sigh. ''Thank you for your patience with an elderly woman.''

Jo knew she'd been dismissed and rose to her feet. "I'm so sorry for your family's troubles."

Grandmother Puripong shrugged. "That is life, full of trouble. We shall endure."

The Youngest Granddaughter appeared from the kitchen to walk Jo to the door and open it for her.

"We are women, and women always survive, yes?" the Youngest Granddaughter ventured to say.

Jo thought of Selena Mellow and the two female McLowerys—baby Anna and Michael's mother. "Not always," she said softly, then the door quietly closed between them. Jo stood on the porch for a few seconds to compose herself, then rejoined the waiting men.

CHAPTER NINETEEN

Fleet Hospital, parking lot
1430 hours

THE *WHOOM, WHOOM, WHOOM* of artillery echoed throughout the valley as Michael climbed out of the car into the overpowering heat. Shimmering mirages seeped up from the sticky black asphalt and shivered in the Santa Ana wind, while dust eddies formed over bare compound areas. Michael ignored the heated air, his anger overtaking and overpowering his every thought. Even that dissipated as the dangerous calm of the stalking warrior took over. A small part of his brain registered Jo and Daniel striving to keep up with his rapid pace.

"Wait here with her, Lieutenant," he said, his clipped tones making the words an order. Jo protested, but Chaplain Preston did not. Michael left them and made his way to the compound gate's guard shack. There he strapped on a pistol and mustered Jackson and two other male MAs. Jackson immediately fell in next to Michael, her head snapping around at his "Find Puripong. We're placing her in custody."

As they marched into the compound, he registered the students staring at his grim face and at the three guards with their rifles-at-the-ready position, unlocked and loaded with real bullets. The sailor students knew they were witnessing not a training drill, but the real thing. Michael's mind and body went into an even higher gear of battle readiness. He tensed, ready to spring into action at the slightest hint of trouble.

The male sailors preceded him into the canvas opening to Fleet Hospital. Michael started to enter, as well, but Jackson shook her head and silently pointed toward the Triage opening on the other side. Michael nodded his understanding. Before Jackson had time to take the lead, Puripong flew out of the Triage entrance and climbed the six-foot-high fence.

"Stop her!" Michael cried. Too late. Except for Jackson, Puripong had surprised everyone. She avoided the highest barbed wire and set out over the facing hilly terrain. Jackson ran out the guarded main entrance and around the fence to the hill, unable to climb easily with her rifle. Michael slipped the safety on his pistol and added the over-the-gun holster strap, then raced for the fence. He climbed quickly, ignoring the sudden swipe of barbed wire on his cheek. He jumped over, a few paces ahead of Jackson as she rejoined him. The race was on.

Puripong had the lead. For a small woman, she ran surprisingly fast. She scurried over the terrain and nimbly avoided the brush, rocks, trees and other obstacles. So did Michael McLowery. Every tour-stationed sailor or Marine at Camp Pendleton had jogged through the tough desert scrub during numerous physical training stints. But desperation drove Puripong farther, and she didn't have the added burden of a rifle in her arms. She ran faster, her arms pumping.

Jackson, a stranger to the terrain and carrying a rifle, started to fall behind. Michael slowed to keep pace with her, then ordered, "Hold up, Jackson."

"Captain, I can get her! We're so close! Unless..."

Jackson held the rifle up and pointed it at the woman's calf.

Michael shook his head. "Hold your fire. This is where the artillery range begins."

"Sir?"

"We're in no-man's land." He scanned for and found a warning sign off in the distance, and pointed.

Jackson muttered an ugly expletive, scowling in frustration. "She's gonna get herself killed!"

"Puripong! Stop!" he yelled. "You're in the firing range!"

She slowed, then stopped right in front of another warning sign. The three adults faced each other, Jackson with rifle now aiming at the other woman's chest. Michael left his pistol in its holster, ignoring blood that dripped down his torn cheek, saying, "Hands up, Commander! And keep 'em up as you head back to me."

Puripong raised her hands but remained in position. Michael ventured forward until he could hear her more clearly, trusting Jackson to cover him. A large distance still separated the two.

"You're here to arrest me," she said during the quiet between artillery hits.

"Yes—for the murder of Selena Mellow."

"I'm sorry about your cousin's death, sir."

Michael continued to advance, then stopped just outside the danger perimeter.

"How did you find out?" she asked.

"The chaplain, the reporter and I went to your home. Jo spotted the nursery—the crib, the diapers, the baby clothes—when she asked to use the bathroom. You didn't take the nursery down."

"The nursery..."

"That's what gave you away—leaving it."

"My sister wants more children. None of us thought it necessary to dismantle everything. As for Darrell…" She let the words trail off.

"I understand your motive, Commander. But I don't understand how you tied my computer into this mess or what this has to do with the illegals."

"I didn't do anything to your computer. I had no part in the hiring of aliens. I strongly suggest, Captain, that you let that problem slide. As I also strongly suggest you let the true nature of Selena Mellow's death slide. The Navy doesn't want adverse publicity, and my death will solve your quest for revenge."

"It won't bring back my cousin!"

"Nor will it bring back my sister's unborn child or punish Darrell for that child's death. But it will save my family from disgrace and give yours a certain sense of justice." Puripong sighed. "You have no evidence to prove your theory. Tell my family I took care of everything, as I always have."

Puripong slowly dropped her arms and started walking backward, moving farther into the artillery area.

"Commander, no!" Jackson yelled. "Come back!"

McLowery removed his holster with gun and spare ammo, and dropped it on the ground, safe from any shrapnel hits and sudden detonation of bullets.

"What are you doing?" Jackson demanded.

"Going after her," McLowery said. "Get on the horn and have someone stand down the shelling."

"Are you insane, sir? You'll get yourself k—"

The screaming whistle of an approaching shell pierced the air.

"Incoming!" Michael threw himself at Jackson and covered her as they hit the dirt. Jackson lost her breath. Michael covered his ears.

Puripong ignored him. She lifted her chin before he ducked his own. The artillery shell landed with an ear-splitting massive *whoom,* exploding shrapnel tearing apart dirt, plants and Puripong.

When the cloud of destruction settled and abated, only lifeless bare rock remained.

Michael rolled off Jackson. Neither of them had sustained any injury save temporary deafness. By the time Jo, Daniel and other uniforms had arrived, the deafness had worn off. One of the approaching staff made a radio call that halted the artillery exercise while Jackson stared at Michael, then at the bomb site. Daniel reached for his pocket Bible, body detail approached, and Jo hugged Michael, trying to stem the bleeding from his badly torn cheek with a bandanna.

"That'll need stitches," she said.

A few minutes later silence reigned as military personnel sorted out the situation, doing tasks quickly and efficiently. Michael merely watched, Jo on one side of him, Jackson on the other, her rifle safely locked and hanging by a strap from her shoulder.

"Dumb-ass fool of a pea-brained officer!" Jackson spat out dirt after the words.

Michael shook his head. "She lived and died for family. Don't dare judge her, Jackson. Not in front of me—not in front of anyone." He stared at the hole in the ground and silently grieved at the waste.

"I have to notify the next of kin, sir. Permission to leave?" Daniel asked.

"Granted. Jackson, have someone radio my office and track down the Commanding General. Send a message that if he isn't personally available to see me this afternoon, I go to the media without him—courtesy of Ms. Jo Marche and Associated Press."

Despite the smell of death, carbide and sweat in the air, he was sharply aware of Jo's fragrance as she stood next to him.

"Wait in my office, sweetheart," he said, his voice gentle. "I'll find someone to give you a ride to Sunshine's and meet you back there."

"Mac, your face…"

"I'll see the corpsman. But you go ahead. I have business to take care of."

The Ranch Area, Camp Pendleton
Commanding General's home
1700 hours

HIS CHEEK NEATLY STITCHED, McLowery and the General faced each other in the main room of the old home that had once been occupied by residents of the former Pendleton Ranch. Named a historical building, the ranch house was appropriately furnished to bring out a relaxed, old-California atmosphere. That atmosphere affected neither man as McLowery spoke and the General listened.

"That's the story of my cousin's murder, General," McLowery concluded. "Now I'd appreciate it, sir, if you'd tell me about the illegal aliens."

The General was silent for a moment. "You know," he began, "the American people have gone soft. They're overfed, underworked and as materialistic as they come."

"Sir?"

"It isn't like the American Revolution or the World Wars. Hardly anyone wants to join the military anymore, let alone make a career of it. Aliens are hungry for food, shelter and medical care. What's more, many of them are uneducated and, in a battle, relatively expendable."

McLowery's breath caught at the bald words. "That's your opinion, General. Not mine."

"Actually, you'd be surprised how many of my superiors subscribe to that thinking. However, if such a plan were in effect, the Navy could hardly go public with it, could they, Captain?"

"No, but a civilian reporter could," McLowery said calmly.

"That wouldn't be wise," the General warned. He pulled out a cigar and clipped the end. "Not wise at all." He reached for his lighter. "Do you mind, Captain?"

"I do mind, General. I mind a lot of things."

The General set down his unused lighter, but continued to roll the cigar between his thumb and forefinger. "What kind of spin would make you...mind less?"

Dammit to hell—I'm gonna be either the hero or the scapegoat here. McLowery thought of Selena, Sunshine, Paul—Selena's fiancé. He thought of Daniel Preston, Mia Gibson, the surviving Puripongs, Jo Marche—especially Jo—and thought quickly.

"Obviously you want me to ignore the escape of the two aliens. That won't be hard, since they're probably back in Mexico by now. We'll never find them. Puripong's death can be ruled an accident, not a suicide. She didn't notice the artillery signs while doing her daily jog. Her family gets survivors' benefits."

"Even though students are restricted to the compound?" the General argued.

"She was helping me in the investigation, as was Chaplain Preston, whom I released from Fleet compound restriction. Naturally, others will assume I released Pur-

ipong from that restriction, as well. The students will be
told the escapees were all part of the exercise. Only a
few of my staff know the truth. I'll make sure the knowledge stops there. Selena's death distracted most of them,
anyway.''

The General nodded. "Go on."

Michael considered his next words carefully, eyes nar-
rowing. ''Darrell Wilcox tampered with my computer.
According to his records, he stole only the high-end
models and therefore can be assumed to know something
about computers. He planned to break into my parents'
house and steal it, check my files and see if he could
rob the computers at Fleet during the commotion of this
exercise.''

''Weak, but it'll hold,'' the General said, finally light-
ing his cigar with a quick glance at Michael.

''Not weak at all, General. I'm betting Darrell had
something to do with our alien inductions into the Navy.
He and his gang speak a total of five different languages,
including Spanish. But Darrell didn't use his skills for
his country. He used them for himself.''

The General puffed on his cigar.

''My parents' computer wasn't stolen, merely tampered with—soon after Darrell got a lucky break when
Selena took the bullet meant for him. Darrell knew his
life was in jeopardy and he knew who was gunning for
him. He found someone to hack into my computer, probably from his gang of associates, and throw suspicion
onto me. What burns me up is that you sat back and just
watched him.''

''*Me*, Captain?''

''You, sir. Your staff also found out that Darrell had
decided to branch out and sell false citizenship papers
to illegals. You discovered that the three Mexican sail-

ors—all students at my compound—had acquired counterfeit papers from him. He initially operated on a word-of-mouth basis, but as your computer records indicate, he got greedy and started looking for more customers. He placed a carefully worded ad in a Mexican newspaper. You knew all this, but instead of sharing the information with me—and possibly preventing my cousin's death—you conducted your own private investigation to see if FHOTC was involved. Darrell had figured that out—which is why he tried to make me look guilty of Selena's murder by breaking into my network and planting phony clues."

"Now you're reaching."

"No, General, I'm not. You see, I had my computer man break into Darrell's records. He found enough evidence to ask my permission to investigate further. Then he broke into *your* records. He's very good."

The General almost dropped his cigar. Michael went on.

"I have reason to believe that in the course of a routine robbery, Darrell tried to rape Puripong's pregnant sister and caused her to miscarry. Puripong ordered Gibson—not the brightest of my staff—to 'kill' Darrell, but my cousin switched places with him and the wrong person died. During the two days of class, before they were isolated in the hospital compound, she changed Mia Gibson's copy of the scripted exercise."

"Careless of you to let a student steal one of the scripts from your office," the General observed.

"I didn't. Puripong stole the civilian reporter's script from her backpack in the hospital. All my script changes went to my staff—except for Mia Gibson. Puripong wrote Selena's murder into that stolen script and got it to Gibson. She used one of the three aliens as a courier—

I'm not sure which. Any of them would be very nervous about disobeying an order from a high-ranking officer, even to the point of ignoring the lockdown protocol and leaving the hospital compound. Puripong had all the student gate guards under her thumb—with the exception of Jackson. Puripong had it all planned. I also believe that you yourself let this happen to see how far it could go. To test military security at the risk of our own people.''

"I can neither confirm nor deny that statement. However, these are dangerous times we live in. Our own people, as you put it, are the very ones who are duty-bound to prevent such information—whether it be top security codes or personal computer diaries—from falling into the wrong hands. Better to risk a few American soldiers learning our security weaknesses than to suffer another terrorist-instigated disaster. Your cousin's death could not have been prevented, Captain.''

The General reached for the lighter, but McLowery stretched out a hand and swept it off the end table and onto the floor.

"You don't know that!''

"I know we plugged some of the leaks,'' the General said seriously, "and thanks to you and your staff, we'll plug the rest. I know we're damn lucky the only people who took advantage of Darrell's citizenship papers were from Mexico.'' He shook his head. "We were definitely keeping an eye on who contacted Darrell and his crew once they'd spread the word through their various contacts. Fortunately for him and for us, the only sales he made were to a few dozen hardworking Mexicans—so it could be said that the Navy benefited there, as well.''

"I've got enough for CNN to pick up this story—starting with Darrell's lenient sentence and his release from the brig tomorrow. If he's freed, then I swear this whole story is going public, including that double-talk statement you just made to me.''

The two men stared at each other until the General said, ''I'm still waiting for the rest of your damage control.''

McLowery carefully reined in his anger. ''The report should say that Darrell is charged with treason—tampering with military computers and stealing sensitive information. Our cover story will be that Selena discovered that Darrell had targeted the computer and the high-tech electronics at my parents' home for one of the gang's robberies. They were next on the list, so Selena was killed for knowing too much. Perfectly understandable motive. So, as I said, Darrell gets charged with treason, and Gibson gets an honorable discharge under the condition that she remain silent. That officially ends it.''

''So Darrell becomes the fall guy? What if he won't cooperate?''

''We won't give him a choice. Treason is usually a death penalty offense, so if he values his life, he'll definitely cooperate.'' Michael shook his head. ''He started all this. My cousin is dead because of his actions. Puripong, too. Standing by and doing nothing makes you responsible for Darrell's deeds, which led to attempted rape and a miscarriage caused by trauma. Or didn't you know about that, either?''

The General said nothing.

''Puripong dragged Gibson into it and tried to kill Darrell. Puripong's dead, Gibson just followed orders, Selena's dead, and that only leaves you, me and Darrell who know the whole truth. Darrell's responsible for a bona fide death—the younger Puripong's unborn child.

He can be the official Navy scapegoat who pays for all the repercussions of your silence.''

"There's a certain convoluted justice in it,'' the General said thoughtfully. "And as a bonus,'' he added, "Puripong's family won't pursue the matter.''

"Neither will the reporter. Or my parents. You can't control civilians, General. They'll want justice. This will take care of that urge. They'll let the matter rest.''

The General bent over and retrieved his lighter, then lit his second cigar. "Write it up, Captain, and sign it.''

"No, sir. I won't validate using American military personnel to test security.''

"Terrorism is a fact of life in this country, Captain. I have no problem testing base security with one of our own.''

"Selena Mellow was one of *my* own. I'll write up your report, but *you* sign it. Not me, and not any member of my staff. I won't sign a deliberately falsified report, nor will anyone from FHOTC suffer repercussions from signing such a document. Do I make myself clear, General?''

The General puffed calmly away.

"There's more—officially. I want four promotions. One for my Chief—Valmore Bouchard—one for Master-at-Arms Jackson and one for Chaplain Daniel Preston. They get assigned the number-one duty-station choice on their dream sheet.''

"And the fourth one's for you, I presume.''

"You presume wrong!'' McLowery spat out the words. "I'd never cash in on my cousin's murder. Ever.''

"It doesn't matter. You corrected the breach in security with admirable speed and skill. The Navy needs men like you, McLowery.''

"Skip the flattery. I'm not finished yet. Puripong has a brother in the Navy. Puripong's sister has a Navy husband. Get the oldest promoted. I'd ask for double promotions, but it would look suspicious. But do get both men stationed stateside. It'll ensure that the Puripongs aren't evicted from military housing. Before the memorial service would be fitting, General."

"Good PR for the Navy, too. I'll have someone write it up for the press with your cover story."

"Don't. I already have a reporter in mind. She's a fair hand at fiction, I understand, and knows most of what's going on, anyway." McLowery rose, his stitched cheek throbbing, his body weary. "I'm taking the rest of the day off, sir. You'll have your report tomorrow." He didn't wait to be dismissed, but turned and headed for the door.

"Captain." The General spoke in a quiet voice that didn't disguise his authority and power. "Your cousin died in service to her country. However, you do understand that the military's part in not shutting down Darrell and his civilian gang—so we could test the limits of base security—doesn't leave this room?"

McLowery did a sharp about-face. "I don't understand a damn thing, sir. But I'll keep quiet if you keep your part of the bargain. I assume you don't want a promotion memo on the aforementioned staff?"

"You assume correctly. I'll remember."

"So will I, sir. Count on it."

For a moment McLowery held the power, but only for that moment.

"Dismissed, sailor."

McLowery met the other's gaze full on. "Sir, with all due deference…"

"Yes?"

"You're a disgrace to the uniform."

CHAPTER TWENTY

McLowery home
8:30 p.m.

JO ANXIOUSLY WAITED for Michael's return. In the living room Sunshine and her husband busied themselves with their late-evening routine while Jo paced in front of the window. Patrick read his newspaper, occasionally rustling it as he turned the pages. Sunshine checked off orders on a ceramic supplies form. Jo had nothing to occupy herself with except fear.

"Could I get you something to eat?" Sunshine asked.

Jo shook her head. "No, thank you. Maybe later."

"Get her a drink, Sunshine," Patrick said irritably. "Make it a double. Then maybe I can read in peace."

"I'm sorry. How can you sit there so calmly?" Jo asked.

"Because I know my son. He said not to worry. He had to swing by the General's place for a briefing, and then…" Patrick cocked his head, lowered his newspaper and replaced his reading glasses in his shirt pocket. "That's him now."

Jo jumped from her seat and ran outside, meeting Michael as he climbed out of his car. He took her in his arms and held her tightly, so tightly she couldn't draw a full breath. She didn't care.

"Are you okay?" she asked, still held against his chest. She lifted her hand to rest it on his undamaged cheek, the other red and raw with unbandaged stitches.

"I will be if you promise to marry me."

If Michael hadn't been holding her, Jo would have fallen, so great was her surprise. A proposal was the last thing she'd expected. "But—"

"Yes or no. And believe me, my love, a negative answer is definitely unsat."

"Yes! You want me, you got me!" As Michael kissed her, Jo honestly thought she could float ten feet above the ground.

"It's time to get out of here."

"Are we going to a hotel?" Jo asked, beaming. "And a negative answer is unsatisfactory there, too."

"We are, but first things first. Get your things, Ms. Lori-Jo Marche-Sepanik. Have I got a story for you."

His cell phone rang, and he stayed outside on the porch to take the call. Jo was left to hurry inside alone. As she ran breathlessly up the stairs, she missed seeing Sunshine and Patrick exchange a look of understanding. Racing back down with her backpack, she slowed just long enough to say in one huge breath of joy, "He says the investigation's over, we're going to a hotel, he wants to marry me, I said yes, I'll have him call and answer all your questions later—bye!"

She dashed out the door, happiness speeding her feet. She didn't hear Patrick's last remark as he put on his reading glasses and opened the newspaper again. "About damn time. My son might end up happy yet."

"Michael knows a good thing when he sees it." Sunshine wiped happy tears from her eyes and hurried over to kiss her husband's forehead. "Just like me."

Patrick refused to respond verbally to such sentimentality, but he didn't get back to his newspaper for a long, long time.

Carlsbad Hotel, California
11:30 p.m.

Jo SIGHED CONTENTEDLY and stretched her naked body with pleasure. Michael lay beside her, his head propped up and supported on his elbow. He ignored the covers and sheets at the bottom of the bed, tangled and twisted from their lovemaking.

"You're still going to marry me?" she asked, rolling toward him. "Because ring or no ring, you're stuck with a lifelong lover."

Michael gathered her close again for a kiss. "I am, if you still want me. Although technically I'm no longer a gentleman, just an officer. Maybe not even that if the General decides to sink my career."

"I'll sink *him* if he dares to try," Jo said fiercely. "I'll go public with the whole story. You poor man— you've really been through the wars since you met me. I'll let you sleep while I stay up to work on my story. Hell, and I thought writing for the tabloids was a crock."

Jo felt a small damper on her happiness. Michael had told her what the General wanted in the "official" version. Jo had the feeling he hadn't told her everything— especially when it came to the General—but wisely left her questions unasked. She could fill in some of the blanks herself, and for those she couldn't, it didn't matter. She had Michael, and as an extra reward, the most whopping tabloid story she could ever have dreamed up—to be released as legitimate to any media source she wanted. "It's gonna take some time to get all the lies straight."

"Not tonight," Michael murmured. "You need your rest, too."

Only somehow their presleep cuddle turned into a second lovemaking session. Finally he kissed her again and said, "You are so beautiful. Thank you, Lori-Jo."

"Don't thank me," she said, suddenly sitting up. "I just remembered a loose end!"

Michael groaned. "What?"

"What about the third alien? The woman?"

"Taken care of," he said.

Jo rose from the bed. She retrieved the ice bucket, a clean facecloth and made a cold compress. "How?" she asked, holding the white material gently against his stitched cheek, noticing he was too exhausted to wince.

"Daniel called earlier and I told him to do what he thought best."

Inside Fleet Hospital Compound
2100 hours

CHAPLAIN PRESTON said a quick prayer as he passed through the guarded entrance. He hoped there would be less of a scene than the one he'd encountered earlier at Camp Pendleton Brig. At Michael's command, he'd left a happily sobbing Gibson assured that her freedom would come soon with all charges dropped if she agreed to a discharge and didn't discuss Selena Mellow's death. He'd called Gibson's sister and let her know that Mia would be arriving home within the week. Then the sister had started to sob on the phone.

Daniel still felt uncomfortable around crying women. He suspected Escalanta was made of sterner stuff. He quickly located her in the Admin area of the canvas hospital, her hair and uniform immaculate despite the late hour, as she used the old manual typewriter, a must in tent cities, to complete her forms. She stopped typing at his appearance and rose to her feet.

"May I help you, sir?" she asked.

"You don't have to stand for officers inside the working areas of a hospital, Escalanta. Sit down."

Escalanta remained standing. Daniel didn't make her suffer any longer. He leaned over to whisper in her ear, "I'm authorized to tell you this. Stay quiet and you stay in the Navy. *Comprende?*"

Escalanta's eyes opened wide, and to Daniel's dismay, started to tear. *"Gracias, Padre!"*

He whispered again. "Don't cry—and use English with me. You'll draw attention to yourself." Then he said in a normal voice, "Please post a notice saying my nondenominational prayer service tomorrow morning will be at 0630, instead of 0600."

Escalanta nodded, then remembered herself and said, "Yes, sir. 0630." She kept her head upright, barely keeping both joy and tears at bay.

Before she sat down, Daniel leaned over and whispered, "Is Escalanta your real name?" When she shook her head, he said, "Write it down for me. Just your first name, so I can keep you in my prayers."

Escalanta reached for a government memo, jotted on the yellow sheet, folded it, passed it to him and said, "Is there anything else, Chaplain?"

"That's all, Yeoman. God bless, Sister Escalanta." Daniel started to unfold the paper but shoved it in his pocket as Jackson appeared.

"Sir? May I speak to you, please?"

Daniel nodded and put the paper away. Here was another soul who needed counseling, someone who'd seen an officer blown away. "Let's step outside, Jackson," he said.

The moon shone bright and clear. The ocean breeze felt cool and welcome against his face, reviving him a bit. It had been a long day.

"About this afternoon..." Daniel began. "The whole experience had to be...disturbing."

"I'm not here for counseling, sir. I'm here for career help."

"Career?"

"Yes. I don't want to carry a rifle the rest of my life, Chaplain. I've wanted to be an administrative aide instead of a sniper ever since I joined up."

"What's stopping you?" Daniel asked.

"My expert marksmanship. I've got great eyes and great aim. The Navy wants to teach me to ski and enter the Olympic biathlon. Skis, Chaplain! Me, an Alabama native! Sir, you gotta get me out of the sniper gig and into church business. I'm computer literate and I type 120 words a minute."

Daniel froze at the carrot she'd offered and wished he had even half that speed. "I don't have that kind of pull, Jackson."

"You got pull enough to keep that Mexican señorita in there outta the brig, Reverend. Or rather, the CO does, and you're tight with him."

"Have you been eavesdropping, Master-at-Arms?"

"Part of my job, sir. My ears are as good as my eyes."

"So...a nosy woman in my chapel?" he said slowly. "A sneak, listening at doors?"

"Get me in your chapel and you'll see a reformed sinner, Reverend. But until you get me out of here, I'm gonna stick to you like glue." She passed Daniel her personal cell phone. "I'll be in the guard shack when you're done calling the powers that be to swing my new gig. Hit three to page Captain McLowery. The cell phone number's printed on the back."

Daniel blinked. "Cell phones aren't allowed in Fleet exercises. They don't even work. Where did you get this?"

"I come prepared for everything, sir, and it'll work as soon as you get off base. It's also encrypted, so no one can listen in on your conversation. I assume you want privacy for your little chats with the CO." She paused, a slight smile on her face. "Oh, did I mention I sang with our church choir as soon as I got out of diapers, and for fifteen years after that? I have a perfect contralto. My mother's the choir director there. She took over after my Nana, Angela, retired. I'm her namesake, Angelica. You need an angel at your side, Chaplain. That's me." Jackson sung a military marching song in an angelic voice to prove her point, then marched away in time with its beat.

A fatigued Daniel couldn't help smiling. He dialed Michael's pager and punched in the cell phone number. That done, he started to shove the little phone into his pocket, crinkled the memo paper inside from Escalanta, withdrew it, unfolded it.

His weary eyes focused on the neatly printed four-letter name.

Anna.

Carlsbad Hotel, California
11:45 p.m.

JO REMOVED the cold compress from Michael's face and substituted an ice pack. "Better?"

"Yeah, thanks." His arms remained against the soft skin of her waist as she sat on the side of the bed and threw the compress into the ice bucket.

"You look like a pirate with that scar."

"I've got the wench." He grinned. "And thanks to Daniel's phone call, the final loose end is now tied up."

"But...I thought of another. Loose end, that is."

Michael groaned. "Make it quick."

"We've both been so tired and so busy...and then at your mother's house I just grabbed my backpack..."

"And?" he prompted.

"I—we didn't use any protection." The words rushed out.."I wasn't trying to trap you. I mean, I really want you in my life, but when you asked me to marry you, I was so...and then we just got carried away...and...oh, hell. You're not gonna like this." She dropped her gaze. "It's my fertile time of the month, too. Sorry."

Michael took the ice pack away from his face and set it on the end table. "I'm not."

"No?"

"Not unless you are."

"Well, I am thirty-three. I always wanted kids. I'm not getting any younger."

"If Sunshine hints about grandchildren one more time—"

Jo felt her joy return in full force. "Please don't say anything to her yet. I'm not *sure* I'm pregnant and it was only twice."

"Third time's the charm." Michael patted the spot beside him. "Why don't you hit the honor bar's chocolate supply first? Build up your energy..." he said with a quick laugh.

"Sounds good to me." Jo actually had the refrigerator

open before something occurred to her. She paused so long that Michael spoke up.

"My blood tests are immaculate. The military tests medical staff every six months," he assured her.

"No, it's not that."

"You already wipe out the munchies? Or you want something else? I can call room service." Michael reached for the phone. "What do you want?"

Jo shook her head, the cold air of the refrigerator wafting over her skin. She didn't even shiver. "I—I'm not hungry anymore."

"Yeah, *right*."

"No, really." She slowly closed the refrigerator door. The empty aching pit inside, that gnawing hunger that had been hers for as long as she could remember, had vanished. "It's strange, but I'm not hungry," she repeated.

Michael didn't argue. "Well, I am. And not for food, either." As he held out his arms, a beautiful smile crossed her face. Her loving heart beat faster at the love he showed for her. As she hurried back to her hero's side, she suddenly realized that she'd never feel empty or alone again.

MICHAEL'S PAGER BUZZED. He sat up, glanced at his sleeping fiancée, checked his pager, then dialed.

"McLowery here."

"Captain, it's Chaplain Preston. Sorry to disturb you, sir, but…"

Michael listened.

"Jackson wants into the Bible biz?" he asked.

"Seems it runs in the family, sir."

"Won't be a problem. In fact, I already have the go-ahead to okay her dream duty and a promotion. That goes for you, too. Just do up the paperwork and get it to me. Anything else?''

''Escalanta's all set,'' Daniel said. ''I didn't ask for her last name, but her Christian name is…Anna. Thought you might want to know.''

Anna? Michael blinked at the freak coincidence—then wondered if it was a coincidence at all.

''Mac? You still there?''

''Yeah.''

''You okay?''

Michael thought about it and found that he was. ''I'm better than okay, Chaplain. I'm engaged to be married.''

''Knowing Jo Marche, that event was never in doubt. Congratulations, sir. I'll pencil you in for the requisite premarital counseling once Fleet's over.''

''Seems I'm going to Maine for my honeymoon. But I'll be back to finish out my tour here. I have almost a year left, and then I'll request a transfer to the East Coast. Afraid I'm still a career man.''

''Glad to hear it, sir. As long as you're taking care of assignments, I've decided I'd like to work at the Camp Pendleton chapel. That way I can keep—''

''An eye on me?''

''Yeah, and on the woman running your life. I want the same for myself—and for the woman who intends to organize my chapel and my choir. We need to watch each other's backs. Jo may be a civilian and Jackson's enlisted, but they outrank us both—uniform or not.''

Michael actually laughed. ''When this exercise is over, meet me at the officers' club.''

''Sir?''

''I wanna buy you a beer…Daniel.''

''You're on. Good night, Mac.''

Daniel clicked off and Michael hung up the hotel

phone. He marveled at the way Jo immediately reached for him as he lay back, how she felt so natural in his arms. He felt like a member of a family again, like a man who belonged, not just some outsider looking in. This woman believed in him more than he'd believed in himself, and with help from two other people had brought the wrong to justice, and showed the world an unbeatable team.

With duty, honor, courage and love. Most of all, love.

Jo stirred as he gathered her closer. "Everything okay?" she asked sleepily.

"A-OK, Lori-Jo." He re-covered her with the sheet and tenderly placed his uninjured cheek against her head. "Couldn't be better."

Coming in May 2002

**Three Bravo men marry for convenience—
but will they love in leisure? Find out in
Christine Rimmer's *Bravo Family Ties!***

Cash—for stealing a young woman's innocence, and to
give their baby a name, in *The Nine-Month Marriage*

Nate—for the sake of a codicil in his beloved
grandfather's will, in *Marriage by Necessity*

Zach—for the unlucky-in-love rancher's chance to
have a marriage—even of convenience—
with the woman he *really* loves!

BRAVO
FAMILY TIES

Where love comes alive™

Every day is

A Mother's Day

in this heartwarming anthology
celebrating motherhood and romance!

Featuring the classic story "Nobody's Child" by Emilie Richards
He had come to a child's rescue, and now Officer Farrell Riley was
suddenly sharing parenthood with beautiful Gemma Hancock.
But would their ready-made family last forever?

Plus two brand-new romances:

"Baby on the Way" by Marie Ferrarella
Single and pregnant, Madeline Reed found the perfect husband in the
handsome cop who helped bring her infant son into the world. But did his
dutiful role in the surprise delivery make J. T. Walker a daddy?

"A Daddy for Her Daughters" by Elizabeth Bevarly
When confronted with spirited Naomi Carmichael and her brood of girls,
bachelor Sloan Sullivan realized he had a lot to learn about women!
Especially if he hoped to win this sexy single mom's heart....

Available this April from Silhouette Books!

These New York Times *bestselling* authors
have created stories to capture the hearts and minds
of women everywhere.
Here are three classic tales about the power of love—
and the wonder of discovering the place
where you belong....

FINDING HOME

DUNCAN'S BRIDE
by
LINDA HOWARD

CHAIN LIGHTNING
by
ELIZABETH LOWELL

POPCORN AND KISSES
by
KASEY MICHAELS

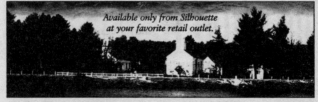

*Available only from Silhouette
at your favorite retail outlet.*

Silhouette®

Where love comes alive™

Visit Silhouette at www.eHarlequin.com

EMERGENCY!

The Family Doctor
by Bobby Hutchinson

The next Superromance novel in this dramatic series—set in and around St. Joseph's Hospital in Vancouver, British Colombia.

Chief of staff Antony O'Connor has family problems. His mother is furious at his father for leaving her many years ago, and now he's coming to visit—with the woman he loves. Tony's family is taking sides. Patient care advocate Kate Lewis is an expert at defusing anger, so she might be able to help him out. With this problem, at least. Sorting out her feelings for Tony— and his feelings for her—is about to get trickier!

Heartwarming stories with a sense of humor, genuine charm and emotion and lots of family!

On sale starting April 2002

Available wherever Harlequin books are sold.

HARLEQUIN®
Makes any time special ®

Visit us at www.eHarlequin.com

HSRE